CW00498891

COMING HOME TO THE HIGHLANDS

LISA HOBMAN

Best wishes

Lisa Hobman

B

Boldwood

First published in Great Britain in 2023 by Boldwood Books Ltd.

Copyright © Lisa Hobman, 2023

Cover Design by Alexandra Allden

Cover Photography: Shutterstock

A CIP catalogue record for this book is available from the British Library.

Paperback ISBN 978-1-80483-666-8

Large Print ISBN 978-1-80483-662-0

Hardback ISBN 978-1-80483-661-3

Ebook ISBN 978-1-80483-659-0

Kindle ISBN 978-1-80483-660-6

Audio CD ISBN 978-1-80483-667-5

MP3 CD ISBN 978-1-80483-664-4

Digital audio download ISBN 978-1-80483-658-3

Boldwood Books Ltd
23 Bowerdean Street
London SW6 3TN
www.boldwoodbooks.com

To my very own Marley. You were the goodest boy that ever was. And the bestest at hugs. Such a sensitive wee soul who knew when cuddles were needed and gave them willingly. I miss you more than words can say, so I wanted to keep you alive in my stories. I hope you're looking across the rainbow bridge with a happy heart.

And to my crazy pup, Wilf. Thank you for helping our hearts to heal.

PROLOGUE

Cheers and whistles rang out round the auditorium and the models at the end of the catwalk applauded world-famous fashion designer, Nina Picarro, as she walked towards them, waving to familiar faces in the audience and blowing two-handed kisses. Once she reached the group of towering men and women, the Italian-born designer was enveloped in a group hug and handed bouquets of flowers. There were lots of air kisses and Nina bowed humbly as Olivia MacBain looked on from the wings with a sense of giddiness and pride fluttering inside her. She had the urge to call her mum, but thanks to the five-hour time difference, it would only be three in the morning back in Scotland. She would refrain from calling now but couldn't wait to call her and tell her all about it the next day.

Seeing her own designs brought to life and paraded before the city's elite at New York Fashion Week had been a huge thrill for Olivia, and a dream come true to boot; something she'd hoped for but had never anticipated *actually* happening when she had left the Scottish Highlands and arrived in New York for her internship at the House of Nina Picarro, six years earlier.

Although born into a noble Scottish family with a long and colourful history, Olivia had decided at the tender age of eight that she wanted to be a fashion designer. At that time, her parents had humoured her, presuming that once she came of age, she would realise the role she must play in Scotland's high society, and would begin to toe the line.

They were wrong.

Six years after Olivia graduated from Glasgow's prestigious School of Art, whilst working at the House of Nina Picarro, her father died suddenly of a heart attack and her world came crumbling down around her. She had been very close to her father and losing him caused a heartache like she had never experienced before and hoped never to again. Losing him made Olivia even more determined that she would follow her own career path. And even though her mother, Lady Freya, had insisted that her husband of thirty-five years Laird Gregor MacBain's heart condition had been something they couldn't have predicted, Olivia knew it was partly the stress of dealing with the day-to-day maintenance of the family seat, Drumblair Castle, in the pretty village of Drumblair, to the south-west of Inverness.

Olivia wasn't in the least bit interested in following in her father's footsteps. Although, thankfully, the tradition was that the eldest son would be the one to carry the mantle, and this particular honour would fall to her older brother, Kerr. At thirty-three, he was five years her senior, public-school educated, and welcome to the title of Laird of Drumblair, as far as she was concerned. He wanted nothing more and had made that patently clear from a young age.

And anyway, now, at the age of twenty-eight, things were finally falling into place for Olivia. Her hard work, at both university *and* during her year-long internship, was paying off. Not only had she been a bona fide design assistant at one of the most prestigious fashion houses in New York for the past five years, but her boss had started to recognise her potential. This latest step of having her designs exclusively included in the show was huge for her career, and she still had to pinch herself when she remembered Nina's response to her drawings

'We simply have to show them, darling,' Nina had said, as if it was the most obvious thing in the world. 'The world needs to know what talent we have here.'

Nina Picarro had dressed royalty, rock stars and movie icons, and her creations ranged from sublime gowns worn to the opera and royal weddings, to the verging-on-crazy outfits that clothed the attendees at the New York Met Gala, but in spite of all this, she remained a down-to-earth, non-egotistical woman who wasn't in the least bit threatened by other talent. In fact, she embraced it wholeheartedly.

* * *

A camera flashed, snatching Olivia from her reminiscing, and she was pulled into a bear hug.

'That was uh-mazing, Olivia,' a distinctly New York accent spoke loudly into her ear. The voice belonged to her best friend and housemate, Harper Franklin. They had met when Olivia arrived from Scotland and was looking for a place to live. Fashion photographer, Harper, had pinned a 'room to let' sign on the noticeboard in the staffroom and Olivia had responded; the rest, as they say, is history.

Olivia scrunched her eyes as she turned to face her friend, dazzled by the bright light. 'I hope you're going to delete that shot. I must've looked completely gormless.'

Harper nudged her playfully and waved her free hand. 'Nah, don't worry. You always look like you totally have *all* the gorm.'

Harper's attempts to decipher Olivia's 'British-isms' were often a cause for giggles. 'Anyways, you must be so damn proud of yourself, Olivia, because I'm so damned proud of you too!'

Olivia nodded, her heart pounding at her ribs and her face beginning to ache from grinning. 'I have to say it was probably the most exciting thing I've ever experienced.'

'You'll be Nina's second-in-command before long. I just know it,' Harper enthused, as she always did about almost everything. Olivia shook her head and rolled her eyes. Michael, Nina's current assistant, was like part of the furniture at Nina Picarro and it was doubtful he'd ever leave, but before she could respond with her reasoning, Harper butted in, 'You do know Michael's getting married soon, right? And his fiancé, Alvaro, wants to return home to Cuba to take over his father's restaurant. Michael won't want to disappoint his new husband now, will he? And who better to take his place as Nina's second than you?'

This was news to Olivia and a rush of excitement flooded her veins in the form of heat, no doubt causing her face to glow like a neon diner sign – an affliction she had suffered since her awkward teenage years when her teeth had protruded a little too much and her gangly legs had made her feel rather like a baby giraffe. She scrunched her brow and made an unladylike snorting noise. 'Pfft, no way. I'm sure there are a dozen people more equipped to fill Michael's shoes.'

'Na-uh!' Harper glanced around in a conspiratorial manner and whispered, 'Between me and you, I overheard Michael talking to Sophie in Graphic Design yesterday. He was telling her that you're going to be a tough act to follow after your work this season.'

Olivia covered her mouth to stop a bubbling squeal from escaping. 'Really?' Harper nodded and Olivia widened her eyes. 'Bloody hell, I've never heard him praise anyone but Nina.'

Harper grinned. 'See? What did I tell you? It'll be your name on that backdrop one day. Now, I'd better go and get some more candid shots of the models backstage for the website. People love that stuff.' She rolled her eyes and shrugged in disbelief. 'Beautiful people acting all natural as if they're human.' She chuckled and raised her brows to feign shock. 'Bizarre but true. They lap that stuff right on up.' Harper leaned in and kissed her cheek. 'See you in about an hour for the after-party. Love you.' Then she dashed away before Olivia could reply.

Nina arrived backstage and made a beeline for Olivia. 'Well, darling, we did it,' she said. She had been in America since her teens and the last remnants of her Italian accent were almost gone unless you knew her well. She held her hands out and tilted her head, her perfect jet-black bob swishing as she moved. 'I looked for you to come and take a bow, but you were hiding.' She shook her head and scrunched her brow. 'Our beautiful Olivia, always too modest.'

Olivia was aware that she was still wearing a grin that resembled a crazed serial killer, but she couldn't help it. 'It was wonderful, Nina. Thank you so much for including my designs.'

Nina drew her into a brief embrace then pulled away and held her at arm's length, fixing her with a sincere gaze. 'I like to promote real talent when I find it. Speaking of which, you and I need to talk. Come to my office on Monday morning at ten.'

Olivia's heart skipped and she struggled to get her brain to remind her mouth to respond. Eventually she spluttered, 'Yes, sure, absolutely, will do.' Her attempts to hide her excitement and intrigue failed miserably.

Nina smiled knowingly before disappearing into yet another crowd of well-wishers, and Olivia had to restrain herself from fist bumping the air. Maybe Harper had been right? Maybe Nina wanted to talk to her about Michael's soon-to-be vacant position.

How on earth would she sleep over the weekend without knowing what fate awaited her in Nina's office?

The exit opened as people began to leave, bringing with it a blast of icy February air, and before the door closed again, from her spot in the warm auditorium, Olivia could see large flakes of snow floating rapidly towards the ground. Her family home jumped, surprisingly, into her mind. Winters in the Scottish Highlands were the most beautiful, yet the most isolating, thing she had ever experienced; at least here the world didn't stand still at the mere flurry of inclement weather. Oh, the many benefits of living in New York and having every amenity a stone's throw away.

Of course, Olivia was expected to attend the after-party and she knew she would enjoy it once she arrived, but she was tired out, exhausted even, from the long hours she had been putting in during the lead-up to Fashion Week. All she really wanted to do was hail a cab and head home to the quaint little two-bed apartment she shared with Harper in Sunnyside, Queens. But considering the discussion Nina wanted to have with her on Monday, she couldn't risk being a no-show. It wouldn't be good for her career if she started to flake after late-night events, considering there could potentially be many more in her future career. That is if Harper's suspicions were true.

* * *

She felt her phone vibrating in her pocket and pulled it out with a huff. She glared at the screen in disbelief as her brother Kerr's name glowed from the handset and a cold shiver travelled her spine as she noted the time illuminated there too. *Ten after 10 p.m. eastern time.* The five-hour time difference had stopped her calling home not so long ago. *What the heck? He never calls me. And certainly not at ten past three in the morning.*

A familiar sinking feeling rolled through her stomach. She hoped he wasn't going to ask her for money again. Last time he had called her, he had feigned this sickly sibling connection that they had regrettably never shared, and then had proceeded to ask her to loan him £2,000; another gambling debt that he was trying to hide from their mother for fear of disappointing her yet again.

The last she had heard from or *about* her brother had been a few months ago when she learned that he was dating the wealthy widow of a former acquaintance of her parents. The woman, Adaira Wallace, was in her late fifties, and Olivia knew full well the reason behind the relationship. The suspicions Olivia held over Kerr's motives had once been directed, by others, at Adaira herself when the former sales assistant had supposedly married 'above her station' and to an aristocrat many years her senior. Adaira had, of course, inherited her older husband's fortune after only ten years of wedded bliss, and was childless. Aiming to get into more than her good graces, Kerr was as mercenary as he was handsome. With their father's striking features that bore a resemblance to a younger Kurt Russell, and their mother's Titian hair, Kerr was quite the hit with the older ladies. Olivia, on the other hand, had inherited their father's mousy brown hair and their mother's natural curls. Although, unlike their mother's, *her* curls couldn't easily be tamed, so she didn't consider herself in any way nearly as beautiful.

When thinking on it further, Olivia was sure Kerr had chosen to date an acquaintance of her parents to throw the cat amongst the pigeons. Especially seeing as their mother had informed him she would no longer be subsidising his extravagant lifestyle; a lifestyle to which he felt entitled as his birthright, an affliction that had never affected Olivia. Sadly, Olivia knew her mother lacked resolve when it came to her first-born and regardless of how many times she insisted she was done helping him, Olivia knew her mother would walk through fire for her children if necessary.

Olivia didn't feel like having her mood blasted which, inevitably, was what all conversations with Kerr seemed to do, but when all was said and done, he was still her brother, and if he needed her enough to call her at such a ridiculous hour of the day... With a great deal of trepidation and an equal amount of reluctance, she tapped the screen and lifted the handset to her ear.

'Hi, Kerr. It's the wee small hours there, is everything okay?'

There was a loud sniffling over the airwaves. 'No, everything is definitely *not* bloody okay.' More sniffling. 'Everything has turned to shit. It's so unfair. I can't bloody believe it. It's utterly ridiculous. What the hell am I supposed to do now?' His words were reminiscent of a petulant child and came out in a slurred rush of, evidently, alcohol-fuelled anger and emotion.

She gave a deep sigh, closed her eyes and rubbed at the throbbing at her temples that had appeared since she'd accepted the call. She presumed Adaira had dumped him, or worse – that he'd once again got himself in serious trouble with a loan shark and his life was on the line. She told him, 'Kerr, please slow down. You're not making any sense. Tell me what's happened.'

'She's bloody dead, isn't she? A stroke. It was immediate, apparently. Totally unexpected.'

Olivia was shocked, as Adaira had always seemed quite young for her age. It just proved that you never knew when it came to such occurrences; after all, she'd heard of healthy footballers dropping stone dead of heart attacks mid-training.

'Oh, Kerr, I'm so sorry. I know you were...' *What's the correct word*? 'Fond of her.'

He snorted. 'Well, I would *hope* so.' There was a strange indignation to his tone. 'I just don't know what I'm supposed to do now.'

Olivia rolled her eyes and the words: *find yourself another sugar mama, probably* rattled around her head, but she immediately bit down on her tongue. She shouldn't be so cruel. Even if it was predominantly about the money, he was evidently fond of Adaira or he wouldn't be crying like this. 'Grief takes time, Kerr. But you'll get through it.' She tried to sound empathetic but realised her words were trite instead.

Another scoffing noise vibrated along the airwaves. 'She was supposed to help me with something pretty huge, you know. It would have made us both so much money. We had so many plans and now that's all gone. So many lost opportunities.'

Olivia closed her eyes and massaged at the crease between her brows with a tensed index finger. So, he'd managed to almost con the poor woman into investing in one of his hare-brained business ventures. Presumably, from his choice of words, she hadn't actually signed on the dotted line.

She struggled for the right words that would appease him on this matter and certainly wasn't about to offer her own finances up for the sacrifice. 'That's a shame,' she said with a cringe, once again knowing her words weren't in the least bit helpful.

'I suppose the one saving grace in all this is my inheritance.' He sighed deeply.

Olivia widened her eyes. 'She's left you something?' *Blimey, he's getting faster at his gigolo craft*, Olivia thought, after failing to hide the surprise in her voice.

'Well, *duh*! I'm obviously in line to inherit everything. I'm the son. That's how it works, Olivia.' Her heart leapt and she felt the colour drain from her face. 'And I can assure you there will be some major changes around the place. Half the staff aren't even needed. And I won't be continuing with the open garden nonsense so that means we won't need any more than two gardeners. I might even sell off the farm cottages and some of the land. I mean, I've got to afford to live, haven't I?'

Olivia swallowed as best she could now that her throat felt as dry as the Sahara. She shook her head. 'K-Kerr... please stop talking for a moment...'

'Charming,' he huffed.

'I'm sorry to be harsh, I just... I need answers, that's all.'

Ker scoffed. 'I bet you do. And I guess you'll be pissed off, seeing as you were Dad's favourite, but what can I say? Tradition is tradition.'

'Kerr!' she snapped. 'Who... who has died? Is it Adaira?'

There was a pause. 'What? No! Don't be daft; Adaira is here with me at the moment. I don't know how I would be coping without her, to be honest. At least she's here and not a gazillion miles away in that god-awful place you call home these days.'

Olivia's nostrils flared and she spoke through clenched teeth. 'Kerr, who. Has. Died?'

'Mother dearest, of course,' he replied with derision. 'In her chair beside her bed, so at least she was at home, I suppose.'

Olivia's leg's weakened and she reached out to steady herself on the wall, feeling as if the air had been sucked from her lungs. 'I'm sorry, *what*?'

'I presumed you'd heard me say at the start of our call that Mum was dead. That she had a stroke. But obviously you weren't listening to me, as usual. Olivia. Our. Mother. Is. Dead. She has shuffled off this mortal coil and abandoned me. I'm an orphan at thirty-three. I can't quite believe it.' He sniffed again and she heard a gentle soothing voice in the background, although she couldn't hear what was being said. 'Thank you, my darling Adaira. I'm so glad you're here with me.'

Ignoring his self-centred pity parade, Olivia shook her head, it couldn't be true. Panic began to flood her veins, sending her heart-beat into a frenzy. 'But I only spoke to Mum yesterday, and she was fine. Y-you must be mistaken. She... she can't be dead, Kerr. She's only sixty-eight.' Olivia felt as though the ground was disappearing away from beneath her feet as the room began to spin and she reached out to steady herself on the wall.

'Well, she is,' he stated matter-of-factly. 'But that's not the worst of it.'

Olivia slid down the wall until her bottom hit the floor and tears welled in her eyes. A deep, thudding ache like the one she had experienced on hearing of her father's passing took hold of her heart. What could possibly be worse than their mother dying suddenly? 'I... I don't understand. What do you mean that's not the worst of it?'

'I've spoken to Alasdair McKendrick, at McKendrick Law.' His use of a mocking tone yet again reminiscent of the spoiled child he had once been. 'You know? Our supposed *family lawyer*. He wouldn't tell me anything! Apparently, Mum made Uncle Innes the executor, so we are beholden to that rat before we can move forwards!'

Feeling anger and abhorrence at his blatant lack of compassion and disregard for the death of their remaining parent, she snapped. 'For goodness' sake, Kerr, our mother has died and all you can think about is money?'

He huffed. 'How can you say such an accusatory thing? I'm broken-hearted.'

There was a shuffling sound, and another voice could be heard. 'Olivia? It's Adaira. I'm so very sorry for your loss, dear. I'm afraid Kerr is so devastated, he's simply not thinking clearly. I'm sure you know how close he was to his mother.' *Close to her purse, maybe*, Olivia thought. 'And this has come as a huge shock to him. Perhaps give him a little time and speak to him again. The funeral is expected to be in two weeks' time. We hope you can attend, but we do understand if that isn't possible due to your work schedule. Be assured that I will help all I can and make sure your dear mother has a lovely send-off. I'll go now, as it's all very fresh and raw. We need time to grieve. Bye, dear.'

The line went dead before Olivia could scream into her handset that of course she would be there. And she was her mother too. And that it wasn't Adaira's place to arrange her mother's funeral. And that Mum's brother, Uncle Innes, wasn't as much of a rat as Kerr clearly was.

She stared at the blank screen of her phone as silent tears cascaded down her chilled cheeks. 'But... Mum... No... no, this can't be right. It just can't be.'

Even after the wonderful experience of the fashion show and the potential of her dream job on the horizon, she hoped more than anything in the world that she was dreaming. She closed her eyes, clenched her jaw and stabbed her nails into the palm of her hand as hard as she could. But when she opened her eyes once again, she was still sitting backstage on the cold floor with damp cheeks, and the weight of loss pressing her down.

1

_____

Monday was so cold, but Olivia was numb. Her hair was piled atop her head in a messy bun, and she sat on her couch in yoga pants and an old T-shirt, a pile of used tissues scattered at her feet and a box of family photos on the arm of the couch beside her. For some reason, thoughts of Marley, her mother's dog, broke her heart further. The Labrador/German Shepherd cross had been a rescue from Glasgow that her mother had fallen for and insisted on taking in, regardless of the fact that he was huge. She had doted on that dog, and seeing photos of her mother and Marley made Olivia sob so hard her body ached. He would be lost without her, but thankfully Uncle Innes had taken him for the time being, so she knew he was in good hands. Harper had eventually left her alone under duress and gone into the office after a great deal of convincing by Olivia that she would be fine. The last thing she'd expected when she was alone and crying in her apartment was for Nina to turn up on her doorstep.

Nina was now sitting beside her, coffee cup in one hand and Olivia's hand in the other. She gave it a squeeze. 'I'm so, so sorry, Olivia. We all are,' she said with sincerity. 'Losing a parent is one of the hardest things to go through. I've been there and I know how tough it is when you're living in the same country, so this must be so much harder for you, sweetie. My heart breaks for you. Truly it does. You must book a flight and go home to Scotland as soon as you can. I'm sure you're needed there just now, and we'll be here waiting for your return. Take all the time you need. You've definitely earned it.'

Olivia wiped her sore eyes for what felt like the thousandth time. 'Thank you for being so understanding. And I'm sorry I didn't make the after-party on Friday night, but I was... I was in shock. When I called Harper, she insisted on calling for an Uber and bringing me straight home. I'm so glad she did. I don't think I'd have got here if it wasn't for her.'

Nina gave a sad smile. 'Hey, a party was the last thing you needed to think about. No one blames you for not going. Especially not me.'

Olivia lifted her head and was met with such a compassion-filled gaze that her throat restricted again, and her eyes welled with yet more tears. 'I'm sorry to let you down like this, Nina.' Olivia's voice wobbled as she spoke. 'I know you wanted to talk to me about something today.'

Nina shook her head. 'That can wait. I suspect you know about Michael and Alvaro relocating to Cuba, so you can probably guess what I was going to ask, but you have enough on your mind right now. The conversation can wait until you're ready to have it.'

Olivia knew that under normal circumstances she would be skipping around the room at the prospect of taking on her dream role but, thankfully, Nina wasn't pushing the matter. She nodded and smiled through her tears. 'Thank you.'

Once Nina had gone, Olivia took out her iPad and located a website Nina had recommended for flights. She booked a one-way ticket to Scotland, as Nina had instructed, leaving the return date open to relieve any pressure she might have felt. No doubt there would be much to do, and she couldn't expect her brother to do it all alone, even if he was heir to the estate.

* * *

Olivia arrived back in Inverness on the Friday of the following week, jetlagged and with puffy eyes from lack of sleep and the abundance of tears she had shed. Harper had been amazing, of course, her one constant in the increasingly tumultuous sea of her life. How could she navigate this whole situation alone? *Thank goodness for true friends*, she had thought to herself over and over since boarding the flight. Harper had insisted that she would follow her to Scotland a week later for the funeral and had received the okay for annual leave from Nina.

Feeling unable to face Drumblair Castle so soon when her mother was no longer there, Olivia contacted Uncle Innes and Mirren, the housekeeper, and explained that she needed a little space before she stepped inside the castle again. They were both understanding, thankfully, and Olivia checked into the Glenmoriston Townhouse, a pretty hotel on a tree-lined street by the River Ness. Her spacious, beautifully decorated room had a river view through a large bay window. The day after she arrived, Uncle Innes met her in the hotel bar for coffee.

'I'm so sorry for your loss, dear Olivia,' he said, embracing her and allowing her to cry into his tweed jacket.

'I still can't believe it's true. I just can't face going home. Not yet. Does that make me a bad person?'

Innes held her at arm's length. 'Not at all. It will be painful, there's no doubt about that. But you will have to face the music sometime. And, of course, there's Marley.'

Olivia's heart ached. 'How is he?'

Innes gave a sad smile. 'He keeps sitting by the door and whin-ing. I think he knows it's different to when I look after him during your mum's trips away. They can sense these things.'

Uncle Innes lived in a farmhouse within the boundaries of Drumblair land. The farm had been taken on by one of the other farmers for his livestock, so Innes was surrounded by beautiful countryside with stunning views towards the castle. A lifetime bachelor, Innes was happy simply dealing antiques from his barn and had made a substantial amount of money from doing so. His work had taken him all over the world but these days he consid-ered himself retired, even though Olivia knew otherwise. He was a workaholic.

'I want you to know that the funeral arrangements are all in hand. I've been able to organise most things already as there was a separate document with the solicitor that was addressed to me as the executor, which contained the funeral details. Your mother requested that a private reading of the will take place once the funeral was over. Kerr has taken it upon himself to be "in charge", but I'm ensuring your mother's wishes are being adhered to. Obvi-ously, now you're here, you can take over if you prefer.'

Olivia couldn't face the thought of that. It was enough to have lost her mum but to have to arrange how and when she said her final goodbye felt too overwhelming. Knowing Innes was doing right by her was enough.

'Thank you, but could you continue on with things? I can't even begin to think about how I'll never see her again—' A sob broke free from her chest.

Innes passed over a handkerchief. 'Of course. It's no bother.'

Olivia dabbed at her eyes. 'Does it make me a coward?'

Innes reached over and took her hand. 'It makes you a grieving daughter. We'll leave things as they are.'

* * *

Inverness hadn't changed much, but then she hadn't been away quite a year yet. Her last visit had been for her birthday the April before, but it felt like so much longer. The sky was heavy with clouds as Olivia walked beside the River Ness to the city centre. Passers-by walking dogs or carrying shopping smiled and said hello in spite of the cold and she was warmed by the knowledge that the city was still as friendly as she remembered. The largely precincted centre still held a certain old-world charm thanks to the architecture. Her favourite was the Victorian Market on Queensgate. The beautiful stone arches and wrought-iron carved interior ceiling supports had replaced the original open-air markets of the city, and then the first closed-in market that was sadly destroyed by fire in 1889. The shops under the arches therein were a range of independent retailers selling a wonderful array of goods from chocolate to jewellery to gifts, and Olivia loved to have a wander and see what she could find.

She had texted her old school friends to let them know she was home for a while, and they'd arranged to meet up at Olivia's favourite coffee shop in the Victorian Market where local artists' work was displayed on the walls and there was a cabinet of hand-made jewellery and artefacts made by local crafters.

After attending the village primary school, Olivia was so grateful to her parents for allowing her to attend a *normal* high school too. Boarding school had been discussed on so many occasions as the best way to finish off her childhood education, but Olivia didn't feel she belonged there. Apart from some bullying issues, she had loved her time at Drumblair Primary School. It didn't seem to matter that she was the child of local dignitaries. She was just Livvy MacBain back then. The teachers had treated her the same as everyone else and she had liked that. When it came to high school applications, she had practically begged her parents to let her attend the high school in Inverness. They had, thankfully, relented under the condition that if she didn't maintain her excellent grades, she would be removed and sent to the boarding school her mother had gone to. Determined not to be sent away, Olivia stuck to her guns and achieved top grades in every subject. Two girls she met at high school orientation, Arabella Douglas and Skye Minto, were also in the top sets and the three had become firm friends from day one. Three was certainly not a crowd where they were concerned.

* * *

When Arabella, aka Bella, and Skye arrived at the coffee shop, the three friends hugged.

'I'm so sorry to hear about your mum, Olivia,' Bella said as they sat at a round table by the window. 'It was such a shock.'

Skye nodded. 'Aye, it was. Freya was such a wonderful woman. My heart broke for you. I know how close you were.'

Olivia fought back tears and squeezed her friends' hands. 'Thank you. I'll let you know the funeral arrangements when they're finalised. My Uncle Innes is just sorting the last few bits out.'

'How's Kerr?' Bella asked with a tilt of her head. 'I imagine he's devastated.' She'd harboured a crush on him since the friends were at high school and they had come to the castle for sleepovers. Apparently, his aloofness had been attractive to a number of her friends; something Olivia struggled to understand, knowing what he was truly like.

Olivia nodded. 'We both are. We just have different ways of showing it, I suppose.' She inhaled a deep, calming breath. 'Anyway, enough of that. Tell me what you've been up to lately. We haven't spoken for ages.'

Skye chewed her lip and glanced around before leaning in and whispering, 'I think Ben is going to propose.'

Olivia and Bella both gasped and let out squeals of excitement before they too glanced around and saw they now had an audience of perturbed café customers. At this, they giggled and returned to their conversation but with *inside* voices.

'So come on, spill it. What makes you think he's going to propose?' Olivia asked, happy to be talking about something positive.

Skye grinned. 'I kind of found a little black velvet box in his coat when I was looking for the car keys.'

Olivia and Bella widened their eyes simultaneously. 'Did you open it?' Bella asked with no less giddiness than before.

Skye cringed and then scrunched her nose. 'No. I got scared and put it straight back.'

Olivia and Bella groaned in unison. 'Oh, Skye! It might have been a pair of earrings or a brooch or something. We could be getting excited over nothing,' Bella said with a harrumph.

Olivia rolled her eyes. 'Ever the optimist, eh, Bella?' She returned her attention to Skye. 'Have there been any other signs?'

Skye's cheeks coloured and she nodded. 'I overheard him booking a table at River House for two weeks on Saturday, and he happened to mention to me that I should keep that Saturday evening free.'

Bella scowled and she appeared to have something to say but was holding back.

'Come on, Bella, out with it.'

She shook her head. 'Pfft... och, it's nothing.'

Skye folded her arms across her chest. 'I know you too well, Arabella Douglas. Come on, I know you've got something to say.'

Bella gnawed at her bottom lip. 'It's just that... Well... have you seen that film with Hugh Grant and Martine McCutcheon?'

Olivia frowned. '*Love Actually*?'

Bella nodded. 'Aye, that's it.'

Skye shrugged. 'I think the whole world and her dog have seen it. Why?'

'Well, there's that bit where Alan Rickman is buying a present for someone and Rowan Atkinson is adding all that fancy stuff to make it look nice, and Alan Rickman is all, "Can you hurry it up, pal?" and then, whatsername finds it in his pocket and it's this gorgeous necklace and she's all "Bloody hell, he never buys me this stuff" so she's dead excited. But when she... you know, erm... the family chooses to open one gift each on Christmas Eve and Emma Thompson – that's her name – asks to open hers because it looks like the box with the necklace in, but it turns out it's actually a Joni Mitchell CD, which means the necklace was for some other woman and she's heartbroken 'cos it means he's probably having an affair. And I never forgave Alan Rickman for doing that to Emma Thompson. She'd already been cheated on by that Shakespeare bloke.' Her words came out in a confusing rush and the other two women stared at her, wide-eyed.

Skye and Olivia both blurted in unison, 'Kenneth Branagh!'

The conversation stopped for a few moments while Skye digested Bella's not so wise words but eventually, now pale and rather wan-looking, she swallowed hard and said, 'Anyway... thanks for that, Bella.'

Bella's cheeks coloured an almost fluorescent shade of pink. She forced a smile, tucked her short blonde hair behind her ears and held out her hands for emphasis. 'I mean, it's just a film.'

Olivia decided to chip in. 'Oh, come on, Skye, don't listen to that rubbish! You and Ben have been together since first year at uni. He absolutely adores you. In fact, I'm surprised he hasn't asked you before now.'

This statement didn't seem to help, and Skye widened her eyes again. 'Shit, maybe Bella's right. Maybe he's going to dump me and take his other woman to River House. Maybe I'm being a total bawbag. Maybe you're right and if he wanted to marry me, he would've have asked before now.'

'That's not what I meant!' Olivia insisted. 'It sounds like he's planning something really special, so give the guy a chance.'

Skye knotted her hands on the table. 'Aye, but what if—'

'I lost my job!' Bella blurted and once again all heads turned to their table.

Olivia and Skye turned to face her. 'What?'

Bella covered her eyes briefly with her hands. 'Sorry. I had to say something to change the subject. I didn't mean to upset you, Skye. I'm just...' She sighed deeply. 'Olivia's right, I'm a pessimist when it comes to love. I've never had a relationship that's lasted long enough for a birthday card, let alone an engagement ring and I need to learn to *haud ma wheesht*. I'm so sorry, Skye.'

'Have you actually lost your job? The one with the PR firm that you've been at for six months?' Olivia asked.

Bella nodded and gave a sad, regretful smile. 'Aye. I made a daft meme and sent it to ma mate. She opened it on her phone and the director saw it over her shoulder while he was standing by her. The timing couldn't have been worse. I was asked to clear my desk and leave the premises. They cited gross misconduct.'

'Oh, no, Bella, that's terrible,' Olivia said, aghast at the story.

'And a bit harsh for a joke,' Skye agreed.

Bella's cheeks returned to their fluorescent pink again and she slunk into her seat. 'Not really. I'd made a joke meme about the director's toupee inviting me out for a drink. I mean, it's got a bloody life of its own, that thing. I'm sure it's alive!'

There was a silent pause and then the three friends burst into fits of laughter as Bella showed Olivia and Skye the meme she had sent. The toupee in the picture had googly eyes and they had to admit it was hilarious but also a disastrous career move.

Olivia reached out and squeezed her arm. 'Something will come up, Bella. You always land on your feet.'

Bella shook her head. 'Well, I'm no' getting a reference from *him*, am I? And there's nothing out there for personal assistants, I know, I've scoured every job site. I might have to just accept whatever I can get now. I might have to move back in with ma folks too.' There was a long pause before Bella continued, 'Oh, good grief, can we change the subject again? So come on, Skye, where would your ideal wedding be?'

* * *

The following day, Olivia walked into Inverness once again, knowing she should really call in on her brother, who lived at the family-owned villa; a grand Victorian detached house in the leafy conservation area of Crown in the city. He had sent several messages summoning her. But before she could face that, she decided to browse the crammed shelves at Leakey's Bookshop. Leakey's was an Aladdin's cave of antiquarian and general second-hand books that had been trading in the city for around four decades from a converted church. She got the same feeling of excitement every time she stepped inside. So many words, so many different lives between the thousands of old, slightly foxed pages.

The walls of the old church were covered in framed antique prints and each level was stocked, floor to ceiling, with every book you could imagine. A spiral staircase joined the two floors and the railings that surrounded the top floor gave the most incredible vantage point to view the place. The stained-glass windows were still in situ and in the centre stood a wood-burning stove that provided the cosy feeling even on a cold day.

Olivia found a book on Victorian fashion and flicked through the beautifully illustrated pages before taking it to the counter and purchasing it to add to her already vast collection. After a little more browsing, she left the sanctuary of the bookshop and paused to text her brother to ensure he was home, and then made her way to Southside Road.

* * *

The stunning nineteenth-century villa that stood back from the road, in an impressive elevated position, had been in the family since before she and Kerr were born. It was, in fact, purchased by her grandparents as a 'crash pad' to use when they were in the city. Olivia found this concept quite ridiculous. This particular 'crash pad' consisted of a large double-fronted building with ten bedrooms and as many ensuites. These days, it was Kerr's home and it had been modernised to his tastes, even though he didn't technically own it. He had butchered some of the period detail and it made Olivia wince when she visited and witnessed the glossy modern kitchen with its high-tech gadgets and abstract artwork. She loved art *and* modern kitchens as much as the next person, but they had their place, and Drumblair Villa was not the house for such things, in her opinion.

At least from the outside nothing much had changed. She climbed the steps to the front door and pressed her finger determinedly on the button for the doorbell, then stepped back and waited.

Much to Olivia's disappointment, Adaira answered the door and almost rugby tackled her into an uncomfortable hug. 'Oh,

Olivia, darling, my sincerest condolences, do come in. Cook is making some tea, so we'll have that in the drawing room.'

Olivia stood there, momentarily confused. 'Cook?' she asked with a slight shake of her head. Kerr had always managed to make his own tea. He was a grown-arsed man living alone, after all.

Adaira smiled. 'I brought my cook from home while I'm staying here for a while. Poor darling Kerr is struggling with the whole situation. I've never seen him so down, poor lamb.' *Ah, okay, that makes sense.* Her brother was playing the wounded orphan and Adaira was lapping it up. Adaira patted her arm. 'You see, you're so much stronger than he is. You moved away, but Kerr has never been able to do that. Always the dedicated son,' she said wistfully, and as if she knew him extremely well – which she absolutely did not.

Dedicated to Mum's bank account, more like, Olivia thought. She resented the fact that Adaira had almost insinuated she wasn't quite as bothered by their mother's passing, but she bit her tongue and smiled sweetly before following the woman into the living room.

When Olivia entered the room, Kerr was standing by the fireplace with his back to her and his head bowed. She felt a small amount of comfort at the fact that this was one of the rooms that had remained true to its period. It reminded her of when Uncle Innes had lived there for a brief time and how much she had always loved to visit him.

Kerr turned quite dramatically, as if he was in some Victorian period drama, and held out his hands. 'Olivia, my dear, dear sister.' *Okay, so I've walked onto the set of* Pride and Prejudice, *have I? I wonder which of us is which.* 'Thank you for coming all this way. We all appreciate it.'

Wondering who the suggested *all* were, she walked towards him and accepted his outstretched hands. 'Of course I came, Kerr.

She was my mother too,' she replied rather indignantly and with a twinge of annoyance inside.

He nodded. 'Of course, of course. We just know that your life is in New York now and this place is behind you. Plus, it's such a long journey.'

Again, bothered by his words, she retorted, 'Again, my mum too.'

Kerr held her at arm's length. 'Why so bitter, Olivia?'

Olivia sighed and closed her eyes briefly before smiling. 'I'm not bitter. I just don't like the insinuations that Mum wasn't as important to me because I moved away. I did so with her blessing and encouragement.'

Again, Kerr nodded and smiled but it all seemed false, forced even. He gave a shrug which indicated what she had said was obvious to him, and that she was wrong in her understanding of his intentions. 'Of course you did.'

A middle-aged woman with her greying hair in a tidy bun, wearing a black dress with a white apron over it, entered the room carrying a tray. On the tray was a fancy china teapot that Olivia surmised must have been Adaira's, and matching cups with saucers, a milk jug and sugar bowl. She silently set it down on the mahogany coffee table and left without speaking. Olivia couldn't help feeling that it was all a little pretentious for two capable, non-working adults to have such an employee. They weren't blooming royalty, for goodness' sake.

'Please, have a seat, won't you?' Adaira said as she sat on one of the brown leather Chesterfield sofas and gestured to the one opposite. Regardless of feeling a little perturbed by her presence and the behaviour that hinted this was not actually Olivia's family home, she did as instructed and Kerr followed suit, sitting beside Adaira.

Olivia waited as Adaira poured weak tea into the cups then lifted hers, simply for something to do with her hands.

'So, you know the funeral details, I take it,' Kerr said as he took a quick sip of his tea and placed it down again.

Olivia nodded. 'Yes... I met with Uncle Innes, and he told me everything. I'm glad it's almost all arranged. I don't think I could've faced that.'

Kerr huffed. 'Yes, I can't say I'm happy at all about Mother's choice of executor. I mean, why *him*?'

Olivia shook her head as it seemed pretty obvious to her. 'He's her brother.'

'*Step*brother,' Kerr sneered. 'They're only related by marriage, which means nothing, if you ask me.'

Olivia sighed; she already knew that Kerr wasn't keen on their uncle. 'Well, it was up to Mum who she chose, so there's no point getting upset about it. And he's been good enough to look after Marley too. I presume you didn't want to take him.'

Olivia was fully aware that Kerr was jealous of the dog. Ridiculous but very true. 'Pfft! Why would I want white hair and mud everywhere? No, thank you. He's welcome to that one thing.'

'Marley is not a thing. He was Mum's beloved companion. And he's not taking it too well, according to Uncle Innes.'

Kerr's face contorted. 'He's a dog, Olivia. Dogs don't have feelings.'

Flabbergasted, Olivia was at a loss for words, so chose not to speak. Kerr continued. 'Oh, I'm sure Innes is all holier-than-thou because of his good deed with that mangy animal. He's used to such things living on that farm. And I bet he loves lording it over us like this. I bet he's thoroughly enjoying the power trip.'

Beginning to regret her visit, Olivia willed herself, once again, to remain calm. 'He lost his sister, Kerr. I'm sure lording anything over anyone is the last thing on his mind.'

Kerr gave a sinister smile. 'Well, I'm only glad that he can't have inherited anything too big. Mum definitely wouldn't have been cruel enough to leave him anything of value that should have been mine... erm, *ours*. And the fact that he's the executor indicates he's not the main beneficiary.'

Olivia knew he was wrong about that; an executor could, in fact, be a beneficiary. Unwilling to hear her beloved uncle berated in his absence any further, Olivia placed her cup and saucer back on the tray. 'Look, Kerr, you asked me to come and visit, so here I am. Please let's not argue about things, okay?'

Kerr opened his mouth as if to protest but Adaira nudged him and frowned when he turned to face her for a moment. It was an unspoken signal of some kind. He took hold of Adaira's hand and turned back to face Olivia. 'Very well. Now, as difficult as this is, we need to discuss the future, Olivia.' Olivia watched as a small smile spread across Adaira's face, like withheld glee. 'Now, I'm sure there will be some provision left to you in the will. I mean, I can't see Mum leaving you with nothing, of course. It may even be that she has left you this old place.' He glanced around the high-ceilinged room and shook his head as if to rid himself of the unpleasant thought. 'But I'm not really sure, as I've been living here for some time now and it will break my heart to let it go.' He paused as if waiting for her to speak. When she didn't, he continued, 'But the main reason I felt we should discuss the future is that I want you to know I intend to make some big changes at Drumblair when I take over.'

Olivia inhaled deeply through her nose with the intention of remaining calm as she spoke. 'Perhaps we should wait until we know what the will document contains. I'm not sure it's appropriate to make such grand plans when we don't know the details. She may have left Drumblair to charity for all we know.'

Kerr gasped. 'She wouldn't do that! Don't be so ridiculous! It's our family home. Our father's ancestral seat. She would never do such a thing.'

Relief flooded Olivia on hearing his vehement response. It was completely unexpected, but at least his reaction indicated his intentions were not to sell the place off.

She decided to humour him. 'Okay, so what changes are you thinking of making?'

He briefly glanced at Adaira and they shared a knowing smile which further irked Olivia. 'Nothing is finalised as yet, but I feel there is definite missed earning potential.'

Uh-oh. I get the feeling I'm not going to like this. Olivia cleared her throat and tried to remain passive. 'How so?'

He shrugged. 'Oh, you know, the land, the cottages. Maybe even the chapel. Chapel conversions are very *en vogue* right now.'

Olivia's temperature began to rise, heating her face, and anger bubbled beneath her skin. She narrowed her eyes at him and held up a finger to halt his words. 'Hang on, you don't mean to sell these buildings off? And you can't sell off the chapel! All of our relatives are buried around there! And the land is farmed already by locals on the family's behalf. You can't just take that away from the people who work the land!'

He crossed his arms over his chest and straightened his spine in apparent defiance. 'Like I said, nothing is finalised. But ultimately, it's my decision.'

She scoffed. 'What happened to "It's our family home, our father's ancestral seat"?'

He scowled and curled his lip. 'You suggested that Mum may have left it all to charity. Why should charity benefit when it's rightfully mine? *I'm* the one who should inherit and benefit, not charity.'

And there you go... Olivia pursed her lips and nodded. 'Oh, I see. I get it. You'd rather sell the place off bit by bit and pocket the cash, while our *ancestral seat* becomes a hotel and spa, rather than a more needy cause, one that our mother supported for example, benefiting from her loss.'

One side of his mouth tilted, and a crease formed between his brows. 'Well, duh! And I think I'm a suitable needy cause, for goodness' sake.'

Olivia stood. 'I knew it was a mistake my coming here. I knew you'd have some half-baked scheme to cash in on our mother's death. My god, Kerr, she's not even in the ground yet and you're planning ways to get rich off of her. It's mercenary, pathetic and totally against anything either Mum or Dad would have wanted. I honestly can't believe you're considering such actions.'

He stood to face her and waved a pointed finger in her direction. '*You* asked about the changes, so what does that say about you?'

Exasperated, she couldn't help raising her voice. 'I presumed you meant replacing the kitchen or updating the heating system like you've done here!'

Kerr's face contorted with incredulity. 'Why would I do all that if I'm going to sell it?'

Olivia widened her eyes, and she stepped back, almost falling onto the sofa again. 'Oh! So now you're selling the castle too?'

Kerr folded his arms once more. 'And what if I am? It has nothing to do with you! You don't even live here in Scotland any more. You swanned off to the US of A to pursue your frock-making dreams! You'd rather be a two-bit seamstress than stay here and look after our poor dying mother!'

Something snapped inside Olivia; she clenched her fists and screamed, 'She wasn't dying! She had a stroke, remember? No one had a clue it was going to happen, Kerr! In fact, it was probably the stress of keeping *you* alive and out of trouble that caused it! And it's about time you dropped this little narrative you've created in your head about being the perfect son and me being the prodigal daughter when it was *clearly* the other way around!' Her chest heaved and her heart pounded at her ribs.

'Get out of my house,' Kerr growled through clenched teeth. Adaira stood, hands on cheeks and eyes wide, just watching the drama unfold.

'Gladly.' Olivia turned and stormed back through the vast hallway where a family portrait hung. She paused to look at it. Her mum and dad sat on the mahogany-framed sofa that still stood in the bowed window of the living room and standing beside them were young adults – Olivia and Kerr – smiling for the artist. Olivia's eyes welled with tears, and she shook her head. 'I'm so sorry, Mum... Dad. I do love you both.' And with those final words, she opened the door and let it close behind her as she left.

2

March continued to wear the same dull and frigid attire as February had donned when it had departed. Even though spring was around the corner, it was as if the trees on the castle estate were holding off displaying their newly sprouted leaves and buds, and the bulbs had waited to bloom out of respect for their dearly departed Lady of Drumblair. Olivia had avoided the castle until the night before the funeral for fear of further arguments with her brother, who would no doubt be around, plotting his takeover. She couldn't stomach watching him planning to deface her childhood home and sell bits off as if it was a car being sold for scrap.

Drumblair Castle was located south-west of the city of Inverness on the shores of Loch Ness, between the villages of Dores and Whitefield. It was a stunning location surrounded by trees and with a backdrop of the loch on one side and an expanse of land to the other which eventually led to a village that shared the castle's name. The castle itself could be accessed by the village and also by General Wade's military road, a network set up in the late 1700s as a way of controlling the locals who had rebelled against the crown alongside the Jacobites.

Olivia remembered going to the loch shore in the summer with her father's handheld telescope and searching for Nessie. She had seen many species of wildlife on her trips but none that she could put hand on heart and confirm as being the so-called monster. She used to picnic down at that same shore with her parents and they would sit by the small chapel and, after much cajoling on Olivia's part, they would regale her with the story of their wedding day; a story she simply never tired of. Such happy times.

The closer Olivia got to home, the more nervous she became. The taxi drove along the tree-lined avenue that led to the castle and Olivia shivered as the majestic building came into view. She paid the driver and as she climbed out of the taxi, a familiar person stood just outside the huge oak doors, waiting to greet her, alongside a majestic cream-coloured dog whose tail wagged a happy rhythm.

Olivia waited as the kind-hearted driver extracted her cases and carried them to the door. Mirren, the housekeeper, pulled Olivia into a warm embrace and her eyes began to well once more as Marley nuzzled her hand, licking at her and whimpering.

'Welcome home, Olivia dear. We've all missed you. I asked Innes to bring Marley home so you could see him,' Mirren told her. 'And I'm so very sorry you found out about your mother the way you did. I was so cross with Kerr.' Mirren had been with the family ever since Kerr was a baby and was originally taken on as his nanny, but her role had evolved over the years, meaning she knew the house inside and out. She was like part of the family after all this time and Olivia adored her.

Olivia sniffed and dabbed at her eyes. 'It's not your fault, please don't worry. I'm used to him after all these years.' She crouched and buried her face in Marley's fur. 'Oh, Marley, I've missed you so much, you poor, poor love. This must all be so strange for you.'

She pulled back and looked at his sweet face and oddly pink nose, then into his eyes. 'We'll make sure you're okay, don't you worry.' Her mind whirred with ideas as to what she could do to take Marley back to New York. She would have to really think it through, and consult with Harper, of course. And check their lease. But the last thing she would do was abandon her mum's beloved friend.

Mirren patted her shoulder. 'Come on in, love. I've just made cocoa, your favourite,' Mirren said as she picked up one bag and Olivia lifted the other one. She followed Mirren into the hallway and inhaled the familiar smell of wood polish and smoke. The vase on the huge round table in the centre of the hallway was filled with an array of coloured roses, her mother's favourite, and as she stepped closer, she closed her eyes to inhale their sweet scent as memories flooded her mind and filled her with emotion.

'You pop on up to your bedroom with your things and I'll reheat the cocoa,' Mirren said with a sad smile.

Olivia picked up her bags and climbed the vast curving stair-case to the first floor, closely followed by Marley, panting as he stuck, limpet-like, to her leg. She paused when her phone pinged. She quickly turned her wrist to check her watch and saw a text message from Harper:

I'm sooo jetlagged! But I made it and I'm all checked into your room at the Glenmoriston. Thanks for keeping it on for me, it's gorgeous. I'm heading to the Brasserie for dinner and then of course the Piano Bar. Cab arranged through hotel reception so I will be with you after break-fast tomorrow. Love ya. H. 🩶

Olivia smiled, happy that she would have someone here to support her, seeing as her brother probably wouldn't. She made her way up to the second floor, past several closed doors and on to her bedroom. After placing her bags down, she closed her eyes and held the door latch for a few moments, summoning up the courage to enter, knowing there would be no little welcome message on her pillow from her mum.

She glanced down at the dog, whose eyes were fixed firmly on her, as if willing her forward. 'We can do this, Marls. We can.'

When she finally entered, she felt a certain amount of stress vacate her body. Home had always had that effect on her, like a magic elixir to eliminate worry and anything that might have been preying on her mind. Even though there was sadness mingled in with her emotions today, and she didn't technically live here any more, it still felt like home. Marley wandered over and took his favourite spot on the rug at the end of the bed and gave a deep sigh as he laid down.

Being back at Drumblair was strange, though, to say the least. It was as if her room had remained in a time warp. It was both oddly comforting and a little disconcerting too that it had been pretty much untouched since she had lived there as a teenager. Back then, she'd been obsessed with an eclectic mix of fashion icons: Vivienne Westwood, Alexander McQueen and Coco Chanel. Posters of slender, overly made-up models wearing quirky outfits she could only aspire to design covered the pale blue walls. In days gone by, she had stared for hours at these statuesque people, who were almost otherworldly in her humble opinion. And as much as she adored the designs, it was her dream to design for every frame size, not just those who could span their waist with their fingers.

A small selection of her own designs were pinned to the notice board above her oak desk, and she could remember drawing each and every single one with passion and excitement. Looking at them now, she was amused at how simple and naïve they appeared, with the exception of one dress. This dress was designed with the family tartan in mind and was subtle and elegant, with a fitted bodice and fit and flare skirt; timeless and simple. She'd often dreamed of having it made up but had never had the connections. Well, not until now, anyway. But she couldn't help thinking that it still wasn't in the league of Nina Picarro.

She left her own room and glanced along the hallway to the opposite side of the corridor. Inhaling a deep breath, she made her way to her mother's bedroom and, once again, paused outside the door. Marley appeared beside her and wagged his tail, as if he was expecting to go inside to greet his owner. This broke Olivia's heart and tears escaped her eyes to leave damp trails down her cheeks.

Once inside the room, Olivia walked over to the window and looked out. Her mother's room had a view of the grounds, down to the chapel and the loch beyond. The water was still and the sky grey. She turned and for a moment watched Marley as he wandered around, sniffing and searching. Olivia wiped at her wet face as she observed the poor dog in his confused state. She perched on the edge of the bed and called the dog. Marley sat in front of her and placed his paw on her leg, he was a sensitive soul.

She stroked his head. 'She's gone, my lovely boy. I'm so sorry.' As if understanding the words, Marley whimpered again and lay down at her feet.

The room still smelled of her mother's favourite Chanel perfume and her make-up and hairbrushes were still laid out on her dressing table as if she was due to return at any moment.

If only she was.

* * *

Once freshened up in her own room, Olivia made her way down the stairs with Marley, to the vast kitchen, where Mirren sat at one end of the battered old pine table. The fire was roaring, and two mugs of delicious-smelling cocoa sat on saucers. The deep, bitter chocolatey aroma made her mouth water and brought back memories of post-hockey match drinks lifted by pink, tingling fingers that had just begun to gain their feeling again.

Marley made himself comfy on his bed in front of the fire and Mirren smiled over at her. 'Come and get warmed up, love,' she told her with a smile. 'And tell me all you've been up to since I saw you last April.'

Olivia explained all about the fashion show and how her designs had been featured and that there was a chance she was going to be offered her dream job when she returned to New York.

Mirren was delighted. 'Your mother would be so proud of you. In fact, she was. Often told me so.' She paused and smiled as she reminisced. 'Aye, Freya was glad you left this place. Sad at the same time, of course, her only daughter was moving away but she knew this wasn't where you needed to be. Not back then, anyway.'

There was another moment of silence when the only noise that could be heard was the crackling of logs in the open fire and the snoring of a sleeping canine.

Olivia soaked up the atmosphere of home. 'I wish I had come home for Christmas,' she said with a trembling chin. 'It was the first one I've missed, and I knew I would regret it. I just didn't know why.'

Mirren reached across the table, a futile exercise as her arms were not long enough for her fingers to make contact, but the gesture didn't go unnoticed. 'Hey, don't do that, my love. Don't start beating yourself up for things you can't change. And anyway, your mum was absolutely fine with us boring staff. We had a right old knees-up.' She chuckled.

Olivia grinned and wiped away a few escaped tears. 'Aye, so I heard. Apparently, Dougie was playing the guitar and the rest of you were singing carols on Christmas night. Mum said the more wine that was drunk, the more the lyrics were being made up!'

Mirren laughed wholeheartedly. 'Och, aye! Tam, bless him, was singing something about "Round John Bergin's mother and child". We were all in hysterics when we asked him who Round John Bergin was and he said that was John from the bible's full name and couldn't understand why the rest of us didn't know!'

'Oh, yes, I heard all about the halls being decked with bras of holly!'

'Yes, that was Celia, Tam's wife! Honestly, they were cut from the same cloth, those two. I mean, *bras of holly*? Have you ever heard such a thing?' Her mirth disappeared. 'They were such an integral part of the team, the pair of them, and the other gardeners.'

'What do you mean *were*?' Olivia asked.

Mirren fidgeted with her mug. 'I'm afraid...' she began but stopped. 'I don't know whether it's my place to say but...'

'Go on, Mirren, it's fine,' Olivia encouraged her.

'Kerr fired most of the gardening team just after your mother passed. I think we all thought it was a knee-jerk reaction because the gardens were her pride and joy, and I got the sense he was angry at her for dying. But...' She shrugged and stared into the dark liquid in her mug. 'He kept to his decision and Dougie's been left to look after the grounds on his own. Well... he *had* been.'

Olivia swallowed hard. 'That's ridiculous! Why would he do such a thing? Is he planning on doing the gardening himself? All two thousand acres?' It was a rhetorical question to which she already knew the answer. 'I can't believe he's begun making his changes already. I thought he might have the decency and respect to wait until after the funeral.'

Mirren nodded. 'Aye, but you know your brother. Not the most patient, nor cooperative, of men.'

'You said Dougie *had* been left to the work. Past tense? Does that mean Kerr has hired someone else?'

'Not exactly. Dougie's son, Brodie, you may remember him from when you were wee. He went off to Edinburgh to live with his mother after she divorced Dougie years ago. He's come back to help out.'

A cold shiver traversed Olivia's spine. She remembered Brodie MacLeod quite well, thank you very much. He was a spotty, annoying teenager, one year older than her at fifteen when she had last seen him. Although she'd actually had a huge, secret, plaguing crush on him until the bullying started. She had towered above him by several inches back then but that hadn't stopped him from picking on her. It hadn't always been like that but at high school he picked on her height and called her names, making fun of her long legs and naturally curly hair. Not to mention her buck teeth. *Goofy Muckle Shanks*, that was it, that was his insulting name of choice, amongst others.

These days, obviously she'd stopped growing, meaning she was no longer spindly, had her teeth fixed and her hair was always smooth and styled perfectly, but she still shuddered as she recalled how embarrassed she had been when Brodie had called her the horrible nickname in front of his school friends. They had howled with laughter and egged him on. They had all thrown leaves and fallen branches at her and made comments insinuating that she could eat the ones from the tops of the trees like all the other giraffes. Then they had guffawed hysterically when they asked if *that's* how she had got such wild hair, by catching the power lines as she ate the top leaves.

Looking back, she knew it could have been so much worse, but at the time it was devastating and so humiliating for her as an already awkward teenager, especially when she dreamed about holding hands with Brodie and being his girlfriend one day. Realising that day would never come had broken her teenage heart. He'd been her first – completely unrequited – love. He'd always been a good-looking boy, despite the teenage acne. She could easily look past that. They had pretty much grown up together and had been such good friends at first. But after the name calling and the way he'd dismissed her friendship when he'd reached fifteen, she had been relieved when he had moved away to Edinburgh with his mother. And now here she was, in the present, wondering why on earth he had chosen to return to this remote, isolated and quiet place when he had been in the country's capital city surrounded by shops, bars and fun. *Why would anyone with no real connection choose to be here, in a place like this?* The concept baffled her. *There must be a serious reason for his return. Maybe he lost his job or his marriage – if he had one – has broken down. If he treated his wife the way he used to treat others, there's no wonder!*

In the back of her mind was the familiar feeling of dread that she would no doubt bump into Brodie during her stay here. *Because that's all this is; a temporary stay*, she hastily reminded herself. There was nothing permanent about this visit. She had a dream career to return to in the Big Apple and nothing was going to stop her.

Realising she hadn't responded to Mirren, Olivia nodded her head. 'Oh, I see,' was all she managed to reply.

'Aye, bless the lad for offering to come back like that and for no pay. Dougie *couldnae* have coped for much longer. He's no getting any younger.'

'So, he did come back by *choice*? Brodie, I mean?'

'Aye, mainly to help his dad. He was fair worried about him.'

'And he's not getting paid?'

'Not a bean. Just shows the kind of man he is now, eh?'

'Indeed,' Olivia replied without much conviction. *Good grief, does this mean he's acquired some compassion in his twenties,* she thought?

She heard a voice coming from the main hall, a one-way phone conversation with a familiar snippy tone, and the hairs on the back of her neck stood on end.

Kerr.

Her stubborn, selfish brother hadn't been in touch since their argument, but Olivia had made no attempt to contact him either. No doubt he'd had imaginary business to attend to – could ruining people's lives be classed as a business? She wondered how many more people he intended to fire. She knew one thing with absolute certainty: if he attempted to let Mirren go, there would be hell to pay. She would simply not allow it. How could she? His desire to radically change their family home was anathema to her. She knew she could protest as vehemently as she liked but ultimately would have no say and this broke her already fractured heart. But the one thing she would put her foot down over would be Mirren.

Kerr appeared in the doorway of the kitchen. 'Something smells good, Mirry – oh! I didn't know you'd arrived.' His eyes widened as they alighted on Olivia and his cheeks coloured pink. 'When did you get here?'

'About an hour ago,' Olivia replied curtly in light of all the new information. 'Adaira not with you?'

He cleared his throat, 'No... no, she's getting her driver to bring her tomorrow morning.'

Driver? Cook? The life this woman leads. I wonder if she can dress herself. 'Oh, right.'

'Oh, I see the dog is back,' he said without hiding his disdain.

Olivia was, as usual, annoyed at his choice of words. 'Yes, Marley is home. I wanted to see him.'

Kerr grunted. 'And isn't that Yankee friend of yours coming over?' he asked with a disinterested tone and a scratch to his head.

'Harper is American and yes, she arrived today. She's getting a cab here in the morning.' She added in a mumble, 'Like normal people.'

He ignored her dig. 'Right. Right. Well, I'll be off up to my room. There's a film I want to watch so...' He turned and left the room and Olivia quickly got up and dashed after him, closely followed by Marley, who had evidently become her shadow and guardian.

'Kerr, hang on a minute, please.'

He huffed and turned. 'What now?'

'Mirren told me you've fired most of the gardeners.'

He curled his lip and shook his head. 'Yeah, so?'

'What happened to waiting for the will reading before any drastic changes were made?'

He pointed an index finger at her. '*You* said that. Not me. And as I said back then, it's nothing to do with you. I'm the rightful heir. My place, my decisions.'

'Who else are you planning to fire? And if you say Mirren, there will be serious trouble, just so you know.'

A sinister grin appeared on his face. 'You really are full of your own self-importance, aren't you, Olivia?'

Olivia scoffed. 'Have you looked in a mirror lately?'

With the grin fixed in place, he replied. 'Oh, I have, and I saw a wealthy, happy, problem-free man.' He held out his hands to exaggerate his point.

Olivia's heart pounded in her chest, and she folded her arms to cover it in case he could tell. 'So... Mirren?'

Kerr made a zipping gesture across his lips and threw away an invisible key before jogging away and up the stairs, chuckling to himself like some ridiculous movie villain.

Olivia growled and clenched her fists. She glanced down at Marley and mumbled, 'Is it entirely wrong to almost hate your own brother?'

* * *

When Mirren had retired for the evening, Olivia and Marley wandered around the ground floor. The stone-flagged corridors were cold, and she wrapped her arms tighter around her body. The castle was more of a mansion house these days with the modernisations that had taken place over the years, but the draughty passageways that linked the house together, like arteries, still held that stark, spooky atmosphere that used to freak her out as a child. More old paintings adorned the walls here except this time they were landscapes and seascapes with the odd portrait of a distant ancestor; mostly oil on canvas and by renowned Scottish artists such as McTaggart, Raeburn and Gillies.

She wandered a little further and opened the large oak door that led to the drawing room, the room they had used most as a family when she was young; the room where the huge Christmas tree had always been placed, surrounded by myriad gold and red-wrapped gifts.

The fire in the grate was still roaring and Marley wandered over to lie down in front of it. It was always that way ever since Olivia could remember. Mirren, or one of the other staff, would check on it regularly to ensure it didn't die out until everyone had gone to bed. A family portrait hung above the carved stone fireplace and in this one she was around eight and Kerr had just become a teenager. She remembered sitting for the photographs that were to be used by the artist and how Kerr kept pulling silly faces to annoy the photographer. Dad had grounded him for his exploits on that particular day, and had made the mistake of uttering the words, 'Why can't you be more like Olivia? Anyone would think she was the older of the two of you with the way you behave.' He hadn't meant anything bad by it, not really, but it evidently hadn't helped her relationship with her brother.

The squashy burgundy velour sofas were still either side of the fireplace and two comfy chairs formed the bottom of the U-shaped arrangement, with a rosewood coffee table in the middle. A huge glass chandelier hung in the centre of the ceiling from a carved rose. Despite the size of the room, it felt cosy and warm, inviting and welcoming, even. Olivia poured herself a glass of single malt from a decanter on the William Trotter sideboard and wandered across to look at the family photographs that adorned the top of the grand piano at the other end of the vast room. Another trip down Memory Lane.

Ornate framed photographs of her grandparents and great-grandparents sat amongst photos of Kerr and Olivia as children. Her brother's mop of unruly red hair stood out so vividly, as did his wide boyish grin. She wondered when he had changed and became so bitter. There was a photograph of her mum and dad on their wedding day as they stood under an arch of flowers outside the chapel by the lake; they both looked so in love and deliriously happy. For a brief moment, she envied their relationship. It was something she aspired to have for herself one day. But up to now, the L word had completely eluded her. She'd had relationships, flings, dalliances but nothing that ever got to the point where she could see a future and that made her a little sad.

Her most recent relationship had been with a New Yorker named Darius. He was ridiculously handsome, swarthy and always smelled amazing. She met him at the bar he was working in when they were on a staff night out. He wanted to be a model and it turned out he had only asked her out because he thought she might be able to help him get a job modelling for Nina. As Harper later said, 'If something or someone appears too good to be true, it's probably because, in reality, they're a lying piece of shit.' How right she was and how clear hindsight was too.

The final straw had come when she had discovered Darius in her bathroom having a conversation on his cell phone in a stupid pseudo-sexy voice, whilst staring at his reflection. He gave what she guessed he thought was a cute chuckle. 'So yeah, babe, I'm thinking of saying something like, "So, gorgeous, how about you hook me up with your lady Nina Piccolo, huh?" What? Well, I have to sweeten her up somehow, baby. But yes, you're my one and only boo. Do you think I'm sexy enough to be a male model, huh, baby?' Another sickly chuckle. 'You do, huh? Well, let's hope she goes for it. Your man could soon be a Nina Piccolo model.' She watched through a crack in the door as he licked his lips and blew a kiss at himself, then bit his lip and chucked his chin. My god did he love himself.

It was embarrassing to watch, and Olivia couldn't help herself, she flung open the door and he almost jumped out of his skin, dropped his phone in the toilet and stood there, staring at her in shock. The cogs were clearly turning as he tried to concoct an explanation, but she wasn't stupid, and she wouldn't fall for his bull crap any longer.

She folded her arms across her chest and said, as snidely as possible, 'It's *Picarro* actually. I think you'll find a Piccolo is a small instrument, rather like what you keep in your excruciatingly tight trousers. Seriously, they are obscene. And Nina wouldn't touch you or your fake tan with a barge pole. Now I suggest you get dressed and get out of my apartment.'

She had watched as he proceeded to reach into the toilet to retrieve his phone, open and close his mouth several times as she simply glared at him, and eventually he had mumbled something about her being an ugly ass bitch anyway, gathered his clothes and stormed out of her flat.

At twenty-eight, she was still relatively young, but having someone to hold her at night would have been wonderful since her mother had passed away. Night-time was always the worst part of her day. Her mind would wander and tell her things that deep down she knew were wrong, like she should have come home more often, or in fact she never should have left at all.

* * *

Shuddering at the memories, she made her way to sit by the fire and sipped at her drink. Marley stirred and relocated himself to lie on her feet. She wasn't a whisky drinker usually, but the smell reminded her of her dad. The heat as she swallowed the drink warmed her from the inside and she smiled. She remembered the first time she had tried it. It had been New Year's Eve when she was seventeen and her parents were hosting a charity ball at the castle.

The ball was held in the long gallery, her father's favourite room in the house. It had been a Georgian addition and was long and vast. At the centre of the plaster-moulded ceiling was a glazed, domed cupola that bounced natural daylight down into the room without shining directly onto the paintings, for their protection. The gallery spread across the back section of the castle and housed her parents' most treasured pieces of artwork, and the family heirloom pieces. It was opulent and beautiful, with sparse seating affording plenty of space for dancing. There was a humongous marble fireplace to one side and a large floor-to-ceiling window to the opposite side that had spectacular views over the grounds, down to the loch and the chapel. It really was the perfect space for parties but on most years prior to this one, Olivia had been sent to bed early and had missed most of the festivities.

On this particular occasion, however, Olivia was allowed to attend the whole shebang and she had worn a navy-blue velvet ball gown with a MacBain tartan sash; she had felt very grown up. Twenty-two-year-old Kerr was already quite drunk and flirting with several of the catering staff who had been brought in for the event. He had to be escorted to his room eventually as he was embarrassing them, himself and Dad. Dad was drinking single malt from a cut crystal glass and chuntering about Kerr's behaviour when Olivia joined him and linked her arm through his.

'I don't think I'm ever going to get drunk,' she had told her father.

He had laughed and shook his head. 'Oh, I've heard that before, Lolly. And I'm afraid I won't be holding my breath on the matter.'

Olivia had gasped in horror. 'No, Dad, I really and truly mean it. I don't like the idea of acting silly and not remembering what I've said to people. It's so embarrassing. I like a glass of wine with dinner, of course, but nothing else.'

With a glint in his eye, her father had handed her his glass. 'Here, see what you make of this. It's a wonderful 1984 Glenfarclas. Very smooth. It has hints of chestnut and pear.'

She had tentatively taken the glass and inhaled the aroma first. She couldn't smell pear, but she could smell *very* strong alcohol. With a turned-up nose, she lifted the glass to her lips and took a sip, swallowed and immediately coughed as it burned the back of her throat. 'Eeeuw, Dad! That's disgusting! It's like drinking petrol or something.'

Her dad had thrown his head back and laughed. 'Whisky is wonderful, take it from a man who knows, especially this one, it's one of the best! But maybe for you it's an acquired taste, eh?' He had nudged her playfully and she had made a very unladylike noise as she shivered.

'Bleurgh! Not a taste I'll be purposefully acquiring, thank you very much!'

Funnily enough, the following Christmas she had drunk the same spirit with her father again as they watched the Queen's Speech and she had rather enjoyed it with a splash of water.

This room was so central to Christmas; the tree was always taken from the grounds and each year one was planted in its place. The pines from the Drumblair grounds had the freshest scent; the fragrance that was the epitome of the festive season as far as Olivia was concerned. It was always traditionally decked in rich red and gold decorations, as well as plenty of the family tartan which was, fortunately, red and green with a hint of white.

Christmas was the one time they all seemed to get on, even her and Kerr. He had bought her some very thoughtful gifts over the years, her favourite being a sterling silver thistle pendant that she had worn for many years. She had so many wonderful memories of her mother sitting at the piano as the rest of the family stood and sang carols. Her mother had had a delightful singing voice and Olivia had loved to listen to her. In fact, she'd often found herself leaning on the piano and just watching her mother play, candlelight glinting in her eyes and a huge smile on her face.

What she would give to see that again.

She left her glass and the drawing room. Thinking about the New Year ball had sparked a need to see the long gallery again, so, along with her companion, she meandered to the back of the castle and pushed through the doors. She flicked on the wall sconces and peered around the once vibrant space. The furniture in here was now covered with dust sheets and the large expanse felt cold. It had clearly been unused for a long while. She struggled to remember the last time there had been a party in here and that saddened her. It had always been such fun to see the place come alive with the splendour and pageantry of the glamorous gowns and the kilts in every clan tartan she could name.

There were still paintings on the walls, although there were gaps where some of the more valuable paintings used to be, and some of the pieces of furniture she had been used to seeing were no longer there; another remnant of her mother's attempts to bail out her brother. A wave of anger washed over her, and she gritted her teeth as she walked out of the room. Her father would have been heartbroken to see the place now. It was as if the heart had been ripped out of it. And all for someone who was ungrateful, greedy and narcissistic.

3

On the morning of the funeral, a mist hung low over the estate grounds that matched Olivia's mood. She stood at her bedroom window as she had done on many occasions before, looking out and watching the deer foraging in the expansive grounds. For most of the year, they stuck to single-sex groups, with the does taking the parenting role over the fawns; however, her favourite time of year was rutting season. Between September and November, there was something ethereal about seeing the fully grown, handsome, majestic stags with antlers poised aloft like strong branches and noses to the breeze as they acted as sentries for the weaker of their herd, or put on displays of bravery to attract the females. This view from her window was a sight she had always loved, but here, on a cold March day, the melancholy it brought, knowing she couldn't share it with her mother, almost made her want to turn away.

When she was a teenager, Olivia and her mum had often sat drinking their first cup of tea of the day on the small balcony outside Olivia's room, watching the young fawns gambolling around in the wooded copse that edged the south of the land, as the sun rose, casting a golden glow over the fields. 'You really do have the best view of the deer, don't you, darling?' her mother had often said. Now, these precious memories were a double-edged sword.

Being back in Scotland under these circumstances wasn't at all what Olivia had wanted. She had anticipated the next time she would visit would be for her birthday in April when the castle grounds would be a sea of bright, cheery yellow daffodils and dusky purple hyacinths, the scent heady and the spring sunshine bringing everything to life once again after the deep winter sleep. She always came home around her birthday and her mother would make a huge fuss of her, much to her jealous brother's chagrin. This year's birthday would be so very different.

She showered and dressed in her black Nina Picarro Peter Pan-collared shift dress with the black diamante rose on the left collar that had been added in memory of Lady Freya MacBain. Nina had gifted it to her for the funeral, insisting it was one less thing for her to worry about. She stood before her full-length mirror and smoothed down the fabric over the curve of her hips. She was no longer a scrawny, gangly teen, that was for sure. Her brown hair, now highlighted with blonde, was neatly tied in a chignon to the right side of her neck and her make-up was, of course, minimal. She didn't much feel like wearing make-up, but she was determined to look smart and presentable and to cover the dark circles that had become a feature of her face lately.

There was a knock at her bedroom door, and she called for them to enter.

'Hello, my love,' Mirren said. 'Harper is here. I brought her straight up; I hope that's okay.'

Olivia turned to face Mirren and smiled warmly. 'Of course. Thank you. Oh, and what's happening with Marley while we're at the funeral?'

'Don't worry, he's staying here in the kitchen in his favourite spot. I didn't think it was wise having him wandering around, knowing how much he sheds, bless him.'

Olivia had the urge to hug the dog tight, bury her face in his fur and forget that today was the day she would say a final goodbye to her wonderful mum. 'Right, yes, fair point.'

Mirren nodded. 'I'll leave you to it. And... you look beautiful. You're the image of your mother,' she said with a distinct wobble of emotion to her voice.

Olivia choked back tears and simply nodded her thanks before reaching for her handkerchief and dabbing at her eyes.

Mirren left and Harper walked in and right up to Olivia, enveloping her in an embrace and allowing Olivia to cry.

When her tears had subsided, Olivia pulled back and fixed her focus on her best friend. 'Thank you so much for coming. It means so much for me to have such a wonderful friend in my life.'

Harper dabbed at her own eyes. 'No thanks needed. We're sisters from another mister, remember? You'd do the same for me. And Mirren was right, you do look beautiful. And you do look just like Lady Freya. I've never noticed how much until now.'

Olivia looked back at her reflection and for the first time she saw the similarities too. She touched her face and smiled. 'I always saw myself as so very plain.'

Harper placed a hand on each shoulder and leaned her chin on Olivia's shoulder as she too addressed their reflections. 'Absolutely not. You're a true beauty. Both inside and out. That's why I love you, anyway... The inside part. You have such a kind spirit and I know you get that from both your parents, but when I look at you now, I see your mom's eyes and smile.'

Olivia took great comfort from Harper's words and the two friends sat on the bed for a while to catch up.

* * *

Later, standing at the graveside, Harper squeezed Olivia's hand reassuringly as they took their places before the other mourners; some other family members, staff and friends. There were not as many people there as there could have been, but Freya had insisted her funeral be an intimate affair, just for those she was close to. Innes stood to the other side of Olivia and rested his hand on her shoulder reassuringly. She glanced over her shoulder and saw Bella and Skye standing together, arms linked, before turning her focus back on the gaping hole in the soil that matched the one in her heart. The vicar's solemn words didn't really register in Olivia's brain as she watched her mother's coffin being lowered into the cold, hard ground. The one saving grace for her was that her parents were now reunited in the family plot at the Drumblair estate cemetery, and in the beyond, wherever that might be.

The chapel's location on the periphery of the grounds of the castle, by the lake, made for a peaceful and tranquil setting. Members of the MacBain family had been wed, baptised and laid to rest there since the castle's construction in the fifteenth century. Remembering Kerr's insinuation that the chapel would make a great conversion to residential use made Olivia baulk. She hoped he would soon realise he could do no such thing when their own parents were laid to rest there.

These days, the grounds of both the castle and the chapel were carefully maintained by the long-serving head gardener Dougie, and his intrepid team, well, before Kerr saw fit to sack most of them, anyway. It was a strange thing to comprehend but the cemetery really was beautiful, and the team of committed workers, the majority of whom were thankfully in attendance despite her brother's protestations, were the sole reason for that. Mirren stood just behind her, with Dougie, relentless tears streaming down her face.

The small stone-built chapel was where Olivia's parents had been blessed in an intimate service after their larger, more formal wedding ceremony at Inverness Cathedral. The photos from the picturesque chapel had always made Olivia think of a fairy-tale wedding and she couldn't understand why it didn't have the same effect on her brother. He clearly had a swinging pound sign where his heart should be.

Although not particularly large in stature, the chapel structure was imposing with its large square turrets at each corner and the clock tower at one end, whose clock hadn't worked since before she was born. Olivia's favourite thing was the arched stained-glass window that caught the sun's rays no matter the season and cast coloured shards of light across the stone floor; something she remembered being distracted by as a child when they attended services for Easter, harvest festival and Christmas.

Kerr was, of course, accompanied to the funeral service by Adaira. Their relationship confused Olivia. Now that their mother had passed away and Kerr was to inherit, he no longer needed her money. This made her wonder if Adaira was, in fact, the hanger on. Perhaps she was after Kerr's money. It would certainly be a first. Despite their lack of nuptials, the glamorous woman with her perfectly coiffed platinum-blonde, Marilyn-esque hair and ruby red lips played the part of a dutiful wife, linking her arm through his, passing him handkerchiefs and rubbing his arm whilst gazing up at him with an almost patronising, piteous stare.

Regardless of his attempts to hide it, the little silver hip flask that had once belonged to their father glinted every time Kerr removed it from the inside pocket of his long black overcoat to take a sip. Evidently noticing Olivia's disapproving glances, Adaira had whispered to her that he needed the Dutch courage to face the horrific truth that his mother was being laid to rest. Everything that woman said was beginning to grate on Olivia and she couldn't help wondering if Kerr's tears were more self-pity than grief, but she berated herself silently for such cruel thoughts. They had *both* just lost their mother, after all. It wasn't a grief that belonged to Olivia alone. And even though Kerr had a tendency to emanate a hard, cold, selfish and unfeeling façade, surely he couldn't deny a deep sense of regret, pain and grief? Even if he was only admitting it to himself.

* * *

The walk back to the castle for the wake after the service wasn't a particularly long one but the biting cold of the Highland air seeped into Olivia's bones as she wrapped her scarf tighter around her neck. Most people walked the gravel path in silence and those who did speak only did so in respectful whispers. The crunching sound of the tiny stones underfoot was, at times, almost deafening.

'Are you doing okay?' Harper asked in a low voice as she squeezed her arm. 'I mean, I know that's a dumb question...'

Olivia turned her face and smiled. 'Thank you again for coming over here to be with me. I couldn't have faced it alone.'

Harper nodded. 'Absolutely. And I know you could have. You can face anything. You moved to the States alone, remember?'

'But I'm better with you here,' Olivia insisted.

They arrived outside the lofty, some might say intimidating, castle building and Olivia stopped to peer upwards. Unlike many castles which displayed a kind of pleasing symmetry, Drumblair had been added to over the years, meaning it now displayed a hotch-potch of parts that surrounded the central, and original, peel tower. The main entrance was arched like a typical portcullis; however, signs of the original metal fortified gate were long gone.

But this was her home and regardless of its imperfections, she still loved it dearly.

As everyone else made their way inside, Harper nudged her gently. '*Are* you okay?'

Olivia nodded. 'I just... I think I need a minute if that's okay?'

Harper hugged her. 'Sure thing. I'll see you inside when you're ready.' She kissed Olivia's cheek and followed the rest of the guests in through the large, ornately carved wooden doors.

Mirren had organised an outside catering company to provide a buffet and staff in the great hall for their return, but Olivia wasn't ready to go inside and deal with people's inevitable condolences yet. She peered up at the exterior stone walls of the immense castle that she had once called home, and immeasurable sadness washed over her, as she recalled many happy hours playing in the long stone corridors and outside in the extensive grounds amongst the trees and walkways. The walled garden to the left of the main building had always been her favourite and she had spent many happy hours as a child pretending to be Mary Lennox from her favourite childhood book, *The Secret Garden*, although deeming herself perhaps less self-centred and mean than the spoiled main character. She wondered what the walled garden looked like now and decided she would take a look whilst she was here.

Eventually, when the bitter March chill became too much, Olivia stepped inside the castle. The decision to stay at her favourite hotel in Inverness prior to the funeral had been a strange one, but necessary. She couldn't bear the thought of returning to Drumblair knowing her mother wouldn't be here to greet her with open arms and hugs. At least today there would be other people around. She wouldn't have the time to be reminded of how both her parents had passed away before she even reached thirty. She wouldn't have a moment to acknowledge the sheer agony of walking through her family home knowing that there was no family left living here.

She glanced up at the deer antlers mounted on the walls that stretched skywards. She had never liked the thought of killing things for sport, let alone mounting the trophies on the walls of her home, and her father had, thankfully, been of the same mind. The antlers mounted here were those naturally shed by the herd in their grounds; their former owners had always simply been for admiring. Sadly, however, hunting had been a tradition that her ancestors had partaken of for many years and there were a couple of stags' heads remaining on the walls in other parts of the house. Her father had insisted on keeping them as a stark reminder of the past and how not to behave in the future.

She moved her focus onto the oil paintings of her predecessors. The familiarity of the faces glaring seriously from their respective canvases reminded her of endless, nerve-racking games of hide and seek. Back then, when their relationship had been a little better, Kerr always told her she could never really hide from him because the paintings told him where she was. For a long while, she was terrified of the paintings, especially at night when she would dash past them with her eyes scrunched tight. But then she remembered learning about the people displayed there from her father when he would proudly wax lyrical about their exploits and involvement in the Jacobite uprising and she realised they couldn't, nor would they choose to, do her harm now.

Her favourite story had been the one about Bonnie Prince Charlie. Legend had it that the young chevalier had been hidden in Drumblair Castle for some time prior to launching his rebellion at Glenfinnan in 1745. She had always tried to imagine the would-be monarch walking through the castle's rooms and sitting before the fire in what they now called the drawing room. She had often wondered what he'd thought of the place. She knew that when he'd been here, there had been secret meetings and plotting a-plenty and she knew the walls must have soaked up so much history that her heart shuddered when she thought of the place being stripped from her family.

4

As she walked into the great hall, Olivia removed her long black
overcoat and a young man she didn't recognise, but presumed was
part of the catering crew, took it from her with a single officious
nod. She made her way towards the huge oak table where the
other mourners had gathered and was greeted by her Uncle Innes.
Olivia had always adored the kind-hearted man. Kerr's own
twisted opinions were something Olivia refused to acknowledge.

Innes kissed her on both cheeks. 'Olivia, darling, how are you
holding up?' Olivia's chin trembled and before she could speak, he
pulled her into his arms and held her. 'I know, I know,' he said as
his own voice cracked. 'Shhh, it's okay. You still have me, you know,
and I'll always be here for you.'

Olivia leaned back and tilted her chin up to look at the grey-
haired man with the kindest eyes she had ever encountered.
'Thank you. That means the world to me.'

He cupped her cheek and smiled. 'I'm so sorry you're going
through this. But you're not alone, okay?' His nostrils flared and he
clenched his jaw briefly before continuing, 'I know you have Kerr
but... well, as I said, you have me.'

There certainly was no love lost between Kerr and Innes. Innes was very much aware of the pain and suffering Kerr had caused to his beloved sister Freya in years past and had stepped in to defend and advise her on more occasions than should have been necessary. Kerr had taken this as Innes trying to get his hands on their mother's wealth. Of course, the truth of it was Kerr's gambling and crazy money-making schemes could have ruined their mother if not for Innes, who seemed to be the only one who could convince her to stop and think about how much she was prepared to dig him out of his messes. It was no surprise that Kerr had an inherent dislike of their uncle.

The food spread out on the antique table looked and smelled divine, if only Olivia had an appetite.

Harper approached her along with Skye and Bella. 'Here, you have to eat something, Olivia,' Harper said, handing her a gold-edged plate with a few small morsels of the buffet arranged on it.

'Harper's right, honey. You need to keep your strength up,' Skye said.

'You don't look like you've been sleeping much,' Bella told her in true Bella style.

'I appreciate you all worrying about me but I'm fine, honestly,' Olivia insisted as she took the plate of food from Harper but the expression on her friends' faces told her they were not convinced.

As the other women chatted amongst themselves, Olivia glanced around the room at the small parcels of people who were talking in whispers as Debussy's 'Clair de lune' played from a stereo system on the beautiful Chippendale sideboard. Her eyes alighted on someone who appeared to be staring at her, but she couldn't quite remember who he was. He looked familiar but try as she might, Olivia couldn't place him. He was tall; very tall, at least six feet four was her guess. His hair was dark and fell in waves that flicked out at the collar above his shoulders. A light stubble graced his chin and strong jawline. He wore a well-fitting black suit and slate-grey shirt with matching tie. When he realised she was looking back at him, he raised his glass and gave a small, solemn bow. She smiled but quickly turned away.

'So, who's the male model giving you the eye?' Harper asked. 'I mean, I know I'm not into guys, but even I can appreciate a good-looking man when I see one.'

Olivia shrugged. 'No idea. He looks kind of familiar. Probably one of Dad's associates.'

Bella chimed in, 'He does look familiar. Maybe we ought to go find out who he is?' she insisted. 'Maybe he's a gate-crasher.'

Skye rolled her eyes. 'I don't think funeral gate-crashing is a thing, Bella.'

Bella scowled. 'All I'm saying is if Olivia doesn't recognise him, maybe he shouldn't be here.'

Olivia felt a hand on her shoulder. 'Olivia, darling, can I have a quick word?' Innes said. Taking the hint, her friends walked away to give them some space.

Once they were alone, Innes cleared his throat. 'I was wondering if you might be available the day after tomorrow to go through the will. I've asked Alasdair McKendrick to come along here to the castle, I hope that's okay.'

Olivia frowned. 'Sure, if that's necessary. Isn't his office in Edinburgh? It's a long way for him to travel for something I presume will be fairly cut and dried.'

Innes glanced over to where Kerr stood with Adaira and a strange expression crossed his face. 'Aye, that's as maybe, but Alasdair recommended he be present. Probably with it being a high-profile matter. Better to dot all the Ts and cross the eyes,' he said with a wink and a smile before turning both his eyes towards his nose. But then his expression changed to one of solemnity again. 'Sorry, not the time for my silly jokes.'

Olivia couldn't help smiling. 'It's okay, don't apologise. My mum always loved your silly sense of humour. So, what time?'

'I've requested Alasdair arrive here for around eleven. Does that suit?'

Olivia glanced across the room to Kerr, who stood holding a handkerchief up to his eyes and dabbing them as his shoulders juddered up and down in what appeared to be fake sobs. She now understood Innes's strange expression from moments before. 'Is Kerr set for then too?'

Innes nodded. 'Aye. Of course, the meeting was originally going to be at noon, but he had to be obstinate about it. Apparently, he has business meetings all afternoon.' He shook his head and a look of disdain flashed across his features this time.

Olivia sighed. 'Figures.' Kerr lifted his chin as one of the mourners approached him and began the whole sobbing thing again as the man patted his arm. *Oscar-winning performance*, Olivia thought.

* * *

As early evening took the sunlight, the mourners began to leave, and Olivia and Kerr stood by the castle doors, hugging people and thanking them for their attendance.

The tall man who she had noticed before was one of the last to leave. He shook Kerr's hand very briefly and with a fair bit of force that seemed to knock Kerr off his game. Her brother's eyes widened, and he opened his mouth to speak but the man glared at him, and he closed it again. He arrived in front of Olivia and took her hand.

He fixed her with a vivid blue, compassion-filled gaze and told her, 'I'm very sorry for your loss, Olivia. You have my heartfelt condolences.' Then with a brief, sideways glance at Kerr, he said, 'Please take care of yourself.'

She opened her mouth to speak, intrigued to discover his identity, but he let go of her hand and walked briskly through the doors before she could form the words. Mirren and the young man from the catering company closed the doors and Olivia turned to Kerr to ask him who the man was but Kerr was already walking away, loosening his tie and heading for the stairs.

'I'll stay here the night and tomorrow but as soon as the will reading is done, I have to leave,' he called over his shoulder. 'I have lots of important matters to deal with and don't have the time to be sitting around making small talk. I'll be in my room with Adaira and we would like to be left undisturbed for the rest of the evening. Today has taken its toll on me.'

'I'm fine, thanks for asking,' Olivia muttered under her breath as she found herself alone in the hallway.

Once changed into her pyjamas, Olivia went to find Marley in the kitchen. He gave excited yips as his whole body wagged in happiness to see her. She crouched to the floor and wrapped her arms around his neck and burst into heavy, heart-wrenching sobs.

* * *

After a fitful night of sleep, Olivia showered and dressed in jeans and a sweater, pulled on her rugged brown boots and folded her woollen wrap around her shoulders.

'Come on, lad. Let's go get some air, eh?'

Marley stood from the bed she had moved in from her mother's room, stretched and yawned and followed her willingly as she made her way down the stairs of the castle, and on to the front door. A quick glance at her watch told her it was only 7 a.m. but there was no point trying to sleep again. Her dreams had been full of arguments with Kerr, and vivid images of bulldozers tramping up the main driveway, ready to demolish everything in sight. At the very end, she was standing in front of a giant machine, hands aloft screaming, 'No!' at the top of her lungs and awoke just before the blade made contact with her body. She had shot bolt upright and found herself covered in sweat, in spite of the chilly temperature of the room. No, there was no point trying to sleep if that was all that waited to greet her. Once the will was revealed, she would have to step away and leave Kerr to wreak his havoc. She knew she couldn't stay to watch; that one thing was certain.

She turned the ancient key in the lock and tugged open the door, which creaked long and menacing under its own weight. The low mist hung across the grounds again and as she stepped outside, her breath clouded as its heat met the cold of the new day. As she walked with Marley down across the gravel, the dog froze and sniffed the air. A stag in the distance raised its head and it watched her suspiciously, only relaxing when she turned to head for her secret garden.

Olivia pushed through the tall green wooden gate and stepped over the slightly raised threshold as a shiver of anticipation shuddered down her spine – or it could have been the cold. Spring flowers were on the verge of blooming now and the tall grasses swayed gently from side to side in the breeze. She had always especially loved this place in summer when the thistles donned their proud purple tufts like the punk rockers of the garden, but even this morning there seemed to be more colours making an appearance than she remembered seeing the day before.

The rising sun shed a golden glow across the place and insects buzzed around, busily getting on with their work, whizzing past her ears and darting in amongst the plants. She crouched and, with her hand in Marley's warm fur, she closed her eyes for a moment and felt her worries melting away as a welcome feeling of peace descended upon her.

She opened her eyes again and stood to survey the garden before her. A higgledy-piggledy path ran through the middle and darted off at tangents into little hidden pockets where there were secrets to discover, although they weren't really secrets for Olivia any more. She knew that a stone bench lay at the end of one path where she used to read as a child, hidden away from any interruptions, and a bird bath at the end of another where you could hide in the bushes and watch wee sparrows splashing around in the water. She wasn't, however, expecting what was at the end of a third path and jumped when she saw a large shape moving around in the undergrowth. Marley barked and lunged forwards protectively.

'Bloody hell!' she gasped, covering her heart as it pounded at her chest.

The person tried to stand rather too quickly and ended up on their back after falling over their own feet. 'Bloody hell, yourself! Are you trying to give me a heart attack?' the man growled as he scrambled to his feet.

'Sorry but I wasn't exactly expecting anyone to be out here at this time of morning,' Olivia snapped in return.

'Aye... well... likewise.' The man came out from the shadow of one of the apple trees and Olivia widened her eyes.

Marley darted over to the man, his tail wagging frantically. 'You?' she said, confusion fogging up her mind as the tall stranger from the funeral came into view.

'You too,' he replied with a shrug. 'Hey, Marley, lad, who's a good boy?' he said, scratching the dog behind his ears, then turning to address her again. 'What are you doing out of your bed? It's only just light out.'

'I couldn't sleep. Lots on my mind,' she replied with a shrug.

He nodded. 'Aye, well, I suppose I can understand that.'

Olivia kept her distance and wrapped her shawl tighter around her body. 'This might be a silly question, especially seeing as you clearly know who I am but... do I know you?' *Marley certainly does*, she thought.

A grin spread across the man's handsome, unshaven face and he ran his hand back over his hair to push it out of his eyes. 'Apparently not.'

She took a step closer. 'But *should* I?'

'Don't I look familiar to you? At all? I mean, I know it's been fifteen years, I suppose.'

She scrunched her eyes as if that would somehow help. 'You do look familiar, I just can't place...'

He walked towards her and rubbed his hands down his jeans. 'I've changed a wee bit. And you were taller than me the last time I saw you.'

The closer he got, the more realisation began to set in. 'No way,' she whispered and her heart skipped as she wondered why on earth she hadn't put two and two together before now.

'Aye, and I've a few less spots these days, thankfully.'

'Brodie MacLeod?' she asked without trying to hide the disdain in her voice.

His expression crumpled. 'You needn't sound so happy about it.'

'I can't say I *am* happy. I'd heard you were back but... you're right, you've changed.'

'For the better, I think,' he said with a stroke to his chin and one eyebrow raised.

Olivia curled her lip. 'Only externally, I see.' She turned to walk away.

'You've changed too,' he said, and she stopped in her tracks, possibly out of some idiotic hope that he might say something nice. 'I think you must have stopped growing not long after I saw you last. No more giraffe legs, eh?'

Okay, so she was expecting too much. What do they say about leopards? She huffed and stormed off in the direction of the gate, closely followed by Marley, of course.

'Hey, come on, I'm only joking around. It's good to see you. You look... well.'

'Gee, thanks,' she replied over her shoulder without stopping, unwilling to accept any kind of veiled compliment from such a hypocrite.

'Hey! What's wrong? Have I offended you somehow?' he called after her, his voice tinged with a little of what sounded like hurt, but she chose not to reply. Instead, she decided to return to the garden later when she'd have more privacy. She wasn't in the mood to be insulted and made fun of.

She was jarringly sent back to the time he had lived nearby and she was reminded of how that rat bag had broken her heart. Brodie MacLeod was someone she had lived without for fifteen years and she would be happy to continue that way.

* * *

At 8.30 a.m., Olivia sat on the bed in Harper's hotel room as Harper checked her passport for the hundredth time.

'So, he was your first love?' Harper said, clutching her hands over her heart.

Olivia made an unladylike snorting sound. 'Yeah, until I woke up and realised what a shit he was.'

Harper tilted her head. 'Allow me to translate; you never got over him and your feelings for him have been hiding in the depths of your soul since you were fourteen.'

Olivia huffed. 'Maybe.'

'So, ask him out! How cool would that be? It sounds like he's changed. Maybe this is your time?'

'You've got to be kidding me. After the way he treated me? No chance. Some things are too hard to forgive.'

Harper ruffled Olivia's hair. 'Nawww. You definitely have the hots for him. It's so clear in the way you talk about him.'

'I certainly don't. He's the last person I'd fancy. Even if he does look like Keanu Reeves and have dimples when he smiles.' She flopped back onto the bed. 'Oh god, Harper, it's useless. Why is he here? He really did break my heart and when you're fourteen, that has a massive impact on your life.'

Harper tapped her thumb to her chin. 'Carrie Cohen was mine. We were both fourteen. And yeah, you're right, you never truly get over it. But she's married with three kids now and she's so wrinkly and real angry looking. I think I'm well out of that.' She laughed. 'Seriously, though, the guy had the decency to attend your mom's funeral. Maybe he's trying to make amends.'

'I doubt that. Anyway, enough about Brodie MacLeod. Give me a hug.' Harper sat and embraced her. 'I wish you'd have stayed at the castle. And I wish you could stay longer,' Olivia said, fighting back tears.

'It didn't feel right to stay there. I know I'm always welcome, but it felt like you needed to be there to grieve. And Kerr hates me. I'm not sure if it's because I'm gay or American. Or maybe it's that I'm a gay American. Anyway, when are you coming home?'

'I'm coming home as soon as I possibly can. I'm already missing work. And I'll miss you more.'

Harper rested her forehead on hers. 'I know, sweetie. I'll miss you too and I wish I could stay longer but Nina needs me back to shoot the fall accessories collection, you know how far in advance these things need to be done. You're needed here for now and

Nina totally gets it, so don't go worrying about rushing back, okay?'

Olivia nodded. 'I know but I want to come back soon. You'll call me when you get home, won't you? No matter what time it is.'

Harper placed a hand on each of Olivia's shoulders. 'No matter what time.' She crouched before her. 'Will you be okay here on your own? I mean, I know Bella and Skye are in the city but... Will you be *okay*?'

Olivia smiled. 'Now who's worrying? I'll be fine. The will reading is tomorrow and then I'll be booking my flight home. I'll stay a few days to catch up with Skye and Bella, but I can't imagine there'll be much point me staying here for longer than a week. I can't say I'm thrilled about the prospect of watching my brother make plans to demolish the castle.'

Harper's eyes widened. 'You don't truly think he'd do that, do you?'

Olivia wished she could confidently answer in the negative, but the truth was she wouldn't put anything past him. 'I think he will do what he thinks is best for him and sod the rest of us. That's why I'll be back to New York as soon as I can get a decent flight.'

The phone on the nightstand rang and Harper answered it. 'Sure, thanks. I'll be right down.' She hung up and turned to Olivia. 'My cab is here.'

The sinking feeling that had become all too familiar to Olivia happened again. 'What time is your flight?'

'Ten after eleven. Then from Heathrow to Boston and onto New York. It's going to be a long-ass day.' She huffed. 'And I'll no doubt look like death when I get back to the office. Jet lag is bound to kick my ass at some point, even after such a fast turnaround.'

Olivia stood and hugged her best friend tightly once more. 'I know and I'm so sorry you're having to make this journey again so soon. But I really appreciate you coming over to be with me.'

Harper reciprocated the hug. 'Hey, I didn't mean to lay a guilt trip on you, sweetie. I wouldn't have let you go through this alone. *Sisters from another mister*, right?'

Olivia smiled as she pulled away. 'Absolutely.' She glanced at her watch. 'I'd better get back to Drumblair anyway. Mirren might need her car.'

'How come you're in Mirren's car?'

'Ugh, because I didn't want to get the driver to bring me in Mum's. I'm not performing a state visit. And I never liked driving Dad's Land Rover. He adored that car but it has no power steering and I don't have the muscles for it.'

Harper nodded. 'Fair points.'

The friends walked down the stairs to the reception area and hugged a final time.

'Take care of you, okay?' Harper said as she tucked Olivia's hair behind her ear. 'And be brave.' The driver took her case and put it in the boot of the taxi.

Olivia nodded and wiped escaped tears from her cheeks. 'I will. I love you.'

'I love you too,' Harper replied before climbing into the car.

Olivia watched and waved as the taxi pulled around the hotel's sweeping driveway and disappeared into the distance, then she walked across the car park to her borrowed vehicle, Mirren's racing green mini. She climbed in and started the engine. As the car's radio sprang to life, she was greeted by Snow Patrol's 'Run'. The lyrics hit a little too close to home and all she could see in her mind's eye was her mother's smiling face. The pain in her heart was too much and stole her breath. She had to sit for a while and allow herself to cry, to let out the anguish and emotion she had been desperately trying to keep in check but failing miserably to do so. Feeling more alone than she ever had, she released the handbrake and put her foot on the accelerator.

It was time to go home.

5

At 11 a.m. the following day, Olivia sat in her father's study, a room she hadn't much been in since his death. Uncle Innes walked in with the family lawyer, Alasdair McKendrick, who had travelled all the way from his office in Edinburgh. Shortly after, Kerr walked through the door, closely followed by Adaira. Olivia glanced up at Uncle Innes and Alasdair, who were exchanging annoyed glances.

Alasdair cleared his throat. 'Mr MacBain, may I speak with you in private?'

Kerr smoothed down his tie and looked at Adaira, who stood to his left. 'No need. You can say whatever you wish in front of my Adaira.' Adaira glanced around the room smugly.

Uncle Innes stepped forward. 'Kerr, this is a family matter. That is immediate family only.'

Kerr snarled, 'So why are you here?'

Uncle Innes's nostril flared. 'You know very well I'm the executor. And I'm afraid Ms Wallace is not immediate family so cannot be a part of this meeting.'

Adaira smiled sweetly at Innes and fluttered her eyelashes. 'I won't make a peep. You won't know I'm here. I'll sit—'

'Look, I'm sorry, Ms Wallace, but you need to leave,' Alasdair said quite forcefully. 'Anything that Kerr wishes to tell you after this proceeding is entirely up to him, but please could both of you have respect for Olivia? This is a family matter and as you are not yet married, that does not include Ms Wallace.'

Adaira huffed and stormed out of the room. Kerr's attention followed her, and once she had gone, he barked, 'Well done! That was completely unnecessary! We already know the outcome of this stupid meeting, so all this is is a confirmation of the obvious. I had no issue with her being here and I'm the beneficiary, so what has it got to do with all of you?'

'Please, Kerr, just sit down and let's get this over with so you can go back to Adaira,' Olivia pleaded.

He glared at her for a moment and then took the seat beside her.

Kerr huffed and mumbled, 'Feels like we've been summoned by the bloody headmaster.' No one replied or acknowledged his petulant comment.

Uncle Innes took a seat behind her father's desk and Alasdair sat on a leather chair slightly further back than her uncle and to the right. Father's old TV still remained on its dark oak stand in the other corner, a TV on which Olivia had watched old family movies from her father's lap. Innes proceeded to spread some documentation across the table, a serious, stoic expression on his face.

'Look, is this going to take long? I'm a very busy man,' Kerr insisted.

'It will take as long as it takes, I'm afraid, Kerr,' Innes replied, fixing him with a determined glare.

'And why is the lawyer here? Surely this is all a formality. As I said, we all know what's in the damned will anyway. This all seems a bit pointless.'

Olivia watched as Alasdair's jaw clenched ever so slightly, almost imperceptible to the naked eye. 'Mr MacBain, I understand you have things to do and so we will keep things as brief as we can, but this is not as straightforward as first expected.'

Kerr rolled his eyes but quietened down and pulled out his mobile phone. He began to tap away at the screen and chuckled every so often at whatever he was looking at. Olivia thought him rude but then he had always been so.

'Okay, so...' Innes began. 'This is a little unusual and frankly something I have only ever seen in films, but along with her signed and witnessed will, Freya has left a recorded message that she has requested you watch first.' He gave a wry smile. 'Of course, it's on DVD and my laptop doesn't have a DVD slot so...' He gestured towards the TV on the stand. 'Anyway, the video contains the same information as the will itself, but Freya felt she wanted to explain her decisions directly. This was filmed last year, just before Christmas, at your mother's request. Once the camera equipment was set up, Freya was left alone to record the message.'

At this point Alasdair interjected. 'Now there is no such thing as a *video will* here in the UK, so this is simply a message of explanation. The will documentation is what's legally binding and I can confirm your mother took all the necessary steps to ensure the legality and authenticity of the document.'

Kerr huffed again. 'Good grief, anyone would think you were right, Olivia, and that she's left the lot to charity!' He chuckled and shook his head. 'I mean, seriously, why all this nonsense?'

'I'd like to see Mum,' Olivia said in a small but firm voice.

Innes smiled. 'Of course.' He picked up a remote control and pointed it at the old TV. It sparked to life and the beautiful face of Lady Freya MacBain could be seen, smiling from the screen. She wore her favourite Nina Picarro dress in deep blue that Olivia had gifted her with her first month's pay cheque. Her Titian hair was streaked with grey and as neatly styled as always. Her make-up was subtle, and she looked every inch the lady that she was. She was seated on the red leather Chesterfield couch that sat in the window of the very room they were in, and Marley was curled up in the seat beside her. Olivia glanced over to the couch and longed to see her mother there now. But, of course, that wasn't to be.

'My darlings,' Freya began with a smile. 'I've seen things like this done on those American movies and always thought it seemed a bit melodramatic, but perhaps this is my way of achieving the dream of being a movie star...' She smoothed down the lap of her dress and her smile faltered before she clasped her fingers together. 'Anyway... I shouldn't joke because if you're watching this, then I'm gone.'

An involuntary sob escaped from Olivia's chest as her heart ached at seeing her mother alive and well, despite her words. She longed to hug her one more time and to see that smile in real life. Tears streamed down her face, and she swiped them away quickly, trying to eradicate the blurring they caused so she could see her mother more clearly. Uncle Innes stood and walked around the table to hand her a pristine white handkerchief. He placed a hand on her shoulder.

Her mother continued. 'Now... you should have been informed that this is not the legal will but simply a message I wanted to relay to explain my reasons and the difficult decisions I've had to make.

'First of all, you will no doubt soon discover that the castle is in a terrible state of disrepair. I want to apologise for not being more honest with you both on this matter. I didn't want you to worry, you see. This is your family home, and you should always be able to return here; to have a roof over your head, no matter what. But these last few years have been the most difficult. There are things that need to be done to the castle to ensure the MacBain legacy carries on. I was hoping to be able to deal with this myself, but I feared that I might not live to see it happen. At the time I'm recording this message, I have just been diagnosed with high blood pressure. Apparently, stress doesn't help, but how do you run a castle without stress, that's what I'd like to know? Anyway, I've been ordered to take things easy but, of course, I won't be doing that. This old place meant the world to your father, and it must remain intact. It simply must.'

Olivia glanced sideways at Kerr as he tugged at the collar of his shirt and fidgeted in his seat. He was clearly feeling a certain amount of discomfort, knowing his own plans for the place, and the changes he had already begun to make.

'Now... Kerr, my dear. I know how much you love Drumblair Villa, and you have made a home there. So, of course, that house and all the furniture is now yours. I hope that you will continue to live there happily and that perhaps one day you may even have a family of your own, so the corridors and rooms are filled with as much love and happiness as we've had there ourselves.'

Kerr smiled and looked across at Olivia. He reached out and patted her hand. 'Sorry, Olivia. I really thought it was going to be yours. But this makes things a little more straightforward, at least. You know you're always welcome to come and stay when you come over to Scotland...' he shrugged, 'if you ever come back over, of course.' He turned back to face the TV.

'Now, my dear Olivia... you always made your father and me proud with the way you stood up for what you believed in. We admired the way you fought for your dream of working in fashion. And we know that's where your true passion lies. So, through a trust fund that was started when you were a child, we have made provision for you to have your own place in New York. The policy matured a while ago and just recently I employed a realtor to find a place. The timing couldn't have been better. I think you'll love it. It's a duplex on the Upper East Side which we were informed was the best location for you to be. Because I don't know at what point you will be watching this, the place may have been sitting empty for a while, but it has been looked after. And this way, you get to continue your dream...'

Olivia gasped and covered her mouth. Her own place just *handed* to her? That's not something she had ever asked for, nor expected. She wasn't like Kerr at all. She knew the world didn't owe her anything. When she left for New York, she did so without accepting the handouts she was offered by her parents. Her mother had tried to insist she bought her a home, but Olivia refused, telling her mother to use the money for something she wanted. Now she knew where the money was going to come from, and things fell into place. But Olivia had always wanted to make it by herself and had achieved so much more than she had ever expected to. She wasn't sure she wanted this.

Freya leaned towards the screen. 'Now, Olivia, I know you're going to be cross with me over this. Your father and I always admired your tenacity and willingness to stand on your own two feet and we were happy to allow this until we were no longer around to support you if you did ever need us. But now we are both gone please, allow us this little indulgence. We will rest easier.' There was a pause as Freya inhaled a deep breath and exhaled it slowly. 'Because it may only be temporary if things go according to plan.'

Olivia scrunched her brow. What did her mother mean by that? It seemed a little cryptic.

Kerr forced a sigh. 'Oh dear, I really thought there would be something permanently in place for you, Olivia. I suppose Dad really was upset that you chose America over your family.' His smug expression didn't go unnoticed. 'Don't worry, though; I won't see you out on the street.' He gave another patronising pat to her arm.

The last thing Olivia wanted was to be beholden to her brother, and she didn't want handouts from anyone. She hadn't needed them up to now. Freya clasped her hands in her lap once again. 'Which brings me to my final wish. Now, this one will be the hardest for you both, I'm sure. I don't think it's what either of you wanted to hear. Many businesses have been keen to get their hands on the castle over the years, but I always said to your father that I would rather leave the castle to charity than let some huge corporation take over.'

Kerr suddenly sat bolt upright, his eyes widened, and Olivia watched in her periphery as his Adam's apple bobbed vigorously in his throat. He was panicking now.

Freya continued. 'This old place needs someone with vision, a passion for what needs to be done; an eye for detail that the rest of us simply don't have. There has to be dedication; a willingness to go against the grain enough but not too much. There has to be drive and a desire to ensure that something of your father's ancestry stays alive here.' There was a pause and Freya closed her eyes briefly. 'Charity seems the obvious option...'

'No! No bloody way!' Kerr blurted. 'How could she do this?' he yelled at no one in particular as he jabbed his hand towards the screen.

But Freya opened her eyes and spoke again. 'And I know this isn't your dream, dear. I know it's not what you hoped for...' Kerr and Olivia shared worried glances. To whom was she speaking now? 'But I know your heart and head will make the right decisions. And so... darling Kerr... this may come as a shock but... I am leaving Drumblair Castle to you... Olivia.'

* * *

The ringing in Olivia's ears wouldn't stop. Her blood sounded like waves crashing against her skull and Kerr's face was beet red. He looked on the verge of a cardiac arrest as Uncle Innes and Alasdair held him back from lunging at her.

'You knew! You bitch! You've known all along, haven't you? That's why you came back here!' Dougie, the gardener, rushed into the room, followed by Brodie, and they joined in the barricade that the men had formed to stop Kerr getting to Olivia.

Tears streamed down Olivia's cheeks, and she realised wiping them away was an exercise in futility. She shook her head vehemently. 'No! I wouldn't have kept that from you, Kerr. I promise I had no idea.'

'What the hell do I do now? Hmm? They'll kill me! And my blood will be on your hands!'

Olivia had no clue what he was talking about. She knew he'd been bailed out of debts many times before today, but his life had never really been in danger, had it?

Kerr yanked himself free from the two men and held his hands up. 'It's fine!' he shouted. 'I'm not going to bloody attack her, for god's sake. What kind of man do you think I am? She's my damned sister!' Clearly unconvinced, the men hesitated and hung back but didn't leave.

Olivia dragged her hands through her hair. 'I don't understand. This is not how this was supposed to go.'

Kerr swung around and glared at her. 'You think? How stupid are you?'

'Hey!' Brodie stepped forward and placed a grubby hand on Kerr's chest. 'Come on now, mate, that's enough, eh? Have some respect.'

Kerr turned his attention to the man who was taller than him, wearing a scruffy pair of jeans and a dirty T-shirt, and sneered. 'Mate? Get your filthy hands off me! Who the hell do you think you are? What gives you the right to talk to me like you know me? Why are you even here?'

Brodie clenched his jaw. 'Because you fired every one of my dad's team and left him to do everything by himself, so we're getting up at the crack of dawn to get stuff done.'

Kerr scoffed. 'I didn't even bloody employ you! You're fired. Get out of my house now!' he bellowed and jabbed an index finger towards the door.

Brodie smiled and shrugged. 'Technically I'm not employed. And if you didn't employ me, you can't fire me.'

Kerr opened and closed his mouth before turning his head towards Olivia. 'Well?'

A little confused, Olivia shook her head. 'Well what?'

Her brother jabbed a finger in Brodie's direction. 'Aren't you going to tell him to get out? It's your damned castle, after all.' Disdain was evident in both his tone and his curled lipped expression.

Olivia widened her eyes and realised both men were staring at her. 'Erm... no. No, Kerr, I'm not going to ask him to leave. He's done nothing wrong. You were behaving in a threatening manner, and he stepped in.'

Kerr shook his head and a sinister grin remained on his contorted, red face. 'Oh, I see. I get it. Right. Well, I hope you'll be very happy together. I should have known you were shagging him.'

Before anyone else could respond, Brodie's fist connected with Kerr's jaw and Olivia watched as he seemed to crumple to the floor in slow motion. She gasped and covered her mouth with her hands.

Kerr scrambled to his feet. 'I'll sue! You wait and see!' he yelled before he dashed from the room, slamming the door behind him.

Brodie rubbed his hands over his face and turned to her with pleading eyes. 'Shit, Olivia, I'm so sorry... I just—'

'Come on, son,' Dougie interjected. 'Let's leave the lassie alone a while, eh?'

Alasdair McKendrick said, 'Yes, I think perhaps Lady Olivia needs some time to process everything.' He led Dougie and Brodie from the room.

Lady Olivia? Oh, my word, that's me now, isn't it? A shiver travelled the length of her spine as the realisation of her position began to sink in.

Uncle Innes walked over and enveloped her in his arms. 'I'm so sorry, sweetheart. I wish I could have forewarned you. I didn't want things to be this way. I told Freya that, but she clearly overestimated the compassion and acceptance that Kerr is capable of.'

Olivia held onto her uncle. 'No, it's not your fault. But I have so many questions.'

He stepped away and held her at arm's length. 'There's another video message just for you. I think perhaps you may get some of the answers you need. Shall I play it and leave you here to watch?'

So many emotions were vying for priority inside of her, but Olivia smiled and nodded. 'Yes, please.'

6

Olivia once again sat in her father's office, only this time she was accompanied by Marley, who sat beside her on the Chesterfield sofa where she was now seated as the TV screen illuminated with her mother's face. Marley rested his head on her lap and her throat tightened and tears stung at her eyes once again.

Freya cleared her throat and gave a brief shake of her head, familiar signs to Olivia that she was trying to put on a brave face. 'Hello again, my darling girl. I'm sure Kerr has stormed off in a foul mood and for that I'm sincerely sorry. The thing is, I have been protecting him for so many years now, from himself, but nothing I do, no help I give seems to make any difference. He won't seek help for the gambling, and the alcohol... well, I'm sure you have witnessed that during your time here for my funeral.'

Freya paused for a moment and shivered. 'Oof, it's strange talking about that when I'm still here, alive and kicking and conversing with a camera. Anyway... Innes says it's been a long time coming and he's probably right, but I think it's time for Kerr to realise that his actions have consequences, however harsh they may be. You see, I overheard him talking to a friend recently... The conversation was pretty disappointing.' Hurt flashed in Freya's eyes and Olivia wanted to reach through the screen and hug her.

'He said he would sell off Drumblair as soon as it was his. Said he was looking forward to the money and a worry-free life without the lead weight of the castle hanging around his neck. He saw it as some posh hotel and spa with a conference centre. He even stated that he didn't care if it was demolished so long as he pocketed the funds for the land.'

She covered her heart and shook her head. 'I think it hit me then how little his ancestry must mean to him. I didn't recognise the man he was at that moment, Olivia. Doing any of that would mean the MacBain family would be totally removed from the place. Cast into nothing but the annals of history just so he can carry on gambling and drinking. I couldn't let him do that to your father's legacy. I hope you can understand that. I couldn't allow him to wipe the memory of your father's family from the face of earth, and certainly not your father himself. I know that might sound melodramatic but it's how I feel about the situation I could be leaving the place in. Your father entrusted Drumblair to me when he died, and I can't settle until I know that it will be protected when I'm no longer here.'

Olivia had only learned over the past few days of Kerr's plans but seeing the pain in her mother's eyes almost broke her again.

Freya continued. 'Now... it breaks my heart to do this to you, to put so much pressure on your shoulders, but please hear me out. I know that this old place was never what you imagined when you thought of your future. Except for visits maybe. But I know how much vision you have. I've seen your clothing designs, so I know how creative you are. I think those skills could be adapted to Drumblair and that's how I know that you're the person to bring this place back to life. To give it a new purpose while still keeping it linked to our family history. There's so much history here. So much wonder. It's been kept hidden for all these years but perhaps that doesn't need to be the case any more.'

She shrugged and Olivia noted the glint of excitement in her eyes. 'You will certainly need to find funding for the works that need to be carried out. And I'm aware there's such a lot to be done. The roof leaks, some of the windows are rotten, the heating isn't up to standard and some of the stonework is crumbling. The farm-land doesn't bring in enough of an income to support the repairs that are needed. Your father was always so generous with his tenants, charging them the smallest rents he could, and he wouldn't change that, but that's what I loved about him. His generosity of spirit. Anyway, we've papered over the cracks for so long now, both literally and figuratively speaking, mainly because we didn't want to worry you. But I know you, Olivia, and I know that once you set your mind and heart on something, you can achieve amazing things. I have faith in you. And so does Marley, don't you, boy?' On hearing his name said by a familiar voice, Marley lifted his head and sniffed the air. Olivia smoothed the fur on the top of his head and smiled. How did she know the dog would be here with her?

Freya continued. 'So, my darling girl... here is my proposal. Your Uncle Innes will have applied for large estate confirmation by now. That's the Scottish version of probate but you may already be aware of that. This can take up to six months to be granted. So, during this time, I want you to leave Innes to handle things. He will take Marley too while you're away. Go back to the USA and continue in your job. Enjoy every minute but use your spare time to concoct some magnificent plan, just like I know you can. Then when everything is handled here, and you are officially the owner, I want you to dedicate two years of your life to the castle. Form a trust and a management team. Look at ways to bring in revenue. Oversee the works that need to be carried out and come up with a way to make the castle sustainable.

'After the two years, go back to the USA and continue with your life there, if you so wish, leaving the trust to run things. By then, you will have the ability to set up your own fashion house. There is provision set aside to ensure that can happen. It's all been taken care of. But unfortunately, I need to ask this of you first. To dedicate two years to the place. To ensure your father's legacy remains intact. I know this is such a lot to ask of you. And if you feel unable to carry it through, Innes has the power to step in and take the work on himself as a guardian or custodian type of thing. I just wanted to give you the opportunity to do this. Because I know you can. You love the place; I know you do. But it hasn't yet met its full potential, Olivia.

'My only stipulation is that none of the place is sold off. It has to remain as the MacBain family's property. *Your* property. But it's up to you how you make it work. You are capable of standing on your own two feet and I know you are more than capable of making a success of this. So please consider it all very carefully. I know it's a huge shock to you right now. It must be. And I know you may be very angry with me.' Freya's chin trembled and her eyes welled with tears. 'But I hope that you find it in your heart to forgive me. This was my only way of ensuring the old place wasn't left to ruin, or worse, your brother's crazy ideas for making money. The residents of Drumblair village need a casino on their doorstep as much as they need a rubbish dump.'

She forced a smile and dabbed at her eyes. 'Please know that I love you and I'm so very proud of you. And so was your father. You were his proudest achievement. I know he would never tell you that for fear of appearing like a bad parent having favourites, but it's true. He always said you had gumption. You knew what you wanted, and you were determined to get it by yourself, no handouts, and no nepotism. He admired that about you so much. He said you reminded him of himself when he was younger. And this is how I know you can make a change here. You can be the difference between the MacBain name remaining or disappearing into oblivion. But know this... I will still be proud of you no matter what you decide. I love you, my darling Olivia. And know that wherever I am now, I'm missing you so very, very much.'

She blew a final kiss at the screen before it turned black, and Olivia was once again left in silence, tears streaming down her cheeks and an ache in her heart the likes of which she had never experienced before.

* * *

Later that day, Olivia sat in the walled garden on the secluded stone bench that stood at the end of one of the winding paths and Marley sat at her feet with his tongue lolling out. The weight of everything she had recently learned was pressing down on her and she needed a little peace and quiet to think, plan and make decisions she had never anticipated having to make. Thankfully the early spring sunshine was warm now and she tilted her head skyward to let the rays heat her skin.

Someone cleared their throat, making her jump and causing Marley to get to his feet. She opened her eyes and looked in their direction and when her eyes settled on the intruder, she smiled. 'Oh, hi, Brodie.'

He smiled briefly in response. 'Hey. I just wanted to check you were okay after...' He gestured towards the castle.

She nodded. 'That's very kind of you, thanks. I'm okay. A little bewildered but fine.'

'I can imagine. I've never heard about your brother being an aggressive man. What's his problem?'

Olivia crumpled her brow. 'He isn't usually aggressive. He can be an arse, yes, but that was a whole new side to him for me. And... you don't know what happened?'

He shook his head. 'Only that we were in the kitchen getting tea and we heard this shouting and swearing so we headed towards it.'

'Quite the hero, eh?' She was aware how sarcastic she sounded and immediately added, 'I really appreciate it. Thank you.'

His mouth curled up at the corners and his eyes lit up; they were a vivid blue shade that seemed even brighter in the sunshine. 'No worries.' He paused and appeared pensive for a moment. 'I didn't understand what he meant, though, about it being your castle. He's the heir, isn't he?'

She didn't reply and he widened his eyes. Holding up his hands, he said, 'Sorry, absolutely none of my business. I apologise.' Again, she didn't speak. She wasn't entirely sure what to say. Thankfully he changed the subject. 'Look... this may not be the best time to ask but... The other day when we were chatting... you took off and...' He rubbed at the stubble on his chin. 'Well, I wasn't sure why. If I upset you, I'm sorry.'

'That wasn't a question,' she replied with a wry smile.

He crumpled his brow. 'Eh?'

'You said *this may not be the best time to ask but...* then didn't actually ask me anything.'

His face flushed and he reached up to rub the back of his neck. 'Oh... aye... I mean... *Did* I upset you?'

She shook her head. 'Not really. I walked away before you said anything really cruel.'

He opened and closed his mouth for a few seconds; a crumple of confusion creased his brow. 'But... I *wasnae* meaning to be cruel. I was just...'

'Kidding around?'

'Aye.'

She nodded. 'Hmm. Well sometimes, in the past, at least, your kidding around was extremely hurtful.'

His eyes widened and he sat on the bench beside her as Marley nudged his hand for attention, which he dutifully gave. 'It was?'

'Yes. I didn't appreciate being likened to a giraffe back then, and it's not that nice being reminded of it now either.'

He winced. 'Shit, I'm sorry, Lady Olivia. I was sincerely only messing.'

Hearing her official title again didn't sit easily with her and she snapped, 'Why did you call me that?'

His brow crumpled and he shrugged. 'I... erm... After all that kerfuffle, Mirren said there'd been changes and we should address you as Lady Olivia now and that solicitor bloke called you it when he saw us out.' She had forgotten about that. 'Sorry if that's not right. I presumed you didn't like how familiar the staff were being with you, so I didn't want to rock the boat. And I can assure you that I didn't mean any harm in my comments the other day. I really was only messing.'

Olivia stood, suddenly thrown off guard. 'Yes, well, as I said, your idea of messing is others' idea of bullying.' And with that final comment, she walked away from him, clicking her fingers so that Marley followed. As she reached the end of the path, her stomach knotted with guilt. He had stepped in to help her and this was how she was repaying him? She turned and made her way back to the bench, but Brodie was nowhere to be seen. He clearly knew a secret way out that she wasn't aware of. She made a mental note to apologise when she next saw him.

* * *

After the strange and surreal goings on of the morning, Olivia
spent several hours wandering around the grounds of the castle
while Marley napped on the stone steps. She was familiarising
herself once again with her childhood home; chasing memories of
games of badminton in the garden with Brodie in the roasting
summer sunshine, picnics lovingly prepared for them by Mirren,
and hide and seek with the gardeners during their lunch break.
Helping to plant the oak trees on the driveway to replace the ones
felled in a bad storm. Building snowmen and raiding her father's
wardrobe for tartan caps and scarves; they really were the best-
dressed snow people in Inverness-shire, that one thing was
certain.

So many memories could be called to mind of happy times in
the castle, but the death of her father stood out as one of the most
painful until now. She had not long since graduated from university and was home with her family for some quality time before
she went travelling. His death had happened suddenly, with no
prior indication or warning that he was sick, just like her mother's.
The memory of her mother's pained cries when she found him on
their bedroom floor created that same ache in her chest again that
she had felt when the news of her mother's death had sunk in. She
paused and closed her eyes, trying to conjure up something happy
again to replace the awful memories assaulting her temporal lobe.

Using her phone, she snapped photos of the old structure of
the castle and its grounds from many different angles, catching the
way the sun's rays highlighted the stone and the carvings thereon.
Looking at the place through fresh eyes, she could see many of the
flaws her mother had mentioned, and worry niggled at the back of
her mind. Was she capable of dealing with that? Or should she
walk away and let Innes take over?

As the sun began to set, Marley rejoined her and she caught
sight of the deer making their first appearance of the evening off

in the distance by a copse of pine trees. She remembered how Kerr had always called them stupid animals when they were younger. He said they should go back to hunting them for trophies, return to the sport of their ancestors like real men. Real men indeed. This was the man who at nineteen almost fainted when he'd got a splinter in his pinkie finger at Christmas after deciding to chop some wood for the fire. Of course, Dougie had already chopped plenty, but Kerr was determined to display his bravado. Oh, yes, she could imagine it now if he had inherited the castle, weekend shooting trips at his snazzy hotel and spa so long as he didn't have to actually do anything with, or go near, the carcases. A shiver traversed her spine at the horrific thought.

Kerr didn't see the point of deer except as yet another cash cow, whereas Olivia could appreciate their gentle beauty. She had been fascinated by the does' protective nature over their young and how they kept watch and were on high alert for predators. Not that there were any here these days; her parents had made sure of that. The grounds of Drumblair were more like a sanctuary these days. At least if she took on the role her mother had bequeathed to her, she could rest easy knowing the deer wouldn't become prey for her brother and his idiotic Neanderthal cronies.

* * *

By the time the sun set, Olivia and Marley returned indoors and were greeted by a delicious aroma of home cooking.

As she entered the kitchen, Mirren looked up from the pot she was stirring. 'Ah, there you are. I was about to send a search party.' Her smile was quickly replaced with a look of concern. 'Is everything okay?'

Olivia pulled out a chair and sat at the old kitchen table as

Marley took his favourite spot by the fireplace. 'I presume you know about the inheritance by now.'

Mirren wiped her hands on a pristine cloth and walked over to sit beside her. She took her hand. 'Aye, I do, dearie. How do you feel about it all?'

Olivia shook her head. 'Honestly? Numb. It was a huge shock. I just presumed that Kerr would inherit, and I would carry on as normal but now...'

After a pause, Mirren said, 'You do know you can say no, don't you? No one can force you into leaving your life in New York behind. No one would want you to be unhappy.'

Olivia appreciated her concern. 'I know. But I don't think I can turn my back on the place with such a risk to the future of Drumblair. I just don't know if I'm capable of taking on such a huge task. I'm a clothing designer. I've never even contemplated running a normal house, let alone a castle. This is more Kerr's thing. Well, maybe not as it stands, but I'm pretty sure he'd love the opportunity to get his hands on the place.' She rubbed her hands over her face, suddenly feeling drained.

Mirren squeezed her arm. 'You're right about Kerr but wrong to doubt yourself, you know. Your mother and father knew how strong you were when you left the UK. You have always stood on your own two feet and that's much more than can be said for your brother.'

'Speaking of which, where is he?'

Mirren gave a deep huff of a sigh. 'Oh, he left earlier. Made a big fuss so we all knew it too. Exaggerated the fact that he was going back to the only home he had ever known, the villa.' She rolled her eyes. 'He's so very bitter. And if I may be so bold, I want to warn you to be careful of him, Olivia dear. Spite was oozing from every pore of him earlier. I just worry about what he's capable of. Promise me you'll watch yourself.'

'I will. But he's my brother.' She shrugged. 'I'm sure he loves me really, even if he never shows it. I don't think he would do anything to really hurt me,' she insisted but realised as she spoke that she wasn't entirely confident in her own words.

Mirren stood and shared out the aromatic beef stew onto two plates and Marley was suddenly awake again and at Olivia's side.

'Are you okay to still eat in here with your old friend?' Mirren asked with a smile.

Olivia scoffed. 'Of course I am. I'm still me.'

Mirren shook her head. 'You're Lady Olivia now.'

That shiver of dread juddered down her spine again and she remembered Brodie calling her that earlier on in the day. 'Don't remind me. Poor Brodie...' she whispered as she remembered her snippy reaction.

Mirren placed two plates of food on the table and took her seat again. 'Aye, I hear he came to your rescue when Kerr kicked off about the will. Seems he's learned some manners, eh? I remember how he used to be so mean to you when you were both wee.'

'Hmm. I can't believe I ever had a crush on him.' She closed her eyes briefly as she realised she had said the words out loud. She glanced up at Mirren who simply smiled.

'Don't think we didn't notice that, hen. Och, the way you used to follow that boy around. You had this starry-eyed expression.' She shook her head. 'Then he hit puberty and turned rotten for a while. Good thing he's changed back.'

'I suppose it is.' She didn't mention that she used to dream about marrying him in the chapel by the lake. And how they would live in her room at the castle. But then again, those dreams had started when she was ten.

'Shame his wife didn't follow him here, though. He must be *awfy* lonely.'

Olivia's ears pricked up and her heart seemed to plummet to her shoes. 'Brodie's married?'

'Aye, apparently so. Four years now.'

Olivia wondered why this fact saddened her a little but pushed the thought aside and tucked into the mouth-watering food on her plate, closely observed by a drooling canine.

7

Olivia awoke to the sound of her phone ringing. She reached over to where it was charging and saw Harper's face smiling from the screen. She realised that with everything that had happened, she hadn't even contacted her best friend to tell her the news. It was only 7 a.m. now, so in New York it was 2 a.m. After a long flight, Harper must have arrived back at their apartment.

'Hey! Are you home?' Olivia asked as she pushed herself up to a sitting position and rubbed her eyes.

'Yeah, but only just. It's been a nightmare, there were delays so... Anyways, how did the will reading go? Are you okay? Has Kerr started to knock down walls already?'

Olivia pinched the bridge of her nose; her eyes ached through a lack of quality sleep. She stifled a yawn. 'Erm... no... it didn't go quite as I expected.'

'Really? How so?' Concern laced Harper's voice. 'Are you okay? Should I come back over? Because I can do that if you need—'

'N-no, no, I'm fine, honestly. It's just that... Kerr didn't actually inherit the castle after all that drama.'

There was a long pause and Olivia could almost hear the cogs of Harper's mind whirring. '*You* did, didn't you? Oh my god, tell me you inherited it!'

Olivia inhaled a deep, shaking breath. 'I did. It's crazy, Harper, but I'm now the owner of Drumblair Castle. Me... I'm officially Lady Olivia.' Saying the words out loud made Olivia a little light-headed. The name sounded strange coming from her mouth, alien somehow. 'Well, I will be once the large estate confirmation comes through.'

'What's that?'

'It's like probate but the Scottish version. It takes around six months, apparently.'

'Oh, my word. So, you're Lady MacBain now, huh?'

'Not to you I'm not. And not to anyone else either if I have any say in the matter. Plain old Olivia is just fine.'

Harper's voice softened. 'But you've never been plain old Olivia, honey, only to yourself.' Her excitement quickly ramped up. 'But this is huge! What are you going to do? Shit, does this mean you won't be coming home to New York?'

Olivia gave a deep sigh. 'I honestly have no idea which way is up right now. I have a lot of thinking to do but... the hardest part is that Mum asked a huge thing of me and I don't know if I can do it.'

'Oh... what did she ask? Can you tell me? I totally understand if you can't.'

'No... no, it's fine, I can tell you. Maybe you can help me decide what the heck to do.'

After explaining the conditions of the will to her best friend, Olivia fell silent for a moment to let her news sink in.

Harper hummed and hawed but eventually said, 'When all's said and done, you have to do what makes you happy, Olivia. And if bringing that beautiful old castle back to life is what will do that, then I support you 100 per cent, even if it means I don't get to see you that often. There's Zoom and FaceTime and email and phone calls. You have to do what you *want* to do. I don't think I can really help because when you think about it, no one can make this decision for you. And you can't make this decision for anyone *but* yourself.'

* * *

There were so many things to do. So many decisions to make, yet Olivia found herself frozen in some kind of overwhelmed state where thinking straight was just not an option. Once again, she wrapped herself up and headed out into the grounds with Marley. She took her sketch pad in case the surroundings triggered design ideas, and walked along the line of oak trees that she had helped to plant twenty-two years earlier. Now they towered over her at around twenty-five feet tall and fresh green growth was visible on the branches, more signs of spring. As Marley snuffled around on the hunt for goodness knew what, Olivia lowered herself to the ground and flipped over her sketch pad. She heard a rustling and turned to see a young red squirrel dashing up the trunk of one of her trees as Marley sat with his head cocked, watching intently. The squirrel's little ears were tufty and its bushy tail, as long as its body, bobbed behind it as it scuttled. The russet colour of its fur brought to mind autumn leaves and suddenly a design based on the rough bark of the tree trunks and the red of the little creature came to mind and she sketched it out, making notes around it of colours, textures and fabrics.

Once she was done with the rough design, she held it aloft and smiled, more than happy with the result. The squirrel was now far out of reach, much to Marley's yips of disapproval, but Olivia could just about make it out. She held up the design and said, 'Thanks for the idea, little guy!' The animal remained statue-still, watching them from its safe spot. It was good to know the place still inspired her. And the trees still held a special draw for her; a sentimental one. She could remember the planting day like it happened yesterday; her father, with his pristine white shirt, returning from some important meeting, had asked his driver to stop on the long driveway. He had climbed out of the car, rolled up his sleeves to the elbows, grabbed a shovel and said, 'Right, my little Lolly, what are we up to?' He was the only one who had ever called her Lolly and it was special for that fact. Like a gift he had given her.

'We're planting hoke trees, Daddy!' she had told him with her typical six-year-old bouncy exuberance. 'Look!' She had held out a handful of acorns. 'They started like this and growed into these!' She lifted up one of the little saplings.

'That's wonderful! I do love oak trees, how fantastic! Can I help you to dig?' he had asked with a bright smile.

'You can!' She held the shovel just below his hands and he let her think she was doing all the hard work but, of course, she wasn't.

One of the things she had loved more than anything as a child was doing things with her dad. They had often gone fishing together at the lake, his huge hands guiding her tiny ones when they cast their lines. But they had always placed the caught fish back in the water in case they missed their own daddies and mummies. They would often go for long walks around the grounds where her father would point out his favourite places that he'd loved as a boy, the best den-making areas and his favourite treehouse that stood in ruins but that he always said they should rebuild. Sadly, they had never got around to it. He would talk and Olivia would listen in awe and wonder. She was most definitely a daddy's girl.

She remembered placing the little saplings in the ground and patting the soil around them under her father and Dougie's watchful eye. Another memory appeared; seven-year-old Brodie had been there, too, helping her to carry the next sapling to its new home. They had made up a little song to encourage the oaks to grow big and strong and had giggled as they danced around the newly planted trees holding hands, much to the amusement of their respective fathers. She had always loved to see her dad smile. Brodie was much sweeter when he was younger; for her birthday after the tree planting, he had given her a little silver acorn pendant on a chain. It was so beautiful and very grown up. She had treasured it for many years until it was lost, and she was heartbroken. That was all before he got in with the crowd of boys who were mean to most people, including adults. But back then, when they were little, Brodie had treated her like a friend. Strange how she remembered things in fragments, almost like pieces of a jigsaw puzzle.

'We did well, didn't we?' a familiar voice asked from behind her. She turned to find Brodie standing there, his clothes covered in dirt and grass stains once again. Marley rushed to greet him and jumped up to add muddy paw prints to his already filthy attire. Brodie scratched the dog behind his ears.

Olivia stood and brushed leaves from her jeans. 'We did. It's hard to believe it was over twenty years ago.'

'Aye. They've grown a bit bigger than average for their age. Must have been our childish enthusiasm, or maybe it was the dancing and the wee song we sang to them.' He chuckled at the thought.

Olivia felt heat rise in her face and she laughed. 'Oh, gosh, yes, I was just thinking about that. I'd forgotten all about it until a few minutes ago. Both our dads were in hysterics.'

'Aye. Happy times.' He paused for a moment before narrowing his eyes. 'Do you still have the pendant I gave you? I remember shopping with my mum for your birthday gift and seeing it in the jeweller's window. It felt like kismet. I had to get it for you.'

Olivia chewed her lip. 'I'm so sorry, Brodie, but I lost it years ago. I loved it so much too. It was my very first piece of proper jewellery and I didn't take it off. I think I might have lost it at the swimming pool. I was devastated.'

'Ah, that's a shame. See, I did used to be nice. But it's strange how we tend to remember the bad stuff people have done first, eh?'

She returned his suspicious gaze. 'What's that supposed to mean?'

He took a step closer. 'I was mean to you back then, wasn't I? Well, when we were a bit older, I was, I see that now. Hadn't really thought about it until the other day when you made some comment about me saying hurtful things. I know I was a little rat bag when I was a teenager.' He rolled his eyes. 'Always trying to look cool with ma mates. But I didn't mean any of it. Not really. I was just a kid.' He shrugged. 'But for what it's worth, I'm sorry for hurting your feelings.'

Guilt washed over her. She really had remembered the bad stuff he'd done to her as a teen when they had actually been good friends as younger children. But twenty years had passed. They were adults. He was married, for goodness' sake; you couldn't get much more grown-up than that.

She smiled and shook her head. 'I think my emotions have just been raw since I got home. I've taken everything to heart. But it was such a long time ago now, I think I can forgive you.'

He grinned and held out his hand. 'Friends?'

She took his dirt-covered offering and for a split second had the urge to tug him into that dance around the tree for old time's sake and a giggle, but instead simply nodded. 'Friends.'

'Fancy a coffee?' He gestured behind himself. 'I've a flask over by the wheelbarrow. I've even got some of Mirren's Dundee cake too if you fancy.'

Olivia's stomach gurgled at the thought of Mirren's best cake recipe, filled with succulent fruit and crunchy almonds, and she nodded enthusiastically. They walked back to where Brodie had left the wheelbarrow and sat on a couple of old stumps as Brodie poured coffee into the two small cups that came with the flask and Marley went back to foraging in the undergrowth. Brodie handed a cup to Olivia, followed by a chunk of fruit cake wrapped in a paper napkin.

They sat in companionable silence for a moment, surrounded only by birdsong, the gentle spring breeze rustling the leaves of the ash and beech trees behind them that made up a decent-sized copse, and Marley's eager snuffling.

'How are you coping since... you know, since the will reading?'

Olivia lowered her gaze and watched a spider scrambling over the mud. 'So, you've heard all about it now then?' Her question was rhetorical. It was obvious that everyone would know by now.

He cringed as he spoke. 'Sorry, I don't mean to pry. Mirren explained everything this morning and it's just that it's a pretty huge thing so...'

Olivia lifted her chin and smiled, hoping to put him at ease. 'It is rather. I'm still coming to terms with it, to be honest.'

'I can now see that's why Kerr was so angry the other day. He didn't take it that well.'

Olivia sighed and shook her head. 'That's a wee bit of an understatement. He's certain in his mind that I've somehow conspired against him. But I love my life in New York and had no intention of being here permanently again. It's thrown a huge spanner in the works. And all this talk of me being Lady Olivia doesn't sit comfortably.'

'Aye, I can imagine it's been pretty hard for you. But you know you should do what's right for you, don't you? I know it's easy for me to sit here and spout that, but life's too short for you to be unhappy and trying to squeeze into a mould of someone else's making.'

'You sound like you're speaking from experience.'

He smiled, but it was void of happiness. 'Not really. Well not in the same way. I just know that you can't force yourself to be happy in a life that doesn't feel like it belongs to you.'

His words were somehow insightful. Olivia wondered what had caused him to be so introspective. Feeling a heaviness descend upon them, Olivia decided to change the subject. 'So, what have you been up to since you left Inverness? The last thing I heard was that you'd moved to Edinburgh with your mum.'

He took a sip of his coffee before speaking. 'I did. We lived in a rented house out by the Royal Infirmary. Can't say it was easy or fun if I'm honest. It was okay at the start but then Mum met someone new, and he was a dick.' He held up his hand. 'Pardon my French.'

'I'm sorry to hear that.'

He raised one shoulder and scrunched his nose. 'It is what it is. I escaped, though. Went to uni and never returned.'

'What did you study?'

He beamed. 'History, specialising in Scottish history.'

Olivia widened her eyes. 'Really? Oh, wow. Fascinating stuff.'

He glanced back towards the castle. 'Aye, and all thanks to this place. I was always fascinated by it. So, I decided I'd try and make a career out of it.' He seemed wistful. 'I used to come back to visit, you know. I guess I loved this place so much I couldn't stay away for long. So, I'd come and stay with my dad just to be near the castle again.'

This surprised her. 'You visited? How come I never saw you?'

He smiled and picked at the grass. 'I kept out the way. Our lives had taken such different paths. We'd become so... unlike each other. You were like this... like this medieval princess. In fact, you reminded me of Stevie Nicks in a way. I'd watch you dancing in the garden from behind one of the trees. Your hair all long and flowy. You were so graceful.'

Olivia felt her cheeks warming. 'Me? Graceful? Are you taking the mick?'

He smiled and shook his head. 'Not at all. I used to love to watch you dance. You'd have your headphones on and just move around like a ballerina. I imagined you were listening to Fleetwood Mac's "Gypsy" or something kind of dreamy and all ethereal like that. It was as if that song had been written about you. I don't know why you didn't take up dancing.'

Olivia laughed. 'Because I had my own left foot and one belonging to someone else.'

He shook his head. 'Not from where I was watching.'

'Stalker,' she said, teasing him.

He held out his hands. 'Guilty as charged.'

'How often did you come back? I still can't believe I never saw you. And your dad never said anything. But then again, I didn't exactly converse much with your dad.'

'A couple of times a year. It got less when I went to university.'

'So, what were you doing before you returned here to Drumblair?'

He munched on a mouthful of cake as if buying time and made a show of swallowing, holding up his finger in a pausing motion. Eventually he took a sip of his coffee and said, 'After I graduated, I was working in the archives at the university. Then I got a job working with Edinburgh Castle. It was brilliant being surrounded by so much history.' His smile disappeared. 'But... things didn't quite work out.'

With her interest piqued, Olivia tilted her head. 'Oh? How come?'

Brodie's face flushed and he laughed. 'Bloody hell, I feel like I'm being interviewed. Have you got a tape recorder stashed away in your pocket? Because I can assure you my life isn't that exciting.'

Olivia cringed. 'Oh heck, sorry I didn't mean to interrogate you. I'm just fascinated, that's all.'

'Aye, well, I should probably get back to what I was doing. Plenty to keep me busy.'

'Yes, I can imagine, although rest assured the first thing I'll be doing is reinstating the gardeners who want to come back, so you'll be able to return to your own life.'

He smiled. 'That's great. Dad will be pleased. Speaking of whom, he'll be wondering where I've got to. And why his cake and coffee are missing.' He gave a small laugh.

She gasped and lifted her hand to her mouth, her eyes wide. 'I've eaten your dad's cake?'

Brodie leaned closer and whispered. 'I won't tell if you don't. Anyway, better dash. Nice chatting to you, Lady Olivia.' And there it was again, that name that separated her from people, like she was somehow special. Trouble was she didn't feel it and didn't want to be.

8

Uncle Innes was checking in regularly to make sure Olivia was okay after the events at the will reading, and of course to ask after Marley. She was grateful for his support and glad to know there were people on her side, even if one of them wasn't her elusive, crabby brother. Kerr had apparently made comments within earshot of staff that he was looking into challenging the will, although he hadn't had the guts to say this directly to Olivia. Uncle Innes had assured her that he didn't have a leg to stand on as tradition wasn't considered in legal matters and claiming such a thing was the only real weapon he had in his arsenal.

She had called him a couple of days after the reading to check that he was okay, as the words he had blurted about his life being in danger had really scared her. They didn't get on, but she certainly wouldn't wish any harm to him.

The conversation had been brief, and ended with him informing her, 'I'm fine now, no thanks to you and your cronies. My darling Adaira has helped me. It's good to know I have someone who actually cares whether I live or die.' Olivia hoped he was simply being overdramatic but was relieved nonetheless to hear that he was now safe. But knowing his past reputation, for how long would that be the case?

Knowing that the local rumour mill would begin turning soon, if it hadn't already, Olivia made a group video call to Bella and Skye and informed them of the results of the will reading. They were both shocked and excited for her whilst a little cautious and concerned about what it would mean for her life going forward.

'What do we call you now?' Bella asked.

'You call me Olivia. I'm still just me. I don't want anyone to think of me differently now. That's my biggest fear, that you'll all start treating me like some kind of aristocrat. I've never wanted that. I didn't want this either—'

In Bella's true no-filter style, she informed her, 'But technically you are an aristocrat.' Then she added thoughtfully, 'You know, I never realised that was a word that was linked to humans. I thought it was just from that Disney film with the cats.'

Skye rolled her eyes and shook her head at the screen before turning her attention to Olivia. 'But your mum trusted you to do the right thing, honey. She wouldn't have done this if she hadn't felt it absolutely necessary. She knew why you left for New York, and she knew what your dreams were. That's why I feel that she had no choice.'

Olivia sighed. 'I know. But... I feel under so much pressure right now. The grief of losing her plus what she's asked me to do... It's just so much.'

'Do you know what you need?' Bella said.

Hoping for some pearl of wisdom, Olivia asked, 'What do I need, Bells?'

Bella brought the camera close so that just one eye could be seen. 'A night out with the girlssss.' Skye and Olivia giggled. 'And you'll be happy to know I have a job interview first thing in the morning, so I'm driving.'

'Fantastic! What's the job?' Olivia asked.

'Oh, it's just an admin position in the city. Nothing flash. Anyway, Skye and I will pick you up at seven in Fifi.'

Olivia grinned at the mention of Fifi. 'I can't believe you've still got that bloody car! It's ancient.'

Bella scoffed and feigned anger. 'Hey, don't you *dare* dis Fifi! She's vintage, thank you very much. And she drives like a dream. So... what do you say?'

'Oh, what the heck. I'm in!' Skye replied.

Olivia sighed but followed this with a smile. 'I suppose I could do with cheering up.'

* * *

Later that same evening, Olivia got ready for her girls' night at the Drumblair Arms. She slipped on jeans and a plain teal sweater, determined to blend in rather than stand out. She curled her highlighted hair and applied minimal make-up. She didn't really feel like socialising. It felt quite wrong to do so, seeing as she had only just laid her mother to rest. But on the other hand, she wanted to show the world that she was still herself and that no airs and graces had suddenly descended upon her since the will reading. And Mirren fervently insisted that her mother wouldn't want her to put her life on hold.

At 7 p.m., the girls arrived and waited for Olivia outside on the gravel driveway. Mirren appeared in the drawing room to let her know and she grabbed her leather jacket, scarf and purse and made her way outside where her two friends waved excitedly from the car. The sky was darkening and there was a chill to the air, so, under a little duress, she hurriedly climbed into one of the rear passenger seats of Bella's ancient... sorry, *vintage*... Citroen 2CV and off they went.

The short drive once again reminded Olivia how picturesque the village of Drumblair was with its old-fashioned lantern design streetlights and whitewashed cottages, interspersed with stone villas. Most of the buildings faced onto an expanse of green at the village centre and most windows glowed a warm amber from within. The village green had a children's play area at one end and a monument dedicated to local fallen soldiers in the centre. Beyond that was the village kirk that she had attended as a child with her classmates for Easter, Christmas and harvest festival services.

The Drumblair Arms was a huge whitewashed building on the main road just past the village green, dating back to the 1700s. It had once been a carriage stop on the route north for travellers. It still held much of its charm and that's what Olivia liked the most about the place. The small windows meant that draughts were kept at bay, and many were the original rippled and bubbled glass. The archway that had once led coaches and horses through to the yard now led people through to the beer garden.

When Bella had parked the car, the three friends climbed out, walked around the front of the pub and pushed through the main entrance door. The place was bustling with lively chat and laughter and the atmosphere was light and welcoming. According to an A-frame Olivia had noticed by the door, there was to be a local band playing later on and Olivia was looking forward to having a relaxing drink and forgetting about her predicament, even if only for a short while. She had made a condition of coming out for the evening that the castle, the inheritance and her newly acquired title should not be discussed. At all. Olivia wanted a simple, quiet night out with her friends where she could enjoy some live music and still feel like a normal human being who hadn't just inherited a grand country estate, and whose deceased parents weren't hoping for her to continue their legacy.

Once they had purchased their first round of drinks, the three friends sat at the only free table left, by the bar. Many long-term locals stopped by the table to pass on their condolences and chat about what a lovely woman Olivia's mother had been, and she found herself welling up on more than one occasion. She was deeply touched by their kind words, which only served to reiterate how loved the family were, despite their enviable wealth and supposed station. It was both reassuring and comforting but, in some ways, contributed to the pressure she was feeling to stay in Scotland.

When the last of the visitors to their table had gone, Olivia turned to Skye. 'So, come on, missy, what's going on with Ben and the proposal? It seems to have all gone quiet. Have there been any further developments?'

Skye sighed deeply. 'We had to cancel our dinner at River House. Ben got a horrible stomach bug so... well, you know.'

Olivia was disappointed for her friend. 'Oh, no. So has anything else been said?'

Skye's expression was despondent. 'Not yet. He's only just getting over it so I'm guessing he might rearrange or—'

'Or what?' Bella and Olivia asked in unison.

'Or he's changed his mind.'

Olivia scoffed. 'Don't be daft, Skye. Like I said before, he adores you, it's so obvious. Just give him some time. I'm sure he'll rearrange things when he's better.'

Skye shrugged, seemingly not convinced. 'Maybe. But the ring box isn't in his pocket any more. I'm worried he's returned it to the shop.'

Bella reached and squeezed her arm. 'Well, if he has, I'm sure you'll find someone even better.'

Olivia glared at Bella. 'Really? Those are your wise words of encouragement?'

Bella shrugged. 'I just mean that if he *has* changed his mind, he's more of an Alan Rickman than we thought.'

At this comment, Skye laughed. 'You can't just use that poor actor's name as the general term for *cheater*. It was a character he played and he's dead now, so it feels a bit mean.'

Bella's eyes grew wide. 'Alan Rickman's dead?'

Olivia and Skye gave a collective groan and then both giggled. For a few minutes, it felt just like old times for Olivia; the banter with her friends, Bella making some innocently inappropriate comment that had them in hysterics...

Bella's expression changed to one of annoyance. 'What? I don't like watching the news; it's depressing so I don't always keep up with current affairs.'

Skye reached and patted her arm. 'Not that current, babe. He passed away in 2016.'

Bella's brow crumpled. 'Oh... right.'

There was a long pause before Bella spoke again. 'What will Kerr do now he hasn't inherited the castle, do you think?' Her question came completely out of left field – nothing new for Bella, really. She was promptly whacked on the arm by Skye and turned to her friend, rubbing her arm. 'Ow! What was that for?'

As if Olivia might not hear, Skye spoke in a loud theatrical whisper. 'We're not meant to talk about any of that stuff, remember?'

Olivia smiled, knowing it was ridiculous of her to ask them not to talk about it. They were her closest friends, after all. She sighed, almost in defeat. 'It's fine. Don't worry.' She paused and thought of her brother. She imagined him sprawled dramatically on the Chesterfield at Drumblair Villa in the city with his head in Adaira's lap, sobbing about his lost opportunity to cash in on her mother's death, all *woe is me*. Her stomach churned and she wished that things were better between them. That they could share their grief like normal siblings, instead of being locked in some kind of fictional combat of her brother's making.

Eventually she replied, 'Honestly, I'm not sure. I think he's very hurt and I know he's angry with me. He's under some misguided illusion that I had a say in all this, so he's keeping his distance, for now, at least. Licking his wounds, I suppose. I mean... this wasn't exactly what I expected either. And it's not like I asked for any of this. Believe me, it kind of changes my future in a way that I didn't want or need.'

Realising that the topic was back on the table again, Skye tentatively asked, 'Aren't you a tiny bit excited, though? I mean, it's a castle. A huge, beautiful fairy-tale-esque castle and it's going to be all yours.'

Olivia rolled her eyes. 'It's only like you inheriting your family home.'

Bella scoffed. 'Yeah, right, only our family homes are a detached 1970s box on a housing estate with a postage stamp garden, and a terraced cottage on a main road with a bus stop right outside the lounge window.'

Skye added, 'Aye and the only wildlife we get are sparrows or, in my case, Roger from next door when he's pished and tries to get into the wrong hoose on a Saturday night!' They all laughed as Skye mimicked her middle-aged drunken neighbour trying to get his key in the door.

Olivia tapped her arm playfully. 'Hey, you know what I mean. It's just home to me. Well, it was. Now it's a bit of an albatross around my neck.' Realising she sounded ungrateful, she added, 'A huge, beautiful, *fairy-tale-esque* albatross obviously. But it's all rather terrifying, to be honest.'

'What will you do about New York? Things were going so well for you there,' Skye asked with a tilt of her head and pity in her eyes.

'Aye and there was going to be a promotion for you, wasn't there?' Bella added.

Olivia nodded. 'Yes. I think so, anyway. I'll go back for a while. Until I've decided what to do in the long term. I have six months until it's all official, so I want to make the most of it. I don't want to let Nina down when she's given me so many amazing opportunities. And I do love New York.'

'Evening, Lady Olivia. Good to see you out and about. Although I didn't think this would be your kind of place these days.' Olivia stopped talking and lifted her chin to see Brodie standing there. Gone were the dirt-covered T-shirt and ripped combat trousers of earlier. Now he was wearing dark blue jeans and a black shirt, sleeves rolled up to the elbows and open just a little at the neck, so his black rope necklace was visible. He looked like he'd walked off one of her catwalks.

Olivia scowled and cleared her throat. She was about to speak when Bella chimed in, 'Let me stop you there, Brodie MacLeod, it's just Olivia, actually. No need for the airs and graces. And anyway, that topic is off the table tonight. She's having a normal girls' night without thinking about all that stuff, aren't you, Liv?' She winked at Olivia in an 'I've got your back' manner, but Olivia felt bad for her friend's snippy retort, although she knew Bella was trying to protect her.

Brodie's expression turned serious, and he gave a swift, curt nod. 'My apologies. Okay... well, ladies, I'll leave you to your evening.' He turned back to Olivia and simply said, 'Olivia,' before walking away.

'Shit, did I say the wrong thing?' Bella asked. 'He looked upset. I didn't mean to upset him. Do you think he looked upset?'

Olivia smiled. 'No, it's fine. I'm not comfortable with the title thing yet.'

Skye was staring at his back as he left. 'He's a bit gorgeous, isn't he? I can't believe how much he's changed since school. I honestly didn't recognise him at all. In fact, don't you think he looks like a younger version of that actor... what's his name... Really handsome, quite a philanthropist. Ugh, do you know who I mean?' Skye asked.

Bella interrupted. 'Oh, yeah. Ted somebody, isn't it?'

Olivia also watched Brodie as he walked over to a group of men at the other side of the pub who were talking with members of the band. 'Keanu Reeves,' she said absently. 'He played Ted in *Bill and Ted's Excellent Adventure*, Keanu Reeves, not Brodie, obviously. Oh, and Brodie's married, by the way.' Olivia wasn't sure why she'd added that snippet to the end of her sentence.

She found herself watching as the men greeted each other with manly, back-slapping hugs and fist bumps and she almost smiled at their friendly exchange. That is until she recognised one of the men as being from that horrid spotty, obnoxious, bullying cohort from their school days and she shivered. Brodie glanced over at her and then at his friends as if he had noticed her disdain. He shrugged, an action she was a little baffled by, then he raised his glass to her as he had done on the day of the funeral before turning back to his friends.

Later in the evening, the pub had filled up so much they'd had to relinquish their table and stand with everyone else. The band clearly had a huge following and everyone fell silent as the group of four twenty-somethings took to the makeshift stage area at one end of the pub and introduced themselves.

'Evening everyone! How yous all doin'?' A cheer travelled the room. 'We're David's Tenants and we're happy to be here to entertain yous all tonight.' A raucous applause and piercing whistles ensued, and Bella almost snorted her Diet Coke.

Her expression was wide-eyed and so innocent. 'Oh my god, that's so weird! There's an actual real-life actor called David Tennant!'

Olivia tried not to choke on her wine and Skye rolled her eyes for what must have been the hundredth time that evening as she grinned. 'I think that's the point of the joke, you daft loon.'

When Bella burst out laughing, Olivia couldn't help joining in.

Bella cackled. 'Oh, hell, and I've no' had any alcohol either.'

The band played an eclectic selection of music, and the evening was turning out to be great fun. Olivia couldn't remember feeling this relaxed in far too long. One song ended and the lead singer chatted to the audience for a few moments.

'So, ladies and gents, I've had a request for a specific song from one of the audience members who wishes to remain anonymous. It's not a song that's usually in our repertoire but apparently someone is celebrating some rather amazing news just now. So, this next song is dedicated to a person who I have on good authority is in the place this evening. Everyone, I give you the newly crowned Lady Olivia MacBain of Drumblair. Please accept our congratulations, your grace!' The pub lights suddenly illuminated, and all eyes turned to Olivia as the opening bars of Tom Jones's 'She's a Lady' began to play.

Olivia felt a furnace rising beneath her skin as she realised the group of men Brodie was with were all looking at her. It was clearly a joke to them, and they clapped and whistled as the singer recited lyrics about a 'little lady'. Every direction she turned, there were more eyes on her. The wine she had been drinking had mingled with the heat in the place and she felt sick and dizzy, her heart rate had increased until it felt like the organ was bouncing around in her chest like a basketball. She glanced over at Brodie, who appeared to be loudly joining in and singing the lyrics into the ear of one of his friends. She felt betrayed, hurt and embarrassed beyond measure. He knew how she felt about the whole situation. She had confided in him. Well, that had clearly been a mistake of epic proportions. One she wouldn't be repeating again. She turned away and pushed her way through a crowd of people she didn't know, clearly fans of the band, and shoved through the door into the cold evening air. She gasped for breath as tears came.

Skye appeared beside her, quickly followed by Bella. 'Shit, I think she's having a panic attack, Skye!'

'Was this that bloody mud guzzler's doing? Was it? Eh? Was it that bloody gardening Keanu Reeves lookalike who did this?' Skye shouted, gesturing back to the pub. 'Doesn't he realise that after what Bella said to him this was totally inappropriate?' All the questions were rhetorical, which was just as well, seeing as Olivia was unable to form a coherent sentence in between sobs. She had never been so embarrassed, well, not since the giraffe jokes at school, anyway, and the fact that she should never have come out so soon after her mum's funeral rattled around her head, proving her right again.

'Come on. I'm taking you home,' Bella said as she stormed towards the car. 'I should never have suggested this. It's too soon and people are idiots. I'm so sorry, Olivia. I really am.'

They hurriedly climbed into the car and Bella started the engine. All the emotion Olivia had been bottling up since the will reading erupted and she sobbed uncontrollably. As they pulled out of the car park, Olivia glanced over her shoulder to see Brodie standing in the car park, his hands scrunched in his hair.

9

Mirren and Marley sat on Olivia's bed until her tears had subsided and she was emotionally drained.

Mirren stood and leaned down to place a kiss on her forehead. 'Try and get some sleep, dearie. Marley will stay and keep you company, won't you, lad?' Marley gave a single wag of his tail as if he understood completely. 'I'll check on you in the morning.'

'Thank you so much, Mirren. For always being here.'

Mirren paused at the bedroom door and smiled. 'No thanks needed. I wouldn't want to be anywhere else.'

Olivia lay awake for what felt like hours, regardless of how exhausted she felt. Marley had lain directly at her side on the bed, with his head on the spare pillow and his paw on her arm. He was such a comfort and the thought of leaving him again broke her heart, but she decided that she needed to fly back to New York as soon as possible and try to get some normality back into her life, even if it would be short-lived. She knew Marley would be well cared for by Uncle Innes again. And she would see him again soon. But the thought of saying goodbye still made her heart ache.

She would arrange a meeting with Uncle Innes and set the

wheels in motion for what she felt was the best way forward for the castle until she returned. She grabbed her sketch pad and made copious notes on the ideas she'd had about Drumblair and its future, and her involvement in it. Then she placed the pad down and lay silently, stroking Marley's soft fur and replaying the evening's events over and over and over... She eventually must have drifted off as she awoke to her mobile pinging. It was a text from Bella. There was one from Skye too. Both concerned and apologising about dragging her out when she wasn't ready.

Olivia replied and tried to reassure them that they weren't to blame and then she showered in the hope it would make her feel better. A short while later, she wandered down to the kitchen with Marley to find Mirren baking shortbread and she sat at the table to watch her work. They talked over the events at the pub again.

'I just don't understand why he would do that. Especially after I'd told him how I was feeling about everything. It was so embarrassing and made me feel so stupid. Clearly leopards don't change their spots.'

'Well, just say the word and I'll make sure Dougie tells him to leave. We can't have that kind of behaviour. It's not funny and I don't see how he can have thought it was.'

'So you don't think I'm overreacting?' Olivia asked with genuine concern.

'I certainly don't. After what you've been through this past few weeks, he should've known better.'

Olivia paused as she remembered him standing outside the pub as they left. He looked upset. Angry too, maybe. But did he look like someone who'd played a prank that had gone horribly wrong? She wasn't sure. But she had seen him singing along, hadn't she?

'Do you know why his wife isn't here with him?' Olivia asked Mirren out of the blue.

Mirren paused and glanced over at her. 'Actually, no. Dougie wasn't very forthcoming. Although maybe he doesn't know. Not all families share what's going on in their lives.' Her brow crumpled. 'It is strange, though. When he arrived, it looked like he was here to stay. He'd enough luggage to suggest it was more than a holiday.' She returned to rolling the shortbread dough. 'But don't you go worrying yourself about all that. He clearly can't be trusted. Maybe his wife discovered that too.'

Olivia pondered on that for a moment. 'Don't ask him to leave. I'm going to head back to New York anyway. I need to start and think everything through.'

'Aye, dear. You've a lot ahead of you, that's right enough. But it'll all come good. I'm sure of it.'

* * *

Olivia met Uncle Innes at the Glenmorriston Townhouse Brasserie for lunch and to chat to him about her plans to go back to New York. She took her sketch pad with the notes she had scribbled in anger the night before.

He read through them very carefully. 'Are you sure about this? It seems extreme... it's a lot of work and risk too.'

'If you'd rather not take it on, I totally understand,' she told him with a squeeze to his arm.

'Oh, no, not at all, Olivia dear. I will help in any way I can, and we'll stay in regular contact throughout the funding application process and everything else too. I just hope you know what you're letting yourself in for.'

Olivia shook her head. 'Not in the slightest.' She smiled.

He patted her hand where it rested on this arm. 'Well, we'll muddle through together, eh?'

'That sounds like a plan.'

Innes tilted his head and regarded her with concern. 'So, Mirren tells me your flight is booked?'

Olivia nodded. 'It is. I fly out on Friday.'

'Any word from Kerr?'

She shook her head. 'Not a dickie bird since I called him the day after the will reading.'

'Ah. Just as I expected. Foolish man.' Olivia didn't reply. She didn't know what to say. Innes sighed. 'So... it's the last week in March now, meaning you will be back in Scotland...'

'Around the last week in September, I think.'

'So, that just leaves tomorrow for you to say goodbye to your friends again. You haven't been home long and I'm sure they'll miss you.'

Olivia shrugged. 'I'll miss them too. But it's only six months. It'll fly by. I think I'm more worried about poor Marley.'

'Ah, yes. Poor mite. But you know I'll take good care of him back at the farmhouse and he'll have a whale of a time with me.'

'That's good to know. He's been like my shadow the whole time I've been here. It'll break my heart again to leave him. It's like having a piece of Mum still around.'

Innes gave a sympathetic smile. 'I know. I feel the same.' There was a short silence before he continued. 'Oh, you'll be home in time for Laird McPherson's annual charity ball, so that's nice. It's the first weekend in October. Your mother always attended; great for making connections. You know, networking, as you young folks call it.' He made air quotes and Olivia had to try not to laugh, it looked so bizarre on such a serious man.

Olivia made a dismissive noise. 'Oh, balls aren't really my thing. A night at the cinema with a bucket of popcorn and I'm your girl but dressing up like the Queen of Sheba... not so much.'

Innes's expression became one of seriousness. 'As Lady MacBain, I'm afraid you will be expected to attend. It'll be frowned upon if you don't. These are the things you need to take into consideration.'

'Lucky that I have six months to dwell on that delightful thought, then.'

'I'm happy to accompany you if you like? I attended with your mother a few times after your father's death. I could show you the ropes. It's not as scary as it seems right now.'

'Thank you. I may just take you up on that if you wouldn't mind.'

'I'd be honoured. The thing is, *Lady Olivia*, you will still hold the title, even if you don't stay to oversee the castle. There will still be expectations placed upon you, which will be difficult, but they come with the territory. I know you didn't ask to be born into this. And you certainly didn't expect to be in this position at all, but now that you are... I'm afraid it's something you will have to learn to deal with. Look at Prince Harry, he left the country but can't leave the royal connection behind.'

Olivia smiled. 'My situation is hardly comparable to Prince Harry's, Uncle Innes.'

'I'm afraid there are probably more similarities than there are differences. You are the heir to a Scottish legacy. And you will have to decide if you will spend the rest of your life here as Lady MacBain or in New York as the same person. It's a hard decision to make when you've set down roots in the Big Apple. But you have to understand that wherever you live, your title will remain.'

Olivia knew he was speaking the truth and as much as she didn't want to admit it, the whole matter terrified her. 'I know. I think I've pretended up to now that if I stay in New York, I'll just be Olivia MacBain, fashion designer, but deep down, I don't think I ever will be *just* anything ever again.'

* * *

Saying goodbye to Skye and Bella had been emotional.

'I can't believe you're going already when we've only just got you back,' Bella said, dabbing at her eyes. 'What has it been? Two weeks? I hope it's not because of what happened at the pub. I'll never forgive myself for that.'

Olivia hugged her. 'Don't be daft. I need to get back to work.'

'You will keep in touch plenty, won't you?' Skye asked.

'Don't I always? And you must let me know what happens with you and Ben, okay?'

Skye nodded. 'I may be an old maid before he decides to propose now. But we'll see.'

Olivia narrowed her eyes. 'Nah. You wait. You'll be engaged by the end of the summer.'

Skye's chin trembled. 'But you won't be here to celebrate.'

Olivia grappled Skye into a hug. 'We'll celebrate when I come back! It's six months. It's not that long, really.'

Saying goodbye never got easier but she had Harper and her other friends waiting in New York. She had a new apartment to move into. One where she had the space to have an office to plan the changes to the castle, to apply for funding, and even create some designs for Nina. She had offered Harper a spare room, but Harper had decided to remain in her own apartment. It had belonged to her grandma, so Olivia could understand her sentimental attachment to it. But she couldn't imagine not sharing breakfast with her best friend every day, nor could she imagine the journey to work without their conversations.

Olivia sat in the kitchen, waiting to leave. Uncle Innes had insisted on her mother's driver, Spencer, taking her to the airport. She had refused at first, saying a taxi would suffice, but he wouldn't back down, so she eventually acquiesced. Of course, there had been no contact from Kerr. He had no doubt yet to forgive her for the things she had supposedly done wrong to ruin his life. She considered extending yet another olive branch but on reflection thought better of it. She wanted to leave Scotland with as positive a frame of mind as was possible under the circumstances.

She had made the difficult decision to sort through her mother's possessions when she returned, feeling that she might be in a better position emotionally to do so then. She had cuddled Marley for the hundredth time, nuzzled his fur and inhaled his scent, sobbing uncontrollably as the poor creature licked at her tears and pawed at her. Innes had collected him and now that he was gone, she was bereft.

She was mid-WhatsApp chat with Skye when someone cleared their throat at the kitchen doorway. She turned to see Brodie sheepishly standing there.

'Oh. It's you. Come to make more jokes at my expense?' she asked bitterly before she returned her attention to her phone. Even so, she was very much aware of him standing behind her.

She heard him step forward. 'Lady... erm... Olivia, look, Mirren told Dad you were leaving, so I came to explain... that is, to apologise. Although technically I did nothing wrong.'

She turned and scowled at him. 'You do understand how apologies usually work, don't you?'

He rubbed at his now fully bearded chin. 'Aye, aye of course, but the thing is I'm not apologising on behalf of myself.'

Baffled and a little irked, she turned to fully face him now. 'So, it wasn't you who humiliated me in front of a pub full of people then? After everything I had said to you about how I was feeling about this whole bloody matter?'

He stepped closer, sinking his hands into the pockets of his combat trousers. 'Actually, no, it wasn't.'

Confusion niggled at her, and she shook her head. 'I don't understand.'

'It was one of the lads. You know Angus Buchan from school? Your favourite of my friends,' he said without hiding his sarcasm.

'The one with the thinning hair? The one whose ear you were singing into as I left the pub under a cloud of embarrassment?'

'Lady Olivia, you're mistaken. That is, Olivia... it was Angus who got the band to play that song. What you witnessed was me shouting expletives into his ear as you left. He already knew about your inheritance. But not from me, I hasten to add. News travels fast around here, as you know. And he'd made some derogatory comment about you being privileged and snobby. I defended you and said that actually it wasn't something you were hoping for or comfortable with, but he said I still had a crush on you, so I was blinkered. Then he spoke to the lead singer and then *that* happened. I was mortified. I... I'm embarrassed to say I punched him after you'd left and then I ran out to explain but you'd gone. I would've come yesterday but I had to go to the police station to make a statement about the alleged assault. Thankfully Angus realised he'd been a nob when he sobered up and isn't pressing charges.'

Olivia listened but couldn't quite take it all in. 'Oh... I see. Making quite a habit of punching people, aren't you?'

He lowered his gaze and his cheeks tinged bright pink. 'It's not who I am, especially when...' He shook his head. 'I mean, I'm so, *so* sorry.' There was a deep sincerity to his gaze, and she couldn't help wondering why he didn't finish his sentence.

Mirren appeared in the doorway. 'Olivia, dear, Spencer is here with the car out front,' she said with a brief glance towards Brodie.

'Oh, right, yes, thank you, Mirren. Please could you tell him I'll be right out?' Mirren glanced at Brodie again, nodded and hurried away.

Olivia stood and Brodie lunged for her luggage. 'Here let me get your bags,' he said.

'Thank you,' she replied, still trying to process everything. Silently she followed him out to the car, and he placed her cases in the boot of the highly polished black vehicle.

'Are you okay?' Brodie asked, genuine concern in his gaze.

Olivia nodded. 'I am. Thank you. And... I'm sorry for thinking the worst of you... *again*.'

He shrugged. 'It's *nae* bother. I just wanted to explain before you left, that's all. Didn't want you all the way over in New York thinking I'd betrayed you. Despite what you might think, I wouldn't do that to anyone. Least of all to you.'

Her heart skipped and she wondered what he meant by that, but she didn't have time to contemplate it as the suited driver opened the car door and Olivia climbed in. Just as Spencer was about to close the door, something Brodie had said suddenly gained clarity.

She held up her hand. 'Wait, one second please.' She turned to Brodie. 'Angus said you "*still* had a crush" on me...?'

Brodie's cheeks flushed again, and he fidgeted. 'Oh, that... aye. He used to rib me something chronic about it when we were kids. And when I used to come home to stay with Dad, he'd rib me about watching you in the garden.'

'You didn't, though, did you? Have a crush on me at school? I mean... the name calling... the twig throwing...'

Brodie dropped his gaze and smiled before lifting his chin and locking his eyes on her again. 'What's that phrase about always hurting the one you love?'

Love? Olivia's stomach somersaulted and heat flooded her veins, but it was short-lived. She paused and reminded herself of what she had learned recently. 'And now you're happily married,' she said with a smile.

He nodded but frowned. 'Aye, and now I'm married.'

Olivia inhaled a deep breath and climbed back out of the car. She stood a couple of feet away from Brodie. 'Well, thank you for explaining. It's certainly helped clear things up. I possibly won't see you when I return in six months' time, seeing as the gardeners have pretty much all been reinstated. Your dad will have plenty of help going forward and I'm sure you have better things to do with your qualifications than pull up weeds at a dilapidated old castle.' She inhaled a shaking breath. 'So... I'll say goodbye and wish you and your wife all the best.' She wanted to hug him but instead held out her hand.

He took her fingers and stroked his thumb across them. 'All the best to you, Olivia. I look forward with excitement to seeing what becomes of this place under your care.'

For a split second, Olivia thought he was going to kiss her hand, but he straightened and released her. She climbed back into the car and Spencer closed the door. He climbed into the driving seat and started the engine but as he did so, Brodie stepped forward and gestured for her to open the window.

She did so and looked up at him. 'What is it?' she asked.

'I— I was just going to say that if I *had* asked the band to play a song, it would have been something completely different.'

She tilted her head as her heart skipped. 'Really? What would it have been?'

His cheeks coloured again, and a handsome smile spread across his face. 'It's pointless telling you, really. But it's another song that used to remind me of you when we were younger. It was an oldie even then, but they were my dad's favourite band, so I was brought up on them I suppose. Their music still has a strange effect on me.'

'Whose music?'

Brodie opened his mouth to reply but Spencer, the driver, cleared his throat dramatically. 'Lady Olivia, I'm sorry to interject, but if you're going to make the check-in for your flight, we really need to go.'

'Yes, yes, one second, Spencer. Brodie?'

'The band was the Police,' he replied with a small smile. 'The song... "Every Little Thing She Does is Magic".'

Olivia's breath caught in her throat.

Brodie widened his eyes and his colour seemed to drain rapidly. 'And, and I'm pretty sure that will apply to whatever you do with the castle,' he added as if to change the meaning behind his words. He patted the roof of the car. 'You'd better go. I don't want to be responsible for you missing your flight.'

'Yes. Yes, I should go. Well... thank you, Brodie.' She smiled, despite a sadness that had wrapped around her heart. 'Take care.'

'You too,' he replied.

She pressed the button to raise the window again with the Police's song bouncing around her head as she tried to remember the lyrics, and as the car pulled away, she turned to see Brodie standing there with one hand raised. She gave a single wave and watched until the car turned a slight bend on the long drive, and she could no longer see him.

Once she'd turned to face the front again, she took out her phone and searched for the lyrics of the Police song that Brodie had mentioned. She read them and her heart flipped. *Surely he can't have really felt that way?* she mused to herself and smiled. But yet again, her smile disappeared quickly when she reminded herself that Brodie was, in fact, a married man.

10

Within only a few days, Olivia had moved into her new apartment in a picturesque block on Park Avenue in the Upper East Side of New York. It was a duplex with the bedrooms on a second level, the principal with its own terrace for morning coffee; the view, however, was somewhat different to her balcony back home. Instead of deer, hares and birds, there were the trees that lined the street below and the other blocks that surrounded her. Windows of other apartments narrowly missed having a direct view into hers. If she hadn't lived in New York before, she could've felt quite hemmed in, but it was something that didn't faze her now. She had an abundance of space inside, where it mattered. The rooms were light and airy with white-painted walls and large, comfortable furniture which was all provided already. There was a bright white kitchen with modern appliances and a breakfast bar that she could imagine Harper sitting at as she cooked them pasta.

The apartment was to become her head office of sorts. The Command Centre, Uncle Innes called it. She had her laptop and papers pertaining to Drumblair set up on the dining table that sat at one end of the large open-plan living area, meaning the spare room remained empty in case Harper changed her mind about moving in. Of course, she knew it was unlikely, but she held on to a little hope.

If her mother was trying to convince her to return to Scotland, she had gone the wrong way about it. This place was a dream; so sumptuous and classy. She still didn't understand why her mother had arranged it for her when she was only supposed to stay for six months. Then Olivia reminded herself that she had given her the option of bowing out and remaining in the Big Apple indefinitely. If she chose to do so, she now had the perfect place to live.

Around a week after her return to New York, Olivia met Nina at a coffee shop on Lexington Avenue to talk everything through before she returned to the office. Nina told her what had been going on in her absence – even though Harper had already kept her abreast of the goings on – and Olivia filled Nina in on all the details of her inheritance, nervously poising herself rigid for the response.

Nina leaned forward in her leather armchair and placed her oversized coffee cup on a coaster. Her eyes were wide, and her mouth formed an O. 'Oh, my goodness!' she said eventually. 'You're landed gentry now! Why on earth have you come back to New York when you have all that waiting for you? It sounds idyllic.'

Olivia sighed. 'Because I love my job here. All I've ever wanted to be is a fashion designer. This situation was never on my radar. My older brother was always the rightful heir, so this whole thing has thrown me for a loop. But now it's happened I'm... *lost*. Part of me knows I will always belong at Drumblair, it's my home, it's my family's history, but an equal part of me knows that here I'm living my childhood dream.'

'Oh, sweetie. It's a lot to take in on top of losing your mamma.

Is there no one else who could take the lead? Did your brother not want the responsibility? What has he said?'

Olivia shook her head. 'Therein lies another tale. He wasn't in the least bit happy that my mother purposely avoided leaving the castle to him. He's... how can I put it? Troubled.'

Nina raised her eyebrows and held up a halting hand. 'Ah. Say no more. Families can be so complicated. But look, you have so many opportunities ahead of you. What's to say you can't get the castle to a point where you know it's repaired and then have your uncle take the reins so you can return here?'

Olivia nodded slowly. 'That's the plan. Well, one of them. I just wanted to be completely transparent with you. I know you wanted to discuss a change in my role, and I don't want to leave you in the lurch.'

Nina rolled her eyes and waved her hand. '*Ciccio*, Michael and Alvaro have gone to make their new life together as a married couple. The wedding was a lavish affair, lots of sparkles,' she added as a side note with a wink. 'But I would love for you to step into Michael's shoes if you think you can handle that *and* everything else you have going on too?'

Olivia gasped. 'Don't you want to interview me? Consider others even?'

Nina smiled. 'Consider this your interview.' She became serious for a moment. 'Look, I've wanted to have you as my second for a while now. I've witnessed you growing and improving whenever you were given the opportunity to fly. But the truth is, Olivia, you're good enough to go it alone. You don't need to stay at Nina Picarro. You could easily start your own label. Maybe that's what you will do eventually, or maybe you will return to Scotland and fully embrace your role as Lady MacBain, I don't know. The truth is, and I know it's selfish, but I would like to keep you on board for as long as I can. You're invaluable to me.'

Olivia smiled but it was tinged with a little of the sadness she felt inside. 'Thank you so much. For everything. For giving me a chance when I first came here. For believing in me. For trusting me. It means so much and I would love to accept.'

Nina sprang to her feet. '*Meravigliosa!*' She hugged Olivia. 'I don't think they sell Champagne here, will another macchiato suffice?' she asked as she waved the waiter over.

* * *

Olivia returned to work at the fashion house after a week of settling into her new place and after many video calls with Uncle Innes to set the wheels in motion for funding for the castle repairs and changes. It was a strange thing to experience, as she had never imagined doing anything other than designing clothing, but dealing with the plans for Drumblair was secretly quite exciting. Invigorating, even.

After her first week back at work, Olivia was sitting at the board room table with Nina, design sketches spread out before them. Olivia could feel Nina's eyes on her and eventually she spoke.

'You've got a glow about you, Olivia, dear. Have you met someone?' Nina asked.

Olivia would've loved to have met Mr Right but there simply were not enough hours in a day. 'No, sadly not. I'm just feeling energised.'

'Well, it suits you, *ciccio*, that's for sure. And these latest designs are incredible. I especially love the texture on this one.' She lifted the drawing that Olivia had started when she was at home, inspired by the red squirrel and the tree bark.

She flooded with happiness. 'I'm so glad you like it! For me it epitomises home, well, my Scottish home, anyway.'

Nina paused and tapped her lips with her finger. 'Can you do more? More along these lines? I think this is some of your best work. It's clear that your home has a positive effect on you.'

Olivia remembered the other sketches she had done while she was at home and nodded. 'Absolutely.'

'Excellent. I can't wait to see what you come up with. I'm thinking next year's fall collection will be amazing.'

* * *

Olivia kept in regular contact with Uncle Innes and Mirren back at home. She had held off asking about Brodie, but a couple of weeks into her return to New York, curiosity got the better of her.

It was Saturday lunchtime in New York and Olivia was munching on homemade quesadillas as she chatted on a video call to Mirren. It was 5.30 p.m. in Scotland and as always, Mirren was busy preparing food for the gardeners and cleaning staff and had her phone propped up against a butter dish as she worked.

'Is Brodie still at Drumblair?' Olivia eventually asked, if a little tentatively.

Mirren stopped kneading the pastry before her, narrowed her eyes and smiled before she began her reply. 'He's back just now but he left not long after you did. Couldn't seem to settle. Told his dad he had stuff to deal with in Edinburgh. Then came back a week or so later and he's been here since.' She paused for a moment, a thoughtful expression on her face. 'Aye, it was a bit strange when he got back. He was wearing dark glasses when it wasn't even sunny. Turns out he had walked into a cupboard when he was back wherever he'd been. He was helping a friend move house, he said. Felt like a right idiot, he said, so wore the sunglasses to cover it up. It was a fair shiner. It's calming now but it did look sore. Wee dafty.'

The old' walking into a cupboard excuse', eh? Olivia was beginning to think Brodie had anger management issues after seeing him punch Kerr, hearing he punched his friend and now this. The thought concerned her. 'Oh, no. That sounds painful. I hope he's okay. Did he... erm... bring his wife back with him this time?'

Mirren scoffed. 'No, but he did bring his *dug*.'

Olivia perked up. She had grown up with dogs and loved having one around. There had been her black Labrador, Duke, who died when she was around eleven. And then of course Marley, who she missed like crazy. 'Oh? I didn't know he had a dog. What kind is it?'

'He's a Golden Retriever. A young 'un too. About a year old and batty as a box of bats.'

Olivia smiled. 'Awww. Has he met Marley yet?'

Mirren laughed. 'Oh, aye. They're like a pair of bookends. The only thing that tells them apart sometimes is Marley's pink nose.'

Olivia grinned. 'Aw. What's his name?'

Mirren rolled her eyes and shook her head. 'It's a stupid name, if you ask me, that's what it is. It's an old man's name, not a *dug*'s. I mean, I know there's a trend of calling *dugs* by human names these days, but what's wrong with Fido and Butch? I mean... who calls their *dug* "Wilf", for goodness' sake?'

Olivia couldn't help giggling. 'Oh, I *love* that! Wilf! It's hilarious.'

Mirren leaned closer to the camera and lowered her voice. 'It's not hilarious when he runs off with your slipper and you're having to shout him and cajole him to bring it back. I feel like a right bampot shouting, "Wilf! Bring back my slipper and you can have a juicy bone instead!" It sounds like I'm calling after some kind of cannibalistic pensioner. The rest of the staff find it highly amusing. I've even been told Wilf must love me, seeing as it's my slippers he runs off with.' She chuckled. 'Wilf... I ask you...'

Olivia laughed heartily as Mirren relayed the goings on at the castle. After what Mirren had said about Wilf sounding like a pensioner, Olivia envisaged her chasing an old man around the grounds with a pork trotter as he tried to keep her slippers away from her.

'It's all right you laughing,' Mirren said with a wry smile. 'But aye, he's a sweet wee pup when he wants to be. Usually when he's hungry or tired. Marley puts him in place when he gets too much. Innes brings him along every time he comes around with contractors. Brodie clearly adores Wilf. And the *dug* follows that man around like a shadow. It's a sight to see, that's for sure.'

A wave of homesickness washed over Olivia and her heart sank a little. It was something she had never really suffered from before. She had settled right into her new city and her new life years ago when she first arrived in America. The bustling metropolis was vibrant and alive with fast-walking people, bright sun-yellow cabs, buildings that seemed to touch the clouds, flashing street signs and a myriad of cultures. It had excited her, driven her and simultaneously carried her along on its waves of momentum. But here she was now, picturing home, the leafy green grounds with their abundance of wildlife, the people who worked together as a team to keep the place going, and the people who she considered family regardless of their lack of blood ties. The cute pair of canine brown eyes that looked deep into her soul and comforted her when she was sad. And her heart ached.

'You've gone a wee bit quiet, hen. Are you okay?' Mirren asked, pulling her back to the present.

Olivia smiled and nodded. 'Oh, yes, I'm fine. Just missing you all. But it's only what... just over five months until I come back.'

'Och, it'll fly by. And you've your birthday soon. What are you doing?'

'I think Harper and I are going to go see a Broadway show. I can't wait. But it will be strange not being home for my birthday this year.'

'How lovely. Well, don't you be worrying about this place. Innes has been keeping things going. He marches around the place muttering to himself and scribbling on his notepad and Marley follows behind like his wee assistant. Had the architect here on Thursday but I *ken* he told you all about that. The plans are looking grand.'

'Yes, he emailed them to me, and I was a little daunted by how much work there is to be done.' She huffed. 'Oh, and before I left, he mentioned a charity ball that he says I should attend in October when I'm home. Do you know anything about it?'

'Och, aye. Your mother always used to go to the McPhersons' ball. It's a good night with good craic apparently. And all for a good cause. Usually a children's charity.'

Olivia stuck out her bottom lip like a petulant child. 'But balls are not really my thing. They were clearly more my mum's.'

Mirren gave her a stern look. 'Well, to all intents and purposes, my dearie, you *are* your mother now. It would be good for you to get into society and do all that *whatsitcalled*? Spreading your net or whatever.'

Olivia tried not to smile. 'Networking. Yeah, I suppose so. I just can't be bothered with all the stuffy folks wandering around like they own the place.'

Mirren chuckled. 'It's at the McPhersons' mansion house and technically they do own it, you bampot.'

'True. Ugh, I just hate all that stuff.'

'Well, if it's any consolation, Owain McPherson will be there. He's a good-looking young man. Single, too.'

Olivia tilted her head. 'Are you trying to set me up, Mirren? Because if you are, don't bother. I remember Owain from when we were kids and I'm pretty sure he will have a string of notches on his bedpost. Anyway, I don't have the time for romance. Maybe when I'm about forty-five, I'll get a window of opportunity.'

Mirren snorted. 'Aye, but by then, your windows will be a bit old and worn looking.'

Olivia laughed. 'Gee, thanks. Although I suppose I could flutter my eyelids at Nina and see if I can wear one of her gowns. It'd be good advertising.'

'Sounds like you're coming around to the idea.'

'I wouldn't go that far. Anyway, have you heard from Kerr at all?'

'No, I was thinking the other day that it was a bit quiet on that front. I heard that Adaira had taken him away for a week or so. Something about avoiding someone in Inverness. You never know with Kerr.'

Concern niggled at the back of Olivia's mind again. She thought that had all been dealt with. 'I just hope he's not in any trouble.'

'Hmm. No doubt if he is, his sugar mama will sort it all out for him. Well, I'd best be off and get this pie in the oven or the gardeners will be eating at midnight.'

'Okay. Speak to you soon. Bye.'

'Bye just now, dearie.' Mirren's face loomed on the screen as she squinted to find the hang up button and then the screen went black.

11

ALMOST SIX MONTHS LATER

Olivia's time in New York had flown, just as Mirren had suggested it would. During that time, Skye had become engaged, finally, after all the worry that Ben had changed his mind. Bella had been for countless job interviews, but the competition had been so fierce, she hadn't yet been successful. She had, however, apparently met someone but was unwilling to share information in case she jinxed it. Harper had met a girl named Summer and things had become fairly serious quite quickly between them. Every time she and Olivia were together, their conversations invariably turned around to something sweet Summer had said, or something cute Summer had worn. Olivia was so happy for her best friend but couldn't help feeling a tiny bit jealous of all her friends' relationships when she had barely been on a single date.

Now on sabbatical from her dream job and following a flight from JFK that included a brief stop at London Heathrow, Olivia exited the interior of Inverness Airport Arrivals on Wednesday, 5 October. The autumnal chill forced her breath to cloud, and she shivered. It was a stark contrast to her cosy first-class flight accommodation where she had been treated like royalty; free-flowing

Champagne, a bed, an à la carte menu. Her recently updated passport, which now showed her newly acquired title, had resulted in an upgrade. This was after she had fought against Uncle Innes, who had tried his darndest to insist she book a first-class flight even though she argued that the family couldn't afford such luxuries.

'It's all about appearances, Olivia dearest,' he had informed her vehemently. 'Fake it until you make it and all that jazz.' She had disagreed just as vehemently and had won that particular argument but had ended up in first class anyway. Oh, the irony.

After boarding the plane, Olivia sat there in her own little capsule feeling a little out of place and like some kind of fraud to begin with, but as the flight took off and she began to see the benefits of first class, she relaxed and began to enjoy the journey. She would accept things as they were on this occasion, seeing as there was little she could do about it, but she would certainly not be booking first class for herself any time soon.

She spotted Spencer, smartly dressed in a long black overcoat and leather gloves, standing just outside the exit at arrivals. Although he drove for other people, including sports stars and actors, Spencer had always favoured the MacBain family and it was good to see his familiar, if a little serious, face. She wondered absentmindedly why on earth he hadn't waited inside when it was so chilly. However, he was standing beside her mother's car, clearly unwilling to leave it, perhaps for fear of damage by other, less careful airport visitors. Her mother had adored that car and even though it was easily fifteen years old, it still looked pristine.

As she approached him, Spencer gave a very brief nod and an even briefer smile and reached for her bags. 'Good to see you again, Lady MacBain. Allow me to get those bags for you.' Now that the name was official, she knew she would have to get used to

being referred to as *Lady*, regardless of how uncomfortable she
was with the title.

Spencer placed her luggage in the boot of the black saloon car
and then opened the rear passenger door for her.

Olivia climbed into the back of the car and heaved a deep,
exhausted sigh. She rarely slept well on aeroplanes, and even
though first class had been enjoyable, it hadn't seemed to afford
her any better slumber. Thanks to this fact, she was completely
drained, and all she wanted now, despite the early hour of the day,
was to get to Drumblair and collapse into bed.

She dropped a message to Harper to let her know she was back
on terra firma and then sent a similar message to Skye and Bella.
Bella didn't reply immediately but Olivia knew instinctively she
would still be sleeping. Skye replied and said she couldn't wait to
see her and show her the ring Ben had given her. Olivia had seen
the ring over video call but seeing it in the flesh, as it were, would
be so much more impactful.

Harper's response came quickly too:

Good to hear. I can sleep now! I've been keeping poor Summer awake
until I heard from you. Love you and miss you. H. 🩶

The message was followed by a heart emoji.

* * *

Olivia dozed for most of the journey but opened her eyes as
Spencer turned the car into the long tree-lined avenue that led to
the castle. She sighed as she peered out of the tinted rear
passenger window. The last time she had been here, the trees were
only just sprouting fresh growth, but now the leaves were turning
russet, orange and brown and beginning to fall to the ground,

blanketing it in all the earthy colours of autumn. She thought back to the autumns of her childhood when she'd been around nine. She remembered the amber glow that seemed to descend over the area which in turn created an excitement that she could barely express.

She had always loved this time of year. Halloween was coming and then Christmas was just around the corner. There was so much excitement ahead, so many things to look forward to. And then a new year, which held so much potential. Things had most certainly been easier back then when, before getting rid of the fallen leaves completely, Dougie would gather them all up into huge crunchy piles and she would dive into them with Brodie and Duke. Duke would bark excitedly, and she and Brodie would fall about laughing as they watched him, tongue lolling out and chasing any leaves that had flown up in the breeze and floated down to earth again.

These were magical memories that she remembered bit by bit with every visit home. She remembered her mother's laugh when she joined them, scooping up handfuls of leaves and tossing them in the air, letting them rain down like confetti. She had a soft Arran jumper she would wear with a pair of rust-coloured trousers and brown leather boots. Even when playing in the garden, she looked chic. Her hair and skin colour seemed to be more vibrant when she matched the colours around her. Olivia's eyes began to well with tears as she pictured her mother out there now, the joy in her eyes as she played with her children. She would have given anything to have the opportunity to see that smile again; to feel her warm arms enveloping her as they walked back to the castle for hot chocolate and whatever delights Mirren had baked. But instead, Olivia would be visiting her mother's grave to lay roses.

* * *

As Spencer pulled the car into the gravelled area directly in front of the castle, Olivia spotted Dougie and her heart skipped. Was Brodie around too? She hadn't communicated with him since the Police song incident six months ago, but it had had a profound effect on her. It was all pointless and stupid considering his marital status, but it did explain why she'd had no interest in dating anyone else. If this was a crush, she needed to rid herself of it immediately. She kept her gaze fixed close to where Dougie was, but there was no sign of Brodie. Although, according to Mirren, he was still in Inverness. She would catch up with him later and hopefully meet Wilf at the same time.

When she thought about it, she put her excitement at seeing Brodie entirely down to the presence of his dog. She would have had a houseful of furry friends if it had been feasible. But of course, living in an apartment in New York and working full-time, and having very late nights, just wasn't conducive to owning a canine companion, hence why she'd had to leave Marley behind. As well as meeting the new dog on the block, the thought of being able to sink her fingers into Marley's fur again and of receiving that unconditional affection he gave was definitely at the forefront of her mind. Not seeing her old childhood friend turned nemesis.

Definitely not.

Spencer carried her bags into the reception hall and Olivia followed, inhaling the familiar smell of woodsmoke and fresh flowers. She was just taking off her jacket when Mirren appeared from the direction of the kitchen.

'Olivia, dearie! It's so good to have you home again. Did you have a good flight? Are you hungry? Can I get you anything? I could do you some scrambled eggs and smoked salmon if you like? Or there's some pâté and oatcakes!' she asked in a rush as she hugged her tightly.

'It's good to be back,' Olivia replied, and meant it. 'To be honest, I really just want to sleep for a few hours. I'm exhausted. So many things whirring around my head just now that sleep continues to evade me.'

Mirren nodded. 'Aye, maybe a few hours' sleep in your own bed is just the ticket. I'll make you some brunch, or lunch when you're ready.'

'Great, thank you. Is Marley here?'

'I'm afraid not. Innes was meeting someone about an antique armoire and took Marley along for the ride, but he'll be along later.'

Just as they were chatting, and Spencer had begun his ascent of the stairs to take Olivia's bags to her room, there was a loud, excited series of barks, a streak of white and a high-pitched squeal as Mirren fell onto her bottom.

Olivia gasped and lurched forward to grab the dog but found no collar and she too ended up in a crumple on the floor. Spencer seemed to be glued to the spot with a wide-eyed expression as he watched the events unfolding before him.

'Wilf! No!' came Brodie's voice from the corridor that led to the kitchen and laundry, and then he arrived, lead in one hand and his other clutching a towel. His pale blue T-shirt was clinging to his body with water and Olivia could see the outline of his toned stomach.

'Ugh! He's wet through!' Mirren yelled, dragging Olivia from her blatant and uncensored ogling and she felt her face heating with embarrassment as Mirren squealed, 'Get him off me!' She swatted the excitable creature away as he licked her face and then turned to Olivia to give her the same treatment.

Olivia laughed and tried to gain a hold of the slippery canine but ended up with hands covered in dog hair. She relented and let the dog greet her.

'Shit! I'm so sorry!' Brodie said. 'I'm so very sorry! Wilf! Here! Come! You wee nugget!'

Wilf stopped what he was doing and mounted yet another lick attack, but this time on Brodie, who also lost his footing on the now damp floor and ended up in a heap. Brodie quickly distracted Wilf by giving him a chew stick from his pocket, which kept the dog occupied enough that he could slip the lead over his head.

When the excitement had died down, Olivia glanced at the other two people where they sat on the floor and then up to Spencer, who had observed it all from the stairs, and she burst into fits of laughter. The others quickly joined in, and Wilf sat there, oblivious to the furore he had caused, tail frantically wagging and tongue lolling out just like Marley's did when he was happy. She was struck by their similarities; apart from the fact that Marley's nose was pink and Wilf was a little lighter in colour, the two dogs could've been brothers.

'What on earth was he doing off his lead and running around like a maniac? You don't see Marley behaving like that,' Mirren said as she leaned on the large round table and scrambled to her feet with the help of Brodie, who stood too.

Brodie then held out a hand to Olivia, who took it and got to her feet while simultaneously trying to ignore the frisson of electricity that shot through her as they touched. He brushed himself off and scraped his hair back from his face. 'I was bathing him in the laundry room because he was in the loch earlier and I didn't want him to stink when Lady Olivia got back. But clearly, even though he seems to love muddy puddles and lochs, he's not too keen on clean water as he slipped his lead and ran off out of there like a bat out of hell. I'm so, so sorry, ladies. Are you both okay?'

Mirren smoothed her hair and her dress. 'Aye, no thanks to that mad *dug* of yours.'

Olivia was still smiling. 'I'm absolutely fine.' She crouched to greet Wilf properly now. 'And you're absolutely gorgeous,' she informed the Golden Retriever, who once again lapped his huge tongue towards her face.

Brodie chuckled. 'I bet you say that to all the four-legged boys you meet.'

Olivia glanced up at Brodie and giggled. 'I think I probably do, actually.'

Wilf made to jump up again, but Brodie managed to stop him before his feet completely left the floor. 'Down, laddie. Where are your manners? This here is the lady of the house.'

'He's a lot lighter in colour than I expected. I always imagine goldens to be... well, golden,' Olivia said with a blush to her cheeks.

'Aye, his parents are both quite light coloured, although some of the litter were more honey than snow.'

'Well, he's just gorgeous, aren't you? Aren't you?' she said to the happy canine.

'Aye, if a little unhinged, eh?' Brodie said with a handsome smile.

Olivia stood and pointed to his eye, which was perfectly healed now. She grinned and said, 'Maybe a tiny bit. You want to watch it with him, or you'll end up with more black eyes like the last one.' She laughed but Brodie's expression turned serious.

He swallowed and his skin seemed to pale. 'Aye. Anyway, I'll go get him dried off.' He turned quickly and tugged on the dog's lead so that he followed.

Olivia frowned and turned to Mirren. 'Was it something I said?'

Mirren shrugged. 'Not a clue. Maybe he's still sensitive about walking into a door like a dafty. Anyway, you go on off to your room and get some rest. You'll need it even more now after all that drama.'

Spencer returned from dropping her bags off and almost broke into a smile. 'Now that I know no one is hurt, I can safely say that was hilarious to observe.'

Olivia tried not to giggle at the stoic man whose face had forgotten to join in with the humour. 'I bet. Thanks for taking my bags up, Spencer.'

He gave a curt nod and, without further comment, walked out of the castle, closing the door behind him.

Olivia made her way up to her room and once the door was closed, she quickly emptied her bags and hung up the stunning gown that Nina had insisted she bring home to wear for the ball at the McPhersons'. It was set to take place on Saturday evening, which was fast approaching, and Olivia was, for once, organised. The dress was stunning. It was a burgundy off-shoulder number with a beaded bodice. The front swept up to just below knee length and the back skimmed the floor. She had elegant high-heeled silver sandals to accompany the gown and was almost excited to attend the ball simply for Nina's exquisite design alone. She had taken up Uncle Innes on his offer to accompany her to it, much to her relief, so at least she wouldn't be attending alone.

Once she was unpacked, she changed into a pair of old joggers and a T-shirt and climbed under the duvet. As she lay there, she pondered on Brodie's reaction for a moment. She hadn't intended to insinuate he couldn't handle the dog and hoped he hadn't thought that's what she meant. She resolved to apologise to him later on and, after that, drifted into a peaceful sleep.

12

Six months of arguments, form filling and tears had culminated in this moment. It was official. Olivia was now formally the owner of Drumblair Castle. There was a lot to do to prepare for her plans to come to fruition and she knew that not everyone, least of all Kerr, would be happy with what she had decided to do with the place, but plans and applications were already in the process of being dealt with or had been approved, and those still outstanding were on the verge of being approved by the council and they would go ahead, in spite of any opposition that would inevitably come her way.

It was the day after she had arrived home and even though she still felt nervous and ill-prepared to a certain extent, Uncle Innes had called a whole staff meeting. Even Kerr had turned up, having heard about things on the grapevine, no doubt. He stood at the back of the dining room, leaning on the wood-panelled wall, arms folded and a look of smugness on his face. She suspected he was there to watch the inevitable sparks fly and was surprised he hadn't brought popcorn to the spectacle.

Olivia stared around the room and swallowed down the lump

of emotion that had become lodged in her throat. She missed her mother with her whole being and would have done anything to turn back the clock so that she could hug her one last time; tell her how much she meant to her; how much she loved her. But instead, she was in the old dining room of Drumblair Castle, in the seat at the head of the Chippendale table; a position her mother had also taken when Olivia's father had passed away.

Her parents' business associates, accountants, lawyer and staff watched her intently as she took her seat; some with a tinge of sadness and some with a hint of pity, but Uncle Innes and Mirren looked on with pride. They knew that she had sacrificed a great deal to return to the Scottish Highlands for the two years ahead, when her heart was still in New York, along with her dream job. They knew that being back 'home' seemed like a punishment rather than a gift, but she was willing to make the best of a bad situation, to honour her mother's memory.

During the six months she had been in the USA, she had discovered, through her research and investigations into the finances, that the castle had been haemorrhaging money for several years, partly due to her mother's inability to say no to Kerr, and something had to be done if her family's legacy was going to remain intact. The newly formed board of trustees had taken on their roles with mixed intentions, and she was under no illusions about the fact. All she hoped was that they could understand her reasons behind the difficult decision she had made and was about to present to everyone. She now realised, however, that certain people had clearly agreed to the funding application because they had presumed she wouldn't be courageous enough to go through with it; or perhaps that funding wouldn't be granted for such an ambitious project.

Kerr had been kept in the loop during the six months Olivia was away, but he hadn't really said much, which had concerned her and made her feel quite uneasy. It was only the night before the meeting that he had truly made his feelings known. Regardless of the inappropriate timing, as she was sitting there waiting to address the room, the intrusive memory of her brother's reaction popped into her head, and she shivered at the recollection of his bitter words when she had spoken to him the night before.

'Over my cold, dead body will you turn this place into a glorified theme park.' Olivia was almost floored by the irony of his words and was about to call him out, but he continued with his tirade. 'You seem to think that just because Mother was mentally impaired enough to hand the reins over to you, that you can do whatever the hell you like with it.' His lip had curled as he'd spoken, or rather hissed. 'Well, sister dearest, you're wrong,' he had seethed, and disdain had seeped from his every pore. 'Just know that I will fight you tooth and nail to make sure your idiotic notions never become a reality. *I* am the rightful heir to Drumblair Castle. Not some jumped-up little dressmaker who pertains to be my sister. No member of this family truly worth their salt would even contemplate this abhorrent idea.'

Olivia had flared her nostrils and fought the tears of anger that had accompanied the fire raging beneath her skin. 'If you hadn't put your gambling before our family and this estate, perhaps I wouldn't have to take such drastic steps to repair the finances and the building itself. Had you considered that? Hmm? If our poor mother hadn't tried her damnedest to help you kick your many self-inflicted addictions by throwing every penny she could at you, perhaps the roof would have been repaired before now. Perhaps the plumbing would have been updated. Perhaps Dad's artwork would still hang on the walls. But no. You couldn't, could you? So don't you dare speak to me of family. You don't know the meaning of the word, you selfish, self-centred arse.' Although she had stood up to her bully of an older brother, she had been quaking in her boots.

But with a smile from Mirren and a thumbs up from Uncle Innes, she stood and walked over to the large screen that had been set up, ready for her to make her presentation.

'Good afternoon, everyone. Thank you for attending this meeting. I know I've pulled some of you in on your days off, but I want you to know you will be compensated for that.' She cleared her throat, feeling each pair of eyes boring into her. 'The following presentation will show you what changes will be made to Drumblair in the coming months. Now, I know this is a little daunting and might not sit comfortably with you all, but in order for Drumblair to be sustainable, I had to make some difficult decisions.'

A scoffing sound came from the back of the room and Kerr chuntered under his breath. Olivia did her best to ignore him and carry on.

'Over the past six months, we have applied for funding and change of use. It's been a very trying time but I'm happy to announce that we now have permission from the relevant authorities to open Drumblair up to the public.' A collective gasp travelled the room and heads turned as people began to whisper to each other. Olivia held up her hand. 'As I said, this wasn't an easy decision to make. It's been my family home for my whole life.'

Kerr coughed and spluttered, 'New York,' defiantly from his place at the back of the room and all heads turned to look at him.

Olivia sighed. 'In spite of what my brother is implying, I have always considered Drumblair to be my home. I've always known I could return here, and I've missed it when I've been away. Now, I don't have to explain my decisions about New York to anyone. My parents supported me wholeheartedly, but I want you all to know that New York was something I needed to do. I had a passion for designing... *have* a passion for it, but knowing that the future of

Drumblair was under threat meant I had to choose.' She inhaled a shaking breath and closed her eyes briefly before opening them again, and with conviction, she said, 'I chose Drumblair.' Mirren began clapping and soon the whole room joined in, that is, except for Kerr.

When the applause died down, Olivia began again. 'We have the most amazing furniture and artwork here and such a rich history that I know people will be excited to come and visit and learn all about the MacBain Clan and its connection to Bonnie Prince Charlie.' A rumble of excitement could be heard now, and Olivia noted the smiles on some faces whilst others were etched with concern.

She gestured to the screen behind her. 'I'll now show you the architect's plans for where various new elements will be such as the gift shop, café and children's play area. There will be deer and bird hides too in the grounds and the gardens will be stunning all year round, thanks to Dougie and his intrepid team. The only part of the castle grounds that will remain private is the walled garden. It was my parents' favourite place, and I would like to keep that as a kind of memorial garden for them. But without further ado...' She turned to the screen, clicked a button on the device in her hand and an artist's impression of the public version of Drumblair appeared in all its colourful glory. 'Tadaaaaaa!' Olivia exclaimed nervously before more applause ensued.

* * *

Olivia's presentation, as she had expected, garnered a range of reactions. The room was now silent, and a heavy atmosphere had descended. She had noted shakes of the head and had heard mutterings as she revealed the plans for the renovations. She had insisted and reiterated over and over that the character of the castle would not change or be spoiled. She wasn't about to put in UPVC double glazing, for goodness' sake. But if the castle was to make money, she had to do something to help matters along. Her father had always said, 'You can't do the same as you've always done and expect to get different results. You have to break a few eggs to make an omelette.' Well, her omelette currently resembled something that had been dropped on the floor and stepped on, and fear had set in. Was she about to lose her entire existing staff?

Alasdair McKendrick, the family lawyer, cleared his throat and stood, smoothing down his tie as he addressed the gathered group. 'So, the upshot is, the funding and permissions are in place and work can begin immediately to get the castle ready for public opening.' He turned and smiled at her. 'And I'm sure I'm not the only one who agrees you have made the right decision, Lady Olivia.' He then glanced around the room with raised eyebrows, clearly hoping for some agreement from his peers.

Uncle Innes spoke first. 'Olivia dear, you know you have my full support. I'm aware that your father never wanted his home to become a zoo, and the things in it – exhibits. But he didn't live to see it heading towards disaster and I'm sure if he had, he would have come to the same decision as you have.' He looked around the room, addressing the whole gathered audience. 'I'm sure you all understand that if Lady Olivia doesn't do something drastic, the place will fall to rack and ruin, which is worse than any idea our dear lady has presented today.'

A mumble of agreement traversed the room and Innes turned back to face Olivia. 'I'm sure your mother would have taken the same route had she lived and maybe been younger, and as brave as you. She was a wonderful woman who cared about this old place. It was in her blood, that much was true. And she put her trust firmly in you, so who are we to argue?' He smiled warmly and relief flooded her veins. The fond mention of her mother had caused her eyes to sting.

'Thank you, Uncle Innes. That means the world to me.'

Alasdair stepped forward. 'I think Lady Olivia deserves a thank you for trying her best to save this castle, not only for the future generations but for every single person employed here now and those who will no doubt be employed in the near future to see these plans come to fruition. Don't you all agree?' He began to clap and one by one every person in the room began to applaud too until everyone was on their feet. She turned her attention to the back of the room and watched as Kerr sneered, shook his head and left.

As the meeting ended and everyone filed out of the room, Uncle Innes joined Olivia and hugged her. 'I'm so proud of you, darling girl. You knocked their socks off. I knew in my own heart there would be some objections, but to be honest, I haven't seen anything but smiles. You were incredible.'

Excitement bubbled under Olivia's skin, and she almost felt like she'd been drinking. 'Thank you so much. And thank you again for taking the reins while I was away. You've done a phenomenal job.'

He held up his fist and said, 'Teamwork,' and Olivia bumped his fist with hers – an action she never expected to share with her ageing uncle.

'I have to say, though...' Innes glanced briefly over his shoulder into the now empty room. 'We must watch Kerr. He's not happy about any of it. Probably because it wasn't his idea. You have my backing, 100 per cent, but you know that Kerr is going to make things difficult for you going forward. He tried to get some of the trustees to reject your proposals. Even resorted to bribery and blackmail. Well, that is to say he *tried*, at least. Thankfully, they are fully aware of his reputation and didn't take the bait. But now that funding is in place and we all agreed to be involved, we have to look forward while keeping one eye on the enemy.'

Olivia had been saddened and a little shocked to hear of Kerr's attempts at sabotage but hoped that he would come around eventually. She would have loved to share this journey with him. But sadly, she knew that it was unlikely.

13

After a night of celebrations with Skye and Bella to finally celebrate Skye's engagement to Ben, Olivia was feeling a little worse for wear. The following morning, she sat on one of the secluded stone benches in the walled garden with her notepad. Marley lay on the ground beside her on a clump of soft phlox. He was snoring contentedly with one paw on her foot. She inhaled the sweet, woody fragrance of her surroundings and the crisp cool air that swirled the fallen leaves around at her feet. Her mind was whirring, and she had hoped that coming to sit here would help calm her. Give her some clarity, perhaps. She peered up at one of the windows and spotted Uncle Innes pointing down towards her as he chatted to one of the architects. He waved and she waved back.

There was so much to do and so few hours available to do it all in. She really needed help, but Uncle Innes was already up to his chin in documentation and meetings on her behalf as it was. She needed help with the organisation of fundraising events for the smaller things that were needed, someone to help her make sure she kept all her appointments with potential funders, builders, local press, *national* press, and so on, and so on. She scribbled yet another to-do list and heaved a deep, frustrated sigh as she gripped her hair with one hand, leaning her elbow on her knee.

'Someone sounds a little fed up,' came a voice from behind her and an excited Wilf came to say hello too, tail wagging as usual. Marley was suddenly alert again and on his feet to greet his canine friend with a good and thorough sniff.

Olivia sat up straight, turned and smiled, relieved he seemed back to normal with her. 'Hi, Brodie, and hi, Wilf! How are you, my gorgeous furry friend?' The dog sat before her as Marley ran to greet Brodie.

Brodie rubbed at his bearded chin. 'Is that your way of saying I need a shave?' He chuckled.

Olivia rolled her eyes and scratched Brodie's dog behind his ears. 'Did you hear that, Wilfy? He thought I was talking to him,' she said in a childish voice. 'Yes, he did. Isn't he silly? Hmm? Silly Daddy.' Wilf stood again and his level of excitement rose until his whole body was wagging along with his tail.

Brodie laughed and sat down on the bench beside her. 'Gee, thanks. Although I am pretty silly where this big softy is concerned.' He stroked the dog's back. 'So, what's up? Why were you looking so glum before?'

Olivia shook her head. 'Oh, it's nothing really. Well, nothing *and* everything. I think I'm in over my head with the castle and the whole *opening it up to the public thing*, and all the stuff that goes along with it. There's so much to do and I've got everyone who's involved spending every hour they have on this project. I could do with an extra few hours in each day, if you know anywhere I can get some.'

He pondered for a moment and then said, 'I don't think you're over your head. I think it's a brilliant idea you've had. But I do think you need a personal assistant. Someone to deal with all the stuff that isn't exactly imperative for you to deal with. You know, fielding calls, arranging appointments and all that. Maybe you should advertise for one? It'd save you some stress.'

Olivia's heart skipped and she smacked her thigh. 'Oh, my word! You're right! And I know just the person!' She wasn't sure why she hadn't thought of it herself. Bella was still looking for a job and she would be *perfect* for this. It might be strange working so closely with her and she was a little scatter-brained, it had to be said, but not where work was concerned. She was organised, thorough and efficient from what Olivia knew of her past jobs, with the exception of the silly email she had been caught sending. And Olivia knew she could trust her, Bella knew the castle, she got on with Uncle Innes and Mirren. Her mum had adored her. It was ideal.

Brodie smiled, creating dimples in his cheeks. 'Well, there you go! I'm glad I could help. Right, well, I think my work here is done. I'll get this nutter back to my flat for the rest of the day.'

Olivia crumpled her brow. 'Your flat?'

His cheeks coloured a little. 'Aye, just an Airbnb. I'm in Inverness for a while, temporarily. I got a few months' work at the cathedral doing research on some documents that were uncovered during some building work. I couldn't really turn it down. Curiosity got the better of me and well... I could do with the work.' He shrugged as if it was nothing. 'It's really interesting and it's nice to be back in Inverness again.'

'Oh, right. But... what about your wife? Is she with you?'

He shook his head and glanced around distractedly. 'Erm... no, Mags stayed in Edinburgh for her own work. Like I said, it's only temporary and I've been going home at weekends.'

Olivia smiled. 'Oh, that's nice. So, where did you meet her?'

He fiddled with Wilf's lead and his face flushed a little. 'Mags? I erm, I met her at Edinburgh Castle. I was taking some tours to help out and she was there with some of her old friends who were visiting from Coldstream in the Borders. We flirted a bit, and her friends were egging us on, you know? I asked her out afterwards and... well, the rest is history, I guess.'

Olivia nodded and tried to ignore the twinge of disappointment that tugged at her. She almost wanted him to say they had split up but realised that was incredibly selfish and cruel of her. She smiled. 'That's sweet. I do love a good romance story.' She scrunched her face as she peered up at the crumbling stonework. 'It seems all my friends are coupling up just now. And here I am, single as the day I was born.'

'Aye, but you've a lot going on right now. Maybe it's not the right time for you? And I'm sure you'll meet someone. Maybe at that ball you're going to on Saturday. There'll be blokes just like you there.'

She scoffed. 'What, stressed and wishing they were somewhere else?'

'Nah, you know, types that you'll fit with and like. Lairds and such. Heirs and that.' He shrugged.

Olivia scowled. 'Jeez, and you think that's my type?'

Brodie shook his head. 'Well, I... I presume so. Don't yous all have to stick together and marry each other?'

She didn't like where the conversation was going. 'If you're insinuating that I'm likely to marry for status, you don't know me very well.'

He gave a small smile that appeared to be tinged with sadness. 'I don't really, though, do I? Not any more. Maybe when we were kids, but now...'

Olivia pursed her lips and her scowl deepened. 'Well, let me bring you up to date, eh? I'm not an aristocrat by nature, only by birth and even then, I hate to think of myself that way. I refuse to marry for status or in order to keep the family line going. That's just not who I am. I know that must seem like a contradiction to what I'm doing in being back here to carry on my parents' legacy, but that's just for the castle. I won't marry someone I don't love for anything. Not even this place.'

He twisted his face and nodded slowly. 'All right. That's me totally put in my place. I stand corrected. Although I didn't mean anything bad by it. I just know from history how these things work usually. Money marries money.'

Olivia snorted. 'Yeah, maybe if you're like royalty or something. Or you actually have money, which technically I don't. And I'm just me. I'm no different to the me I was before all this happened.'

Brodie shook his head and smirked a little. 'No, I see that. You're exactly the same... only now you've inherited a castle and a title.' It was clear there was no malice intended and Olivia supposed he did have a point.

She smiled and fought the urge to stick out her tongue like she might have when they were kids. 'Semantics,' she replied.

His smile widened and he appeared relieved. 'Right,' he said with a jovial wink. 'Well, I'd better be off. See you Saturday, maybe? I'm at the cathedral again tomorrow.'

'Bye, Brodie. And thanks for helping me sort my head out. I'm going to call Bella and offer her the PA job.'

'Bella? Was she at our school? Is she the one who shot me down at the pub about calling you Lady Olivia?' Olivia nodded. He tilted his head and gave an approving bob of his head. 'Grand. At least you know where her loyalties lie. Glad to have helped. Bye, Lady...' He stopped and bit his lip. 'I mean bye, Olivia.' He turned and Wilf ran to catch up with him, then the two of them walked along the path and left the garden by the tall wooden gate.

* * *

Bella arrived on Friday morning at 8.30 sharp. She was dressed in a smart navy trouser suit and white blouse, her short blonde hair styled to perfection. She looked every bit the professional and Olivia couldn't help but be impressed.

'Morning, boss!' Bella said before hugging Olivia. Then pulled away and glanced furtively around where they stood on the gravel area out front. 'Shit, should I be calling you ma'am or something in case anyone is listening?'

Olivia scrunched her face. 'Not if you want me to answer, you don't. I'm not eighty and I'm not the queen. What have I told you?'

'That you're still the *same old Olivia*,' Bella recited parrot fashion.

'Exactly. Anyway, how are you?'

Bella made a snorting noise. 'Ugh, I'm okay. Although I haven't told you that I moved in with my gran, have I?'

The last Olivia knew, she was living with her parents and she wondered why she hadn't mentioned it on their night of celebrations. But then again, that was about Skye. 'Oh, so you've moved?'

'Aye. Not by choice, I hasten to add. I've been sleeping in my brother's room but he's back from uni now that he's finished his degree, so I was going to have to sleep on the couch. Anyway, Granny Isla stepped in and offered me her spare room. Don't get me wrong, I love the woman to pieces, but my god, she can be nosy. I've been there three days and she's already trying to marry me off to her friend's carer. He's a male nurse and he's so handsome according to Gran. But my gran still has the hots for Tom Jones, so you know...'

'Tom Jones is a very talented man.'

Bella huffed. 'Aye, but I don't want to bloody date a lookalike, do I?'

Olivia tried not to giggle. 'It was sweet of her to take you in, though. Better than couch surfing.'

'Hmm,' moaned Bella. 'I just want to save enough cash and get a stable enough job to get my own place. It's not too much to ask at my age, is it?'

Olivia felt her cheeks flush. 'You could have come and stayed here if you'd said, you know. I mean, I have sixteen spare bedrooms.'

Bella's eyes widened. 'Jeez-oh! I'd forgotten there were so many. And anyway, I'm not one to ask for handouts from friends.'

'Well, the offer is there and it will remain open.'

Bella's eyes appeared glassy, and she hugged Olivia without speaking.

Olivia clapped her hands. 'Right, come on, I have *soooo* much for you to do.' Olivia turned to walk away, and Bella grabbed her arm.

'You... you didn't give me this job out of pity, did you, Olivia? I mean, don't get me wrong, I appreciate it and everything, but... I hope you didn't feel obligated or anything silly like that,' she said with a furrowed brow.

Olivia walked back to her and looked into her eyes with what she hoped showed her sincerity. 'Of course not. I gave you the job because you're perfect for it, and in all honesty, without you, I may go insane. I'm worried I'm already heading that way.'

Bella rallied. 'Ugh, we can't have that, Lady O. Shall I go get you a cuppa and then we can go through your lists?'

'Lady O?' Olivia laughed. 'And yes, a cuppa would be marvellous. I'll get sorted and meet you in my dad's old office. I've kind of taken up residence in there. Although fetching me cups of tea isn't in your job description, you know? I'm quite capable and you're not a maid. Just so we're clear.'

Bella smiled. 'Heard loud and clear. But I'm just happy to help. See you in there shortly, Cap'n.' She saluted and hurried off into the castle as Olivia watched her with a giggle. She wondered how many more nicknames Bella would dream up in the days to come.

* * *

Olivia and Bella had just finished agreeing what needed to be done and what Bella would be taking on when there was a commotion in the corridor outside. Marley was barking and sounded distressed, so they both dashed out of the room to see what was going on.

Uncle Innes sat on the stone floor, clutching his ankle with one hand and holding the other one aloft as Marley licked his face and Mirren fussed around him. A broken ladder sat on its side behind him.

'What on earth has happened?' Olivia asked as Mirren muttered something about getting some ice and hurried off.

Uncle Innes glanced up with an ashen face that appeared drained of blood, and through gritted teeth told her, 'I... I was going to move some of these paintings into the long gallery to fill the gaps... so I borrowed a ladder from Dougie's shed but as soon as I got to the top it sort of... well... collapsed.'

Bella stepped forward and crouched beside him to examine his injuries. 'I think it did more than *sort of* collapse, sir. I think you need to go to hospital. Your wrist is swelling up and I don't think your ankle should be that colour.'

Uncle Innes glanced down at his arm. 'Oh, yes, that doesn't look good, does it? And actually,' he held his good hand up to his head, 'I feel a bit squiffy, to be honest.' He began to fall backwards, and Bella reached out and caught him just in time. Marley gave a worried yip and continued his attempts to lick his face.

Dougie came dashing along the corridor, with Mirren following closely and clutching a couple of icepacks.

'What the hell were you *daein'*, man?' Dougie asked Innes with wide eyes. 'That ladder *wasnae* to be used. It was on the woodpile. Did you no see that?'

Innes glanced over at him. 'Ah... no. I did wonder why it wasn't hung on the wall where your ladders usually are. But it didn't look faulty.'

Dougie rubbed his hand over his sparse head. 'Aye, well, now you know that it is. And why didn't you come and find me to ask, you bampot? I could've given you another one, for pity's sake. And you should always have someone to brace a ladder. Preferably someone with two legs, not four. It's basic health and safety. It's a wonder you've no snapped your neck.'

Bella looked up at Dougie. 'I think he needs to go to hospital. I can't quite believe he didn't pass out immediately, looking at his wrist and the colour of his ankle too.'

Mirren crouched and placed a pack of ice on his wrist. 'That'll be the adrenaline. Here you go, Innes, hold that. Olivia, if you can come and hold the one on his ankle. Dougie, can you call for an ambulance?'

'*Nae* point d*aein'* that, lass,' Dougie informed her. 'I'll run him up to A&E at Raigmore. An ambulance will take time to be sent and I can get him there faster. And I... I feel kind of responsible.'

'Oh, no, Dougie, it's not your fault, honestly. It was just a mistake.'

'Not at all, Dougie. I'm entirely to blame.'

'Och, Dougie, you *cannae* be held responsible.'

They all spoke at once, trying to reassure him.

They helped Innes to his feet and out to Dougie's car with Marley in tow for moral support and Olivia insisted that one of them message her when they knew the damage. Then they watched as Dougie drove at speed down the long driveway. Olivia could only imagine the lecture Innes was getting from her gardener. And rightly so. If he hadn't been so badly hurt, she would have been so cross with him.

'Do you think he'll be okay?' Olivia asked no one in particular.

'Aye, of course, dearie. He's a tough old beggar, that Innes,' Mirren insisted. 'But I think that there may be broken bones involved.'

Olivia and Bella turned to walk back inside. But Olivia suddenly realised that her uncle would now be incapacitated and unable to be her plus one at the ball. The last thing she wanted was to go alone.

'Erm... Bella, what are you doing on Saturday evening?' She silently held her breath and crossed her fingers in hope of the right reply.

14

Late Saturday afternoon, Olivia sat in front of her dressing table mirror, sulking. She had, in fact, been sulking all day. Mirren had pointed out that she'd end up souring the milk if she stayed in the kitchen like that for too long. So, after wondering if there was such a thing as a doggy tuxedo and if she could get away with taking Marley as her plus one, she had wandered aimlessly around the grounds with the dog, trying to conjure up decent, believable excuses to get out of going to the ball by herself. She came up with zip. Zilch. Nada.

Bella had plans with her new secret man and was, as yet, still unwilling to divulge any information about the relationship as it was apparently still early days. But he had arranged something fancy for her so she couldn't really rearrange. Olivia totally understood that but couldn't help her disappointment. Skye was away for the weekend, ironically *to* Skye, with her new fiancé, so that was also a non-starter. So, the ball would definitely be a solo event.

If she even attended at all.

Uncle Innes had called her from the hospital the night before where he would be having a pin put into his broken wrist at some point.

'I'm so sorry about all this, Olivia. I'm kicking myself over it. Or I would be if my ankle didn't hurt so much.' He laughed lightly. 'But anyway, I'm sure you have a friend who can go with you?'

'I'll sort something, don't worry.' She realised she had been rather curt and immediately felt bad.

Uncle Innes sighed. 'That means your friends are all busy, doesn't it? I can tell in your tone.'

She didn't want to guilt trip him. 'I didn't mean to sound so snappy. I'm sorry. And no, they're not available but it's fine. I might just give this one a miss.'

There was an almost inaudible sharp intake of breath and Uncle Innes's tone changed to one of seriousness. 'Please don't do that, Olivia. You're expected to attend as your mother's representative. It won't look good if you don't go. Unless it's you with a broken wrist and badly sprained ankle, you really should make an appearance.'

'Now there's an idea, maybe I could go see if Dougie has another dodgy ladder hanging around in his shed,' she replied dryly.

'You shouldn't tempt providence, my dear.' There was a long pause. 'I really am truly sorry.'

Olivia softened. 'Honestly, don't worry. It can't be helped and it'll be fine. You have more important things to worry about just now. Get yourself rested and healed, okay? I need you. You're my right-hand man.'

'Lucky for you I broke my left one then.' He chuckled.

So, there it was. The inescapable truth of her predicament. She was just going to have to put her big girl pants on and go to the stupid ball alone.

Marley had been temporarily banished to the kitchen due to

the dark colour of the dress Olivia was going to wear and was, according to Mirren, sighing continuously and grumbling his disappointment at the matter. She applied the rest of her make-up and sat there staring at the stunning gown Nina had loaned her for the occasion. It was on a padded hanger on her wardrobe door and even there it was absolutely gorgeous. How could she do it justice with her grumpy face? The one saving grace was that Spencer was driving her and had agreed to keep his phone on loud in case she needed to make her escape. And she was pretty sure that would happen after approximately thirty minutes.

She pulled on her gown and took a long look at her reflection in her full-length mirror. Her blonde highlighted hair was fastened in a pretty chignon at the nape of her neck and the fitted dress accentuated her curves. Maybe Brodie was right, and she would meet someone at the event. She did scrub up well when she made a concerted effort, even if she did say so herself. She wouldn't admit it out loud, but she really hoped she did meet someone. It had been too long since she'd had someone to snuggle up and watch movies with – well, someone that wasn't her human best friend or her canine bestie, anyway.

Olivia collected her little satin pouch that was just big enough to fit her phone and lipstick in and left her room. As she descended the staircase, she saw the back of Brodie as he stood by the large round table in the hallway. She was surprised to see him, considering it was Saturday.

'Oh, hi, Brodie. I thought you would be back home this—' As he turned, the words halted in her throat when she realised he was wearing a kilt and dinner jacket with a crisp white dress shirt and tie.

His eyes widened as he took in her appearance and eventually, he said, 'Wow... look at you. You really are beautiful.' As if he wasn't meant to have said the words out loud, he shook his head and cleared his throat. 'I mean... erm... that's a stunning dress. Did you, erm, design it? Is it, erm, one of yours?'

She couldn't help the rapid flutter of her heart as she smoothed down the fabric. 'Oh, no, no, this is one of Nina's. It's just on loan for this evening. W-where are you off to all dressed up?' She frowned. 'You look very handsome, I have to say.'

He glanced down at his attire and scrunched his nose. 'I always feel such a tube in a kilt, but I was told it was that kind of party so...'

Still confused and awaiting his answer, she tried again. 'Which party are you going to?'

'Oh, aye, you did ask before, sorry. Well... the thing is, Dad felt so bad about what happened with Innes and the ladder, and that you were left without a plus one for the charity ball at the McPhersons', that he asked if I'd accompany you. I... I hope that's okay?' He cringed.

Relief flooded Olivia's veins and she walked down the rest of the stairs to stand before him. 'Really? Oh, that's so lovely. No one said anything to me about it.'

'No, no, I said they'd best not in case I couldn't get my kilt dry cleaned in time. Luckily, I have friends in the right places so...' He held out his hands and did a turn on the spot.

Olivia beamed at him. She wanted to hug him and kiss him in such grateful thanks. But she restrained herself, and instead simply said, 'Thank you for being my knight in shining armour, Brodie. I really appreciate it.'

'I don't know about shining armour, but it turns out the moths hadn't eaten my kilt so that's something.' He smiled. 'And I couldn't see you stranded like that. It's my pleasure.'

Olivia's heart ached a little, her crush on him intensifying uselessly. 'How come you're not at home with Mags this weekend?'

As soon as the words had left her mouth, she regretted them. She didn't really want to talk about his wife.

'Oh, I, erm, I told her I was needed here by Dad. Not a total lie. It was Dad who asked me to help you, so...' He shrugged and she wondered why he hadn't told his wife the truth.

'Well, I hope she doesn't mind when she finds out.'

His nostrils flared and he clenched his jaw for a split second. 'She won't find out,' he said rather quickly in reply.

She gestured to the door. 'Well, Spencer will be waiting at the car for us so we should get going.'

'Aye, *nae* bother.' He held out his arm and she linked hers through it. As they walked towards the door, she turned her head and saw that Mirren was watching them leave. She smiled at her, but Mirren's expression was odd. Her brow was crumpled and her mouth downturned. Olivia wondered what she had to be sad about. She was doing her duty as lady of the castle, which is what everyone seemed to want. What more could she do? Or was it that Mirren thought Olivia was getting attached to a man she couldn't have? If that was the case, she would have to prove otherwise.

The drive took them through darkening countryside as the sun had already descended below the horizon. Owls and bats could be seen darting around in the headlight beams and the moon cast a silver edge upon the branches of the roadside trees. Inverness-shire was a truly stunning county, regardless of the weather and time of day or night. A deer shot out into the road before them, its eyes glinting gold in the glare of the headlights, and Olivia held her breath, fearing it would get clipped by the car. Luckily the beautiful creature bounded off into a copse and Olivia relaxed once more.

Brodie and Olivia travelled in silence for a while but to Olivia it didn't feel uncomfortable or awkward. It was companionable. Like the two old friends they were, relaxed in each other's company regardless of the amount of time that had lapsed since they had played together as children.

Eventually Brodie asked, 'So how are you finding your new role so far?'

Olivia heaved a sigh. Her feelings were incredibly complicated, and she hadn't quite figured them out yet. 'It's all a bit strange, really. I still get a kind of sinking feeling when I wake up and realise I'm not in New York. But I'm sure it'll pass. I'm just hoping there won't be a lot of these kinds of things that I have to attend. They're just not me.'

'Aye, it must be hard to have left your new life behind. Do you think you'll stick around after the two years is up?'

Olivia paused for a moment as she pondered his question. She had almost forgotten she had the opportunity to leave the castle again once things were up and running. 'I haven't really given it much thought, to be honest. I suppose I'm still stuck in duty mode for now.'

'But your mum wouldn't want you to be unhappy. And if New York is your happy place, then that's where you should be.'

She decided to change the subject. 'How about you? Are you coping splitting your time between Inverness and Edinburgh? It's a long drive to be doing every weekend.'

She watched his brow furrow and he glanced at her quickly from the corner of his eye. 'Aye, it's fine. I don't go every weekend anyway. So...'

'And Mags is okay with that?' Olivia asked.

'Aye, fine. It's all good.' He turned to look out the window and Olivia took this to mean the conversation was over, for now.

* * *

Eventually Spencer turned the car up a long torchlit tree-lined drive and Olivia knew they were almost at their destination. She hadn't been to the grand Dores Manor House for many years, possibly since she was five or six, and at that time it was for one of the McPherson children's parties. Possibly Owain but it could have been his sister, Clarissa, who was a year and a half younger. She couldn't remember much. All she did remember is that there had been a freaky-looking clown making rather rubbish balloon animals and performing tricks that kept going wrong. She was pretty sure, even at that young age, that his mistakes weren't part of the act, judging by how frustrated he was getting. To top it off, he had terrified most of the kids in attendance and Olivia had had nightmares afterwards for days.

Spencer pulled the car to a stop and climbed out to open the door for Brodie to get out. Brodie then held his hand out to help Olivia. Once again, she slipped her hand into his and tried to ignore how nice it felt.

'I'll be available whenever you're ready, Lady Olivia,' Spencer informed her before climbing back into the car and pulling away.

'Right, Lady Olivia, let's go show 'em how it's done, eh?' Brodie said with a grin.

'Show 'em how what's done?' Olivia asked with a nervous giggle.

He shrugged. 'Balling, I suppose.'

She linked her arm through his offered one and they ascended the torchlit steps to the front of the vast manor house. It was Palladian in design, built around the mid-seventeenth century by some architect who had clearly been heavily influenced by the Italian's work. A pair of Doric columns flanked the huge mahogany doors, and the fenestrations were of equal number on either side, in true Andrea Palladio style. It was a grand property built from pale

sandstone and had been in the McPherson family since the eigh-
teenth century, when, rumour had it, it was won in a card game.

They followed other arrivals and entered the foyer, where they
were greeted by the warming and welcoming scent of cinnamon
and cedarwood. Huge pillar candles stood atop mahogany stands
and the light from them flickered with the breeze from the door,
causing the crystal chandelier to sparkle like a huge disco ball. It
was the stuff of fairy tales and Olivia watched Brodie as he took it
all in. They were shown through to the great hall where a small
chamber orchestra played 'Autumn' from Vivaldi's *Four Seasons*. No
sooner had they walked through the double doors than Olivia was
greeted with a sight she wasn't expecting.

Kerr walked determinedly towards her with a half-smirk on
his face. He was wearing his kilt in their family tartan.

'Well, hello, sis. Fancy seeing you here.' He bent and kissed her
cheek then gave Brodie a look of disdain before turning his attention back to Olivia. 'You could've come alone, you know. I did.'

'Why are you here, Kerr? I had no idea you would be coming.
And where's Adaira?'

'Me not come to a McPherson ball? How long have you known
me? Good food, an open bar, lots of pretty young fillies. What's not
to like? Oh, and my darling Adaira has one of her migraines. I'll
tell her you asked after her. She'll be touched.' There was no
holding back on his sarcasm.

'Fillies, Kerr? Really?' Olivia curled her lip at her brother's
vulgar reference to the women in attendance. 'Maybe if you'd
mentioned you were coming, I could've stayed home,' she
informed him with a huff.

'And let your handyman miss out on a view of how the other
half live?'

Olivia clenched her teeth. 'Why do you always have to be so
obtuse?'

He stuck out his bottom lip. 'Oh, take a joke for once, Olivia. Anyway, I wasn't expecting you to be here. I thought you'd be too busy with your grand plans to take time out for socialising.'

'I don't know why you're wasting your time talking to him, Olivia,' Brodie chuntered in her ear.

'Aww, is your guard dog getting fed up already? Maybe stick him in a corner with a chew toy.'

Brodie lunged forward and Kerr stepped back, laughing. 'Ooh, down, boy!'

Before Olivia could retaliate, Laird Hamish McPherson and his wife, Fiona, approached them.

'Come now, Kerr, don't hog your sister's time, you see her every day!' Hamish said before turning to Olivia. 'Lady Olivia, we're so glad you could come,' he said, kissing her on both cheeks.

'You look stunning,' Fiona added.

'She wouldn't have missed it for the world, would you, sister dearest?' Kerr said with a wink at her.

'Absolutely not.' She glared at her brother in the hopes that looks could actually kill. Then she turned to her hosts. 'Thank you for inviting me. The hall looks wonderful,' Olivia said as she glanced around at the fresh flowers adorning every available surface, and the artwork gracing every wall.

'Oh, thank you. All in aid of the children's ward at Raigmore Hospital this year. And who is this?' Fiona asked, smiling greedily at Brodie.

'Oh, this is the gardener from the castle. We like to involve the staff in everything we do, apparently,' Kerr said, eliciting a kind of under-breath growl from Brodie.

'Ignore him, he's kidding around,' Olivia said with a waved hand. 'Fiona, Laird Hamish, I would like to introduce you to my good friend, Brodie MacLeod. Brodie, this is Lady Fiona McPherson and Laird Hamish McPherson.'

Brodie glanced at her as if unsure what to do but eventually held out his hand and gave a swift nod of his head just to cover all bases.

'You make a very handsome couple,' Laird Hamish said.

Kerr faked a sneeze and muttered 'Bollocks!' as he did. 'Ooh, bless me. Allergies. Pollen, probably,' he said with a smirk towards Brodie. 'Please excuse me, I see a glass of Dom with my name on.' Much to Olivia's relief, he walked away.

Olivia relaxed a little, her shoulders distancing themselves from her ears at last. 'Oh, no, we're not a couple, just friends. We went to school together.'

Fiona's eyes lit up. 'Oh! I see. And what is that you do, Brodie?'

He looked a little embarrassed. 'I'm a historical researcher, I suppose. Working at the cathedral just now. It's only temporary, though.'

'Right, right,' Fiona said with a slight hint of disinterest. 'Olivia, dear, you must come and say hello to Owain. He's been so looking forward to seeing you. Come and I'll take you to him.' She held out her hand.

Olivia hesitated and glanced at Brodie, worried he would be upset at being abandoned so early, but he said, 'Go on, I'm fine. I'm going to grab a drink and listen to this wonderful music.'

She mouthed the words 'thank you' and dutifully took Fiona's hand, allowing herself to be led through the crowd of exquisitely dressed guests with perfectly coiffed hair and enough jewels to fill the Brinks-Mat warehouse.

Owain stood with his back to them as he chatted to some older men who looked vaguely familiar to Olivia.

'Owain, darling, look who I've found!' Fiona told him with a tap to his shoulder.

Owain turned and his eyes lit up when he saw Olivia. 'Lady Olivia MacBain! Look at you.' He bent to kiss both her cheeks. 'I haven't seen you in years. You look amazing. It's so good to see you.'

Olivia smiled. 'It's lovely to see you too.' He was incredibly handsome in his suit and tartan waistcoat, having foregone the traditional kilt on this occasion. He was tall, possibly six feet two, not as tall as Brodie, and his blond hair was short and neat.

'Your delightful brother is here. Have you seen him?' Did she note more than a hint of sarcasm?

'I have, yes. And delightful isn't a word I'd use.'

Owain laughed. 'You too, eh?' He stepped back and looked at her from head to toe but not in a lascivious manner. 'I love that dress. Is it one of your designs?'

'No, I can't claim this one unfortunately. It's a Nina Picarro.'

He widened his eyes. 'Oh, wow. I love her work. I caught her Paris Fashion Week show back in March and wow. Just wow. There was this particular jacket that I just adored. A longline one with buckles down the sleeves.'

Olivia grinned, knowing exactly to which jacket he was referring. 'Oh, yes! That was a masterpiece. I totally agree.'

'Guys, give me a smile.' Olivia turned to see a camera lens a foot from her face.

'Oh! Erm...'

Owain pulled her into his side. 'Come on, Olivia, let's give them something to talk about, eh?' He leaned down and kissed her cheek as the photographer snapped a few shots of them together.

'You guys are such a cute couple!' the photographer said before turning and making his way towards another group of party goers.

'I didn't realise your mother was having the event photographed,' Olivia said as the blotches in front of her eyes subsided.

'Oh, the press always attend. Apparently, my folks are a big deal.' He shrugged and leaned in to say, 'Lord only knows why

having more money than sense makes them interesting. There
needs to be a shake-up of the aristocracy, don't you think? It's all so
bloody pretentious.'

Olivia agreed and laughed at his comment. She spotted
Fiona across the room, directing the photographer who to snap
next.

'So, what are you doing these days?' she asked Owain enthusiastically. He had always been into art, something they had in
common.

He linked his arm through hers. 'Come on, you haven't got a
drink, let's remedy that.' A waiter passed by with a tray of Champagne flutes and Owain grabbed two, handing one to Olivia.
'Much to Mummy and Daddy's dismay, I'm being totally useless
and spending my time painting and sculpting.' She giggled at the
way he'd said Mummy and Daddy in a mocking tone.

'What would they rather you were doing?'

'Oh, you know, running some highfalutin corporation while
my wife and 2.4 kids are being looked after by a Swedish au pair or
something.' He rolled his eyes. 'Don't get me wrong, I know I have
a very privileged life, but all this,' he waved his glass at their
surroundings, 'it's just not me.'

She related so much. 'Yes, I'm just the same. I was chatting to a
friend the other day who was asking me about marriage and if I
was going to marry one of my *own* sort, or words to that effect. I
was horrified. I want to marry for love, and it doesn't matter what
that person does for a living. It doesn't matter how much money
they have either.'

'Great minds think alike, Olivia my dear,' he said in a 1940s
detective show kind of accent that made her laugh. 'Seriously,
though, we need to stick together. Are you free for coffee in the
week? I could show you what I've been working on in my studio.'
He smacked himself in the forehead. 'Good god, did I just invite

you to see my etchings?' He burst out laughing and Olivia joined him.

'I think you did!' she told him. 'And I'm happy to accept. Let me know when you're free and I'll make it work.'

The MC of the evening spoke over the sound system. 'Ladies and gentlemen, please clear the dancefloor for the first dance of the evening, the waltz.'

'Come on, Lady Olivia, they're playing our tune.' Owain grabbed her hand and tugged her towards the space in the centre of the room as the orchestra began to play Strauss's 'The Blue Danube'. He slipped his arm around her waist and pulled her close as they circled the floor in time with the 3/4 beat.

Olivia felt thoroughly swept off her feet. Owain was nimble and elegant as he danced with poise and Olivia found it easy to follow him, even though she hadn't waltzed in years. For the duration of the dance, she completely forgot about poor Brodie, whom she had abandoned somewhere in the room with his glass of Champagne. But she was having too much fun to let her thoughts drift to the man she couldn't have and wouldn't admit to wanting if pressed to do so. Owain was fun, and more similar to her in attitude than she could have ever expected. She abandoned all thoughts of leaving early and at the end of the waltz, she fired off a text to Spencer to say he could return for her at midnight, lest she turn into a pumpkin or however that story went.

A little out of breath, she informed Owain she needed air and to powder her nose and went on the hunt for Brodie. She owed him an apology.

'Ah, there you are,' she said when she found him chatting to a young blonde woman.

'Hey, Olivia, you looked like you were having fun out there,' Brodie said with a genuine smile and Olivia mentally kicked herself for hoping he might have shown a twinge of jealousy.

'Yes, it was brilliant. I haven't danced a waltz in... I can't even think. Probably when I was a kid, actually!'

'Clarissa was telling me how you, she and her brother used to be good friends when you were kids, just like you and me,' Brodie said as he drew attention to the woman standing beside him.

Olivia turned to the woman and widened her eyes. 'Clarissa! Oh, my goodness, I didn't recognise you!' She was in such high spirits she hugged Clarissa and thankfully the embrace was reciprocated.

'It's lovely to see you after all these years. How was New York?' Clarissa asked.

'Oh, it was wonderful. But... now I'm here for a while, which is also good.'

Clarissa leaned closer. 'Your date is gorgeous, by the way,' she said with a coquettish smile in Brodie's direction.

Olivia waved her hand dismissively. 'Oh, no, no date, Brodie and are just friends. He's married actually, aren't you, Brodie?'

'Aye. That I am,' he said before taking a long swig from his glass.

Clarissa pouted. 'For shame! I was hoping we would be hearing wedding bells soon. I haven't been to a good wedding for years.'

'Ah, sorry to disappoint,' Olivia replied with a side glance at Brodie who had his gaze firmly fixed on her and a deep crease between his brows. *Why is he annoyed?*

A dark-haired man came over and took Clarissa's hand. 'Come on, Rissa, you owe me a dance,' he said as he pulled her away.

'Oof! I guess I'm going! Lovely to speak to you! See you later!' Clarissa almost squealed as the dapper-looking man hurried her away and into the throng of dancing bodies.

Olivia turned her attention back to Brodie. 'Are you okay? Are you annoyed that I left you alone for so long? Because I know that was a bit shitty of me and I'm so s—'

'It's not that, okay?' he replied rather curtly.

Olivia scrunched her brow. 'So, what is it then? I've clearly pissed you off.'

He pursed his lips and clenched his jaw for a moment before saying, 'It's nothing. Forget it.'

'No, come on, it's obviously something. Please tell me or how will I be able to make it right?'

He looked around, anywhere but at her. 'Why is it that your first words to anyone about me are that I'm married? Why can't you just say we're friends? Leave it at that? What has my marital status got to do with anything or anyone else?'

His reply irked her. 'I'm sorry but you *are*, in fact, married. Most people don't mind that information being told to others. I presumed you'd be the same.'

'Yeah... well... Being married doesn't define me. It's not who I am. It's just a thing that's part of me. Part of my life. It doesn't have to be the first thing people know.'

Olivia's stomach roiled. 'I'm sorry. I won't mention it again. But... why are you so closed off about Mags?'

He shut his eyes and inhaled long and deep. 'It's... she's...' He shook his head and smiled an evidently false smile that his eyes were not aware was being actioned. 'It's nothing. Ignore me.'

Olivia reached out and touched his arm. 'Brodie, if—'

'Ah! There you are, my light-footed dance partner,' Owain said as he arrived beside them. 'Word on the grapevine is that there's a foxtrot coming up and it's my favourite to watch on *Strictly Come Flirting*.'

She laughed. 'Don't you mean *Strictly Come Dancing*?'

He leaned closer. 'Have you seen how many of those contestants pair off? Come on!' He tugged at her hand, but she stood stock still.

She turned to her plus one. 'Brodie?'

Brodie applied a wider smile to his mask. 'Go on! You can't deny the man his foxtrot, for heaven's sake.'

'Good man!' Owain said with a jovial slap to his shoulder.

Olivia sighed and allowed herself to be pulled to the dance-floor once again, but in the back of her mind, something niggled. Something was definitely not right with Brodie.

15

After the foxtrot, Olivia and Owain danced another waltz and after that, they stood at the side to watch the other dancers and catch their breath.

'You know I didn't want to come tonight,' Owain admitted out of the blue. 'But spending the evening with you has made it worthwhile.' He smiled tenderly.

Her heart skipped. 'I have to say that I wasn't really looking forward to it either, but it's turned out to be great fun.'

He eyed her for a moment and eventually said, 'So, you and Brodie... you're definitely not... you know?'

Olivia shook her head. 'No, definitely not. Married men are not my thing.' *Even if Brodie is...*

He nodded and his smile widened. 'Great. So, when can I see you again?'

Olivia felt her face warming and she touched her cheek. 'Gosh, it's so warm in here.'

'Yup. Mum always insists on the heating being on at these things, even though people are dancing.' He shook his head. 'So come on then... when?'

He clearly wasn't going to let it go. 'I thought we were going to go for coffee already?'

Owain took a deep breath and turned to fully face her. 'Look, I'm not going to beat around the bush here. I'm not getting any younger and I really like you. I mean, what's not to like? You're beautiful, you're from a good family, not that that matters, though, you have amazing taste in clothes, and you design them, you love art as much as me, and you can dance.' He lifted his arms out at his sides and let them drop. 'I get the feeling you like me, too, maybe not quite as much yet, but I think we have the makings of a proper whirlwind romance, don't you? Maybe even more. And let's face it, our children would be adorable.'

She stared, open-mouthed for a few moments as she took in what he'd just said. Then she couldn't help the laugh that finally escaped. 'Wow, erm... What do I say to that?' She scratched her head, genuinely flummoxed. 'I mean... yes, I like you, too, but maybe you could slow down a little, Owain.' She held up a halting hand to reiterate her point. 'Let's just get to know each other and see how it goes. But I'll tell you straight off the bat, I'm not in a rush to get hitched and have babies.'

He placed a hand on both of her arms and smoothed his thumbs over her skin. 'Thank goodness for that because neither am I. But you do want to see where this goes?'

She felt more than a little bamboozled. Her heart was doing the jive in her chest and her mind was trying to catch up. It was all a little fast. 'I think... what I mean is... I mean yes, that'd be lovely.'

He picked her up and spun her around. 'Yes! Okay, I'll pick you up tomorrow evening and take you for dinner at a lovely Italian I know in Inverness, yes?'

Blimey, he doesn't waste time. 'Erm... okay.'

'Bravo! I'll go get us another glass of champers.' He turned and left Olivia reeling from his enthusiasm. Was she wrong to feel a little disbelieving about the whole thing? She decided that no, it had been a long time since a handsome single man had shown an interest in her. And she was going to blooming well enjoy it. You heard all the time about people who met and just clicked. Maybe that's what this was? And surely sometimes if things seemed too good to be true, they could actually just *be* that good. Surely? As her mind fought to process it all, Kerr appeared beside her.

'Fed up of slumming it already, I see. Owain is a marginal improvement, I suppose.'

Olivia heaved a deep, exhausted sigh. 'Kerr, just stop, please. You don't impress anyone with your snide comments and your holier-than-thou attitude. You don't have to look down your nose at everyone, you know,' she snapped.

'Oh, but I'm not looking down my nose at *every*one. Oh, god, here comes Owain's mother. No doubt she'll want to plan your wedding to her son now you're a somebody.' With those harsh words, he scuttled off, probably under the nearest rock, Olivia surmised.

Fiona held out her hand and Olivia took it for a second. 'Olivia dear, you and my darling son seem to have hit it off. I can't tell you how happy that makes Hamish and me,' she said with a squeeze to her hand before releasing it. 'We've been waiting so long for him to meet the right woman. Who'd have thought it would happen tonight?'

Wowsers, his family are like a pack of Exocet missiles too. She hated that Kerr was on the verge of being right. She didn't want to get Fiona's hopes up, nor did she want to sound negative, so she went for as neutral a comment as she could. 'Owain is lovely and such fun. It feels like it's been weeks since we saw each other instead of years.'

'Indeed. You brushed shoulders on many occasions throughout your childhoods. Your mother and I used to joke about you getting married one day. But you were both so young. It's all about the timing, don't you think?'

Olivia couldn't imagine her mum talking about her in that way. She smiled and nodded and suddenly remembered Brodie. She glanced at her watch. 'Oh, no! I need to be going. It's just past midnight and Spencer will be here to pick us up. Can you excuse me?'

Fiona frowned and shook her head. 'Oh... yes, yes, of course. What should I tell Owain?'

'Tell him I'll see him tomorrow evening and please pass on my apologies.' Without waiting for a response, Olivia dashed over to where she had last seen Brodie and hoped that he had managed to avoid further encounters with Kerr. She needn't have worried. Once again, her plus one was chatting to an attractive young woman, a brunette this time. The woman was definitely flirting with him; tosses of the hair, touches to his arms, rubbing her fingers around the rim of her glass, biting her lip, her overtures weren't exactly discreet. Although Brodie wasn't making any attempts to put her off. *So that's the kind of man you are, is it? No wonder you don't want me telling people you're married.*

'Brodie, are you ready to go? Spencer will be waiting for us.'

He looked up and his eyes widened for a split second. *Ha! Caught in the act*, Olivia thought.

He nodded. 'Oh aye, yes, sorry. Excuse me, Matilda, my carriage awaits.'

'No problem, Brodie. It was lovely to meet you. Let's go for a coffee sometime,' Matilda said with a tilt of her head and flutter of her eyelashes before sashaying away in her long black figure-hugging strapless dress that fanned out in a fish tail at the bottom. She had one last glance at Brodie over her bare shoulder.

Olivia made a derisive scoffing sound and Brodie turned to face her. 'What now?'

She held up her hands. 'Nothing to do with me.'

He rested his hands on his hips. 'But you've clearly got an opinion.'

'I just wonder what Mags would think, that's all.'

Brodie shook his head. 'Well, lucky for her she isn't here then.'

They walked out into the cool evening air in silence and Olivia shivered. Surprisingly, Brodie took off his jacket and placed it around her shoulders.

'Thank you,' she whispered, once again feeling guilty for sticking her nose in his business. He knew his wife, she didn't. Perhaps they had an open relationship; it worked for some people. Olivia couldn't imagine how, but she'd seen documentaries.

Spencer was standing by the car and as they approached, he opened the rear door so they could climb in.

Once they were seated, Brodie tried small talk. 'Brother dear was on top form tonight, eh?'

Olivia shook her head. 'I honestly don't know why he hates me so much.'

'Because you're not only successful but people like you too. You're very affable, unlike Kerr.'

'Thank you. He just seems to want to go out of his way to make me angry or upset. I wish we could just get along.'

There was a short silence before Brodie spoke again. 'On a more positive note, you and Owain were getting very friendly. Do I sense that something more is blossoming there?' he asked with a strained smile.

Still a little annoyed with him for flirting with other women behind his wife's back, she shrugged. 'I like him. A lot. We're going on a date tomorrow night.'

Brodie nodded. 'Wow, fast mover. Impressive. Well, I hope you have fun. He seems like a nice guy.'

Olivia turned away and looked out of the window into the blackness of the night. 'He is. He's handsome too. And he likes a lot of the same things I do.'

'Great,' Brodie said flatly.

'Looks like you've had a good time too. Plenty of pretty women to keep you company.' She couldn't help the snide edge to her tone.

He gave a small laugh. 'I didn't go looking for them, believe me. And don't forget you did kind of abandon me back there. What was I supposed to do?'

His comment exasperated her. 'Oh, so your flirtations are my fault?'

'I didn't say that! And I wasn't being unfaithful or anything like that. We were simply chatting. Mostly about stuff I have no interest in, if I'm honest, but I was being polite. The last thing I wanted to do was make you look bad, so I was on my best behaviour, if you must know. I only came so you didn't have to be alone. Although I mean, don't get me wrong, it looks like the evening has paid off for you after all. Owain clearly has a lot going for him. And he's part of your crowd too. Bonus.'

His comment stirred anger up within her and her stomach twisted. She turned to face him. 'My crowd? I've told you before that status doesn't mean anything to me. I like Owain for who he is as a person. Not for his parents' land, house or titles.'

'Aye, you say that because he *has* all of those things.' She gasped, like he had slapped her. Brodie closed his eyes for a moment and when he opened them, he eyed her with a sad expression. 'I didn't mean it like that. I just mean... Look, let's forget it. We've both had a nice evening so let's not spoil it by falling out, eh?'

She didn't speak, instead she returned her gaze to the darkness outside, and a heavy silence descended upon them, and she wondered once more why his opinion of her meant so damn much.

* * *

In bed later that night, Olivia replayed the events of the evening in her mind. Seeing Brodie as she had descended the stairs at the start of the evening had almost floored her. At that precise moment, she had sent up a wee prayer that he was going to accompany her but couldn't quite believe it when he actually said that's why he was there. She hated that she felt that way. It was utterly pointless.

Brodie had looked so gorgeous in his kilt, like he had walked off the cover of a fashion magazine, and what he had done by accompanying her had been so gallant. He really was a sweet guy, and such a good friend for stepping in to rescue her from an uncomfortable night. Although in reality it had been anything but uncomfortable for her in the end, apart from the run-ins with Kerr. It had been good to see Owain again after all those years. He had changed so much. And unlike Brodie, Owain was single. He had similar interests to her. He appeared to feel the same about their social standing as she did. Plus, he made her laugh and they'd had such a fun evening. So why did she feel like going on a date with him was some kind of bizarre betrayal? She wasn't even sure on whose behalf she was sensing the betrayal. It can't have been Brodie's because he was married, regardless of his penchant for flirting with other women. And it can't have been hers because she was single.

She shook off the feelings and decided she would still go on the date as agreed. Brodie had almost encouraged her to do so by the positive things he was saying on their journey home. And perhaps she would, once and for all, be able to put the wasted thoughts of Brodie to the back of her mind.

* * *

16

Sunday morning began with a layer of frost on the ground outside and after observing this from the warmth of her room, Olivia climbed back into bed and wrapped her duvet around herself. Marley jumped up and lay down beside her and she sank her fingers into his thick coat to fuss him before she reached over and checked the time on her phone. It was almost 8.30 a.m., meaning that it was only 2 a.m. in New York. Harper would be snuggled up in bed with Summer, no doubt. She sent a quick text suggesting a video call soon and placed her phone down once more.

She was later woken by her phone ringing and rubbed at her eyes. She realised she must have dozed off again and picked up the phone to find it was now after 10 a.m..

Shit! 'Hello?' she said as brightly as possible without checking to see who the caller was.

'Good morning, sleepy head. Are you hungover?'

'Hi, Owain. No, I'm fine. Just tired, that's all.'

He chuckled. 'That'll be all the dancing. Look, I wanted to check that you actually do still want to go out tonight. I was chatting to Rissa, and she seems to think her big brother has been too full on and pushy. I know I can be like that, but I didn't mean to force you into a date. We can wait and just go for coffee next week like we originally planned if you prefer. Unless my over-exuberance has put you off completely.'

She was a little taken back. 'Oh... I don't really mind. Tonight is good for me. I don't have any other plans.'

'And you don't feel pressured? The last thing I want is to have you feel cajoled into dating me. I know my enthusiasm can be irritating.'

His self-deprecation was sort of charming. 'Oh, no, don't worry. I'm looking forward to it.'

There was an audible sigh of relief. 'Great. That's really great. I'll go ahead and book a table and pick you up at 7.15 if that suits?'

'Sounds good. So, are you hungover?' she asked with a smile.

'Ugh, I was this morning. But then I didn't stop drinking after you left. A few of us went into the drawing room and opened a bottle of Balvenie. I had rather a few too many. Tumbled out of bed about half an hour ago. We've had a huge cooked breakfast and plenty of coffee, so I'm fine now. But I'm finding as I get older, I can't handle it like I used to in my uni days.'

She decided not to tell him she was still in bed and his call had woken her up. 'Oh dear. Maybe it's good that you're driving this evening then.'

'Absolutely. Soft drinks all night for me. Anyway, it'll be nice to be out in casual gear instead of being trussed up like a tartan Christmas turkey. Right, I'll let you go. And I'll see you later. Can't wait.'

Olivia smiled. 'Me too. Bye just now.'

* * *

At 6.30 that evening, Olivia was showered and standing in front of her full-length mirror in jeans and her favourite dusky pink Fair Isle jumper. It was a far cry from the previous evening's ensemble, but just like Owain had said, she was happy to be in more casual attire again. She made her way down to the kitchen to find Brodie sitting at the table reading a book about Bonnie Prince Charlie.

She placed her bag on the table. 'Oh, hi. What are you doing here?' She realised this sounded harsh and immediately added, 'Where's Mirren?'

'Hey, you look nice. Erm... I said I'd come in and stoke the fires seeing as Mirren is out for the evening. Some quiz at the Drumblair Arms, I believe. She and my dad are part of a team.'

Olivia wasn't surprised. Mirren was an incredibly smart woman and what Dougie didn't know about horticulture wasn't worth knowing. She imagined they would be quite the dream team.

'Ah, that's great. Mind if I join you for a while? Owain is picking me up at 7.15.'

'Be my guest,' he said, placing his book down. 'There's fresh coffee if you want some.'

'Thanks, but I'm good.' She pulled out a chair and sat. 'They get along so well, don't they?' Olivia asked with a smile. 'Your dad and Mirren.'

He smiled warmly. 'Aye. They're funny, like an old married couple without the marriage. I've often wondered why they didn't get together officially. It's so clear they adore each other. But then my dad was hurt so much by Mum that I don't suppose it's such a surprise.'

'I think they'd make such a lovely couple,' Olivia said wistfully.

'Me too.' Brodie fixed his gaze on her. 'You never know... Love always finds a way if it's meant to be.' He cleared his throat and took a sip of his coffee. 'So, where is Owain taking you?' he asked with an inquisitive tilt of his head.

'Some Italian in Inverness that he loves.'

Brodie nodded. 'Good choice. If it's the one I'm thinking of, Bella Italia on Stephen's Street, you have to try the mushroom *agnolotti* with truffle oil. It's...' He brought his fingers to his lips for a chef's kiss, 'the best I've ever tasted.'

Olivia smiled. 'Duly noted. So, the Young Pretender, eh?' she said pointing to his book. 'Is it a good read?'

'Fascinating. I've been trying to find out more about the Bonnie Prince's connection to this place.'

Olivia's interest piqued. 'Oh, wow, have you found anything?'

He huffed through puffed cheeks. 'This is the third book I've read, and I've only managed to glean bits, but I'm determined.'

A thought struck Olivia. 'Hey, when do you finish your work at the cathedral?'

'Next month, as it happens. We got through the documents faster than we thought.' Disappointment creased his brow. 'I've been too bloody efficient for my own good.' He gave a light laugh.

Excitement set butterflies fluttering about inside Olivia. 'Look... and feel free to say no, because obviously you have a wife to go home to. But I was wondering how you would feel about making your research here official. I mean, going forward we need pamphlets, display boards and such making up for the castle tours. But they need to be researched and done properly by someone who knows what they're doing. I think you would be perfect to put them together. You could really get your teeth into the Bonnie Prince Charlie connection.'

Brodie sat up straight, his eyes sparkling. 'You're offering me a job? That's what you mean, right?'

She beamed. 'It is. We need someone who can be in charge of the collections too once the castle opens, so it doesn't have to be temporary. What do you think? I mean, obviously discuss it with Mags first because, well, Inverness is a fair distance from Edinburgh and she has her job there but...' She didn't bother to try to stop the smile that spread across her face. 'Maybe some things can be done remotely? Anyway, chat to her about it.'

'I'll... I'll do that. I'll give her a call. But heck yeah! I'd bloody love to do it. It's...' he glanced down and fiddled with his bookmark; his cheeks tinged with pink. 'This is going to sound so corny but doing that job, *here*... It's a dream job to me.'

Olivia placed a hand over her heart. 'Really?'

He lifted his chin and smiled, those dimples forming in his cheeks. 'Really. Thank you for offering it to me, Olivia. It means a lot.'

'That's fantastic. You really are the perfect person for the job with your degree, your passion for this place and your connection.'

The doorbell chimed and Olivia stood. 'That must be my date. I'd better get going.'

Brodie nodded. 'Aye. Have a great night, Olivia.'

She found herself unable to think of anything to say. The way he looked in that moment melted her heart and she so wished it didn't. She smiled and turned to leave.

* * *

Owain had arrived in a taxi, much to Olivia's surprise after his comment about soft drinks. The taxi dropped them off at the edge of the precinct in Inverness and they walked up the hill to the Italian on Stephen's Street. It was just as quaint as Olivia had expected; gingham tablecloths and candle holders made from old wine bottles. Olivia and Owain were seated at a cosy table in the corner of the room. The place was already quite busy and had a lovely warm and friendly atmosphere.

Owain looked handsome in a pair of dark blue jeans and a tan-coloured jumper that matched his boots. 'I was really nervous about this evening,' he admitted as they perused the menu.

Olivia narrowed her eyes. 'Me too. But this place is lovely.'

A waiter arrived and Owain ordered a bottle of Rioja and then gestured to Olivia to place her meal order.

'I'll have the mushroom *agnolotti* with truffle oil,' she said handing back her menu.

Owain's eyes lit up. 'Ooh, that sounds good. Make that two.' The waiter left them to chat. 'You seemed to be sure of what you wanted,' he said with a warm smile.

'Oh yes, well, Brodie has been here, and he recommended it so...'

'Oh, right. You and he are quite close then?' There was nothing accusatory or jealous about his tone.

'I wouldn't say that. We used to be very good friends as kids. His dad has been the castle's groundskeeper and gardener for years now and he lives in a cottage in the grounds. Brodie and I grew up together until he relocated after his parents' divorce. Then we lost touch. I've only reconnected with him since I returned home, really.'

'And he's married, I understand.'

Olivia wasn't sure why he was asking questions about Brodie. Unless he was trying to figure out if she had feelings for him, so he didn't waste his time on her. 'Yes, that's right. His wife is in Edinburgh while he works in Inverness for a while.'

'That must be difficult. If and when I get married, I'm hoping we can't bear to be apart.'

This comment rang an alarm bell. Was Owain one of those clingy types who needed to know where their partner was every minute of every day? Better to find out now. 'Hmm, I think in this case it's a needs must thing. It's just for work. And every couple needs their own space some of the time.'

He frowned but nodded his agreement. 'Oh yes, of course. I think so too. I just mean that if you're married, you should at least live together.'

He had a point. 'I suppose so. But it must work for Brodie and Mags.' *Time for a change of topic*, she thought. 'Anyway, tell me about your artwork. What do you paint?'

'Landscapes mostly and some abstracts. But I love to try new things. Art is such a vast spectrum of mediums that I want to at least try everything once, except portraits. I'm not good at portraits.'

A waiter arrived and placed their wine and two glasses on the table. 'Owain. Good to see you, *amico*,' the tall, dark-haired man said in an Italian accent. Olivia guessed he was in his late twenties to early thirties.

Owain stood and embraced the man. '*Stesso, stesso,* Niccolò. *Come va?*'

Niccolò grinned. '*Bene, grazie.*'

'Niccolò, this is my friend Olivia. Olivia, this is Niccolò. I met him during an artists' retreat in San Niccolò, Florence, believe it or not. We had some great times, didn't we, Nic?'

Niccolò from San Niccolò slapped Owain on the back. 'We sure did. And when I told him I wanted to open my own restaurant, Owain convinced me to come to Scotland because he loves the place so much and so, here I am, years later. Turns out I love it too.'

'Niccolò owns this place,' Owain told Olivia. 'He has such a creative flair for food.'

Niccolò placed his hand on his forehead. 'Stop it before my head explode with embarrassment. Anyway, here is your wine,

Owain, your favourite Rioja and it's on the house. Enjoy your evening.' Owain and Niccolò hugged again and then Niccolò left to go back to work.

Olivia raised her eyebrows. 'So, an artists' retreat in Florence, eh?'

Owain shrugged. 'Sometimes you have to take advantage of your parents' wealth and willingness to get shot of you for a few months.' He laughed. 'Seriously though, I learned a great deal from some really talented people. Niccolò's parents owned the house where we stayed, and he was the chef. We just... hit it off, I guess.' He seemed to drift off for a few moments but then shook his head. 'Anyway, your turn. Tell me about New York.'

The rest of the evening went by quickly and was filled with laughter. Brodie had been right about the *agnolotti* too. It was mouth-wateringly good. But every mouthful made her think of him when she was in the company of a perfectly lovely, attractive man.

Life was so unfair sometimes.

17

Over the next few weeks, Olivia spent more and more time with Owain. She grew to really like him. They had such a fun relationship based on common interests and it felt good and easy to be with him. It was also nice that he hadn't tried to rush things with her. There had been several kisses and lots of snuggling on the sofa in his apartment but there had been no pressure for them to take things to the next level, which suited Olivia just fine. She wasn't ready to be intimate with anyone just yet.

Brodie had accepted the role Olivia had offered him but had returned to Edinburgh to work on the research for Drumblair, and to prepare the map of the grounds, the guidebook and the signposting for the interior. Olivia understood why he'd returned to the capital but missed seeing him. She missed their chats and how he always seemed to know the right thing to say when she needed to hear it. Their brief meetings over Zoom weren't quite the same and had taken on more of an employer/employee tone.

Plans for the castle opening were coming along a lot faster than any of them had anticipated. Uncle Innes was still recovering from his surgery but managing to hobble around with his wrist strapped up and attend meetings.

During one such meeting at the beginning of November, they had been discussing the prospect of holding some trial events. Olivia was keen to get the ball rolling, but winter had well and truly arrived, and she was a little stumped. However, after a thoughtful pause, Bella said, 'You know what we need, don't you?'

'What?' Innes and Olivia asked simultaneously.

'A Christmas gift fayre. Lots of stately homes hold them these days. You get a load of craft makers as stall holders, rope in the local school choir, put on mince pies and mulled wine, alcoholic and non-alcoholic, of course, and you decorate the place for Christmas.' She held out her hands as if it was the easiest thing to arrange.

'Bella, I don't mean to be negative, but we are already at the start of November. Most craft creators who do these kinds of fayres will already be sorted for such events. I don't think we have time. But next year definitely.'

Bella shook her head and grinned. 'You know there was supposed to be one at the village school that had to be cancelled, don't you?'

Olivia had been so busy with the castle that she hadn't a clue what had been going on in the village. 'I didn't.'

'Well, their roof collapsed. Luckily it happened at the weekend so no one was hurt but they won't get it repaired in time, so I think we could offer Drumblair Castle as an alternative venue. We could also put the feelers out and see if we could get a few more vendors.'

Innes chewed the inside of his cheek for a moment, his brow crumpled. 'And you think we have time to pull this off? I mean, we have a matter of a few weeks, that's all.'

Bella straightened her spine. 'Leave it with me. I think the Drumblair Christmas Countdown Fayre will be a great success.'

Olivia grinned. 'Ooh, I'm quite excited about it now. I just wonder if people will come.'

Innes tapped his nose. 'Host it and they will come.' He chuckled.

Olivia snickered. 'All right, Kevin Costner. Okay, Bells, go for it.'

Bella clapped her hands excitedly. 'Yay! I love Christmas!'

The date was set for the second weekend in December and, true to her word, Bella worked her magic. By mid-November, almost all the stalls had been booked.

* * *

It was a Saturday in mid-November when Olivia next saw Brodie in person. She had been to an afternoon screening at the cinema with Owain to see the new Ryan Reynolds movie and they had arrived back just before five.

'Do you want to come in for hot chocolate?' she asked Owain as she gazed up into his deep brown eyes under the newly lit archway.

He kissed her nose. 'I think I'd better go get my beauty sleep. I'm heading to Edinburgh tomorrow, remember. I still wish you could come with me.'

She smiled. 'I know, but I have so much to do. The Christmas Countdown is in just over two weeks and I'm still trying to make sure we have everything we need. You won't be back until Wednesday and that would mean four days where I don't get anything done.'

He stuck out his bottom lip like a petulant child. 'But I might be *wonewy*.'

Olivia giggled. 'I'm sure you'll be just fine. You have your friends to keep you company and you'll be too busy with the Christmas market and afternoon drinking to think about me.'

'I'm going to get you the best Christmas surprise *ever*,' he informed her with a glint in his eyes.

'Oh? Well, I'll certainly look forward to that.' She tiptoed up to kiss him lightly on the lips before opening the door to the foyer and waving goodbye as he returned to his sports car and drove away. As she watched his headlights disappear down the long driveway, she sighed. There still was no spark when he kissed her, and she hated that fact. They had such fun together and he was so easy to talk to. Maybe her expectations of the butterflies whenever they kissed, and the desire to rip his clothes off at every given moment, were unrealistic? She hadn't chatted to Bella and Skye about it yet as she wanted to let things breathe for a while. He seemed to like her. He always complimented her and was kind and thoughtful. She was desperate for the thunderbolt to hit so she suddenly fell head over heels in love with him. Because he really was perfect. He was attractive, talented, funny... so what was the problem?

Once inside the dimly lit entrance way, Olivia glanced around to see several bulbs missing from light fixtures. The old bulbs in the chandelier and wall sconces were being replaced by energy efficient ones but it had meant making some adaptations to the old fittings. It was like stepping into a cave just now, however, and she made a mental note to speak to the electrician on Monday. Suddenly she heard barking and there was the usual streak of white before Wilf and Marley appeared in tandem. Wilf jumped up at her, almost knocking her off her feet again. His tail was frantically wagging and his tongue lolling out at one side of his mouth. Typical Wilf. Marley was hanging back a little to let Wilf get his exuberance out of the way. Such a polite boy.

She scratched the dogs behind their ears. 'Hey, Wilfy, hey, Marley, you're both always so happy to see me! Where's—'

'Shit, I'm so sorry, Olivia,' Brodie said, jogging up from the direction of the kitchen. 'I really am trying to improve his recall, but he just won't listen.'

'It's fine, I've learned to brace myself whenever I hear his claws hitting the floor at speed.'

He gave an apologetic smile. 'That's a good thing. Anyway, I was just dropping some logs off in the drawing room for my dad and now I'm about to wander down to his place, so I'll be out of your hair. Don't want to be a third wheel to the loved-up couple,' he said, glancing behind her and scratching his head.

'Oh, no, you're fine. Owain is setting off for Edinburgh early tomorrow with some friends so he's having an early night.'

Brodie glanced at his watch. 'It's 5 p.m.. How early does he need to be in bed?' He laughed.

Olivia shook her head and rolled her eyes. 'I know. Crazy, right?'

'Things seem to be going well for you two. I'm really happy for you,' he told her with a handsome smile that she wished she hadn't noticed.

Deciding not to dwell on it, she said, 'Thanks, hey, I was going to make hot chocolate with marshmallows if you fancy some?'

Brodie glanced at his watch again and his face contorted a little, seemingly he was weighing things up for some reason. 'Oh, sod it, why not.' They headed for the kitchen with Wilf and Marley trotting along behind.

Once in the light of the kitchen, Olivia grabbed some mugs and scooped five heaped spoonsful of powder into each as Wilf lay beside her feet and Marley took to his usual spot. 'So, what have you been up to today?' she asked as she poured boiling water into each of the large mugs.

'I've been finishing up some of the wording for the signage that's going in the costume gallery.'

Without turning, she said, 'Brodie, it's Saturday. You're allowed a day off, you know.'

'Aye, but I was a wee bit behind, so I just thought I'd try and catch up.'

Olivia turned with the two mugs in her hands and stopped in her tracks with a gasp. 'Brodie! What the hell has happened to your face?' Wilf hurried over to sit by his master as if he needed defend him. He laid down with a whine.

Brodie lifted his hand to his cheek. 'Oh, this? It's nothing. I'm a clumsy wee dobber.' He laughed. 'Tripping over this wee rascal.' He reached down to scratch Wilf's head.

Olivia placed the mugs on the table and slid into the chair opposite him. 'Come on, what really happened? It looks like someone's hit you.'

He reached for his mug and stared at the contents. 'You should see the other guy.' He forced another laugh.

Olivia narrowed her eyes in concern. 'Was there just *one* other guy?'

Brodie swirled the liquid around in his mug and nodded towards it. 'You won't laugh if I get a marshmallow 'tache, will you?' he asked with a smile. "Cause there's a lot of them in here.'

'Brodie?' Olivia said, reaching with her hand on the table but not touching him.

He sighed defeatedly. 'I'm fine, honestly. I've just been a bit off my game. Walking into stuff, you know? I probably just need more sleep. Anyway, was the film any good? Mirren said you were going to see the new Ryan Reynolds one. He's brilliant, isn't he? Such fantastic comedy timing. Would you recommend it?'

'The film was great but... Brodie, are you in trouble? This isn't the first time you've had a black eye.'

He shook his head but didn't make eye contact. 'Trouble? Me? Pfft, nah. Like I said, I'm just accident prone.'

'You do know you can talk to me, don't you? If you owe someone money, I—'

He quickly lifted his head and glared at her. 'You'll throw money at my problems and fix them? Thanks, Olivia, but I don't need or want your money.' She was taken aback by the harshness of his tone and lost for words for a moment. He swallowed hard. 'Look, I'd better be getting back to Dad's. I'm setting off back to Edinburgh after dinner.' He pushed his chair back and stood. 'Thanks for the hot chocolate but if I wait for it to cool, it'll take too long. I'd better go. Come on, Wilf.' He patted his leg and Wilf dutifully jumped to his paws before they walked out of the room.

Olivia rushed to follow. 'Brodie, please, I didn't mean to offend you! I'm—' The main entrance slammed. '—Sorry.' She stared at the closed door, worry niggling at her mind and knotting her insides.

She glanced down to find Marley had followed her and she scratched his head. 'Oh, Marley, I think there's more to Brodie's situation than he's letting on.' Whatever it was he was dealing with, he wasn't prepared to ask for help, so she would just have to step back until he did.

Monday morning was bustling at the castle. It was just over two weeks to the Christmas Countdown and there were so many people wandering around the place, she wondered if this was similar to what it would be like having the general public walking around her home. Her phone buzzed and she glanced at the screen to find an email from Brodie.

Dear Olivia,

Please find attached the final wording for the main rooms. Please let me know if you would like any changes making before I send them to the printer. Innes says they will be displayed behind Perspex so just make sure you go for the anti-glare stuff, or they will be difficult to read with the lighting in the rooms being dimmer to protect the artwork. I'm also attaching the portions for the guidebook. Innes says the photographer has forward the final images and that you're happy with them. That's good news.

Best wishes,

Brodie MacLeod

Olivia stared at the screen. The email was so formal. So staid. And from the contents of the email, it was evident he had been corresponding with Innes on things he would usually contact her about. That was disappointing enough in itself. But the fact he signed off with his full name as if she didn't even know him... that really stung.

At around 11 a.m., Olivia made her way to the row of old farm workers' cottages within the boundary walls of the castle. Dougie had lived in the end of the four cottages for as long Olivia could remember. She walked up the path to the front door through the neatly manicured garden, surprised that it could look so colourful and vibrant even at this time of year. Dougie certainly had a green thumb.

She knocked on the door and waited.

When it opened, Dougie smiled widely. 'Lady Olivia. What a nice surprise. What can I do for you?'

'Hi, Dougie. I'm sorry to intrude but I wondered if Brodie was here?'

Dougie clenched his jaw and a crease appeared in the middle of his brow. 'Erm... no. No, he left yesterday.'

Olivia's heart sank. 'Ah, back to Edinburgh?'

Dougie's mouth twisted as if he was trying to stop words from escaping. 'Not exactly. He's just gone for a bit of space, you know? He does this sometimes. Things get a bit much for him and he takes off for a wee while.'

Olivia was surprised and concerned by his admission. 'Oh, I see. Do you know where he's gone?'

'He usually goes to the same place. Rosemarkie. A wee seaside place on the Black Isle that we used to go on family holidays. But he'll be fine, don't worry.'

'Dougie... do you know what's going on with him? The black eyes... the secretiveness. It seems so out of character. He was always so confident, but these days...'

'Lady Olivia, I mean no disrespect by this but... you're better off staying out of it. It's not my place to tell you things. He'd be upset and I'd be betraying his trust. He's my only son... please understand.'

Olivia nodded as her heart began to pound. 'So, there is something wrong?'

Dougie closed his eyes and sighed. 'Please don't get involved. It'll be worse for Brodie all around if you do.'

Worry needled at her, and she wanted to do more. 'Dougie, he's my friend. He's not replying to my messages and his last email was so formal, it didn't feel natural. I'm just worried. I want to help him. Is there any way I can do that?'

Dougie smiled but it was tinged with sadness. 'Just be here for him when he returns.' He clearly wasn't going to divulge anything, and she couldn't be angry with him for that.

It was clear that something was very wrong but what could she do if Brodie refused to confide in her? She only hoped his wife was helping him through whatever the hell it was.

* * *

By the beginning of December, the majority of the interior work at the castle was complete. There was a gift shop now where the old basement games room had once been and a café in the former stable block. Everything was being cleaned in preparation for the Christmas Countdown and the biggest Christmas tree Olivia had seen, barring the one outside of the Rockefeller Centre, had been placed in the centre of the gravel driveway outside. It was lit with multicoloured lanterns and decorated with giant baubles. The fireplace in the entrance way was now adorned with swags of holly and ribbons and all the bulbs were now in place in the updated chandelier. The pine tree in the foyer smelled fresh and festive and Olivia could close her eyes and be back in her childhood once again. The strings of dried oranges and cinnamon sticks added to that feeling of nostalgia for Christmases past and Olivia was filled with mixed emotions.

She stood in the long gallery that had been cleared of the antique heirlooms in readiness for the gift fayre and peered up at the portraits. She wondered what her ancestors would make of the decisions she had made. She wondered if her mother and father would be proud of her. She certainly hoped so.

Olivia hardly recognised the castle when she walked through the rooms now, but excitement still bubbled up under her skin at the prospect of what the future would bring. The gift shop shelving was all in situ and Bella had been working with Olivia to decide what kind of stock they would hold. She had enjoyed visiting wholesalers and riffling through myriad catalogues and websites, looking at potential stock. Uncle Innes had even begun interviewing staff and Bella had been assisting him.

Eventually, after many conversations between themselves, Olivia and Uncle Innes had put forward the possibility of early spring for the grand opening and the board agreed that Saturday, 11 March would be the official opening to the public of the castle for tours. However, they had decided that seeing as the long gallery was ready and had its own access, they would venture to hold a couple of events prior to this. Bella had suggested getting the local press involved and people from other local tourist attractions, so they were in the process of discussing ideas.

* * *

Following an ideas meeting, Olivia had been in the grounds getting some much-needed space and fresh air when Kerr had approached her.

'How is it all going then, sis?' he asked when he sat beside her on one of the newly installed wooden benches. Marley wandered up to him and Kerr reluctantly patted the dog awkwardly on the head. Probably sensing his disinterest, Marley walked back to where he had been sitting at Olivia's feet.

His question shocked Olivia. 'Oh... it's going well. Thank you for asking.'

He gazed out at the scenery before them. 'That's good. I mean... I'm still not exactly happy about having our family home turned into a visitor attraction but I do understand why. And... I... I think you've done a good job.'

She turned to him and simply stared, dumbfounded.

He gave a light laugh. 'What?'

She narrowed her eyes. 'You're being nice. I'm waiting for the punchline.'

His shoulders hunched. 'I see. I've been such a shit brother that I can't even compliment you without you thinking it's a joke. Great.'

She reached out and squeezed his arm. 'No, it's not that...' He eyed her suspiciously. 'Okay, Kerr, busted, it *is* that. But thank you. It really does mean a lot. It's what I've wanted all along, for us to do this together. We're still family.'

He inhaled a long breath and closed his eyes as he exhaled. 'We are. You're right.'

'So, how's Adaira? Are you two still getting along?'

He gave a deep sigh. 'Ah, therein lies a complicated and laborious story. Suffice it to say that she's been a literal lifesaver.'

Olivia widened her eyes. 'You weren't kidding about the death threats then?'

He narrowed his eyes. 'You think I would make something like that up?'

She shrugged. 'Well, I hoped you wouldn't, but I hoped it wasn't actually true. I don't want to see you get hurt.'

'Okay. That's good to know. But no, I wasn't joking. I'm seeing a therapist now. I'm aware I have issues with drinking and gambling. And Adaira has been very supportive. In fact, she's footing all my bills. So, I guess I'm kind of beholden to her. Not the best way to be, I know. And not something I foresaw, to be honest. I was only dating her to get at Mum. And yes, before you say anything, it was a shitty thing to do. But Mum had cut me off and I was angry. I regret it and beat myself up regularly. But a good friend told me that I should cut my sister some slack. That I haven't exactly been a good brother since Mum died. I realise now that perhaps I've blamed you for things I shouldn't have.'

Olivia was stunned by his admission. 'Wow... I don't know what to say.'

'You don't need to say anything. I know it's not your place to bail me out. So, Adaira will do for now.' He glanced at her and shook his head. 'I know that makes me a rat bag. But I can't just dump her. Not after everything she's done for me. And it's nice to be wanted.

That doesn't happen much in my life. And I know you're a goody two shoes who wouldn't ever use anyone like that, but try not to judge, eh? And maybe keep your opinions on the matter to yourself. I just want to be able to pay her back at some point. Maybe when one of my business ideas takes off, that will be possible. That way, I won't feel as guilty to break things off with her.'

Olivia exhaled a long breath. 'Again, wow. As long as you're safe, I suppose. And no one gets hurt.' She knew that in his situation, someone was bound to get hurt, but he had asked her not to judge, so she tried her best not to.

'So, have you given up on designing pretty little frocks now that you're a one-woman organising machine?'

Olivia decided to ignore his condescending choice of words on this occasion. 'Not at all. I've been sketching through this whole process. In fact, I've had an idea for the press event.'

He turned to face her and raised his eyebrows. 'You have? I heard that you were going to get the press involved. I think it's a good plan. So come on then, what's your big idea?'

Olivia paused for a moment, unsure as to whether to trust her brother with the details. As if reading her mind, he held up his hands and said, 'Look, I'm not going to tell anyone. It's your idea. I was just interested, that's all. But I understand if you don't want to tell me. I mean, I haven't exactly been involved or supportive through all of this.' He hung his head and guilt niggled at her. He was offering an olive branch and she should at least meet him halfway.

'Okay. So… Nina is in London for Fashion Week in February, and I was thinking of asking if she would come north and put the show on again here at the castle. I want to show it as a flexible venue for all kinds of events, as well as having it open to the public. We have plenty of room for the models to stay over a couple of nights and I think it would be something different for people to see, you know?'

He smiled and nodded slowly, letting the idea ruminate for a moment. 'So, a fashion show in the long gallery with a world-famous designer, eh? Big plans. But I think you should go for it. It's the ideal way to put the place on the map.'

Olivia's heart lightened at his comments. 'Really? I mean there's no guarantee that she would agree to it, but I can always ask.'

He nudged her with his shoulder. 'Exactly. And why would she say no? You were one of her favourite and trusted employees. She's already going to be in the UK anyway. Nothing ventured and all that.'

Olivia beamed and excitement caused a stampede of hobnail-booted butterflies in her stomach. 'You're right! I'm going to email her!'

Kerr smiled; it was the first time in ages that she had seen it. She reached over and hugged him.

'Thanks, big brother.' Unfortunately, despite his words and her happiness at hearing them, there was still a niggle at the back of Olivia's mind that he was keeping something from her; not telling her the whole truth; being insincere. But she tried her best to push the thoughts away. After all, it would be lovely to have a real brother for once.

18

Olivia paced around the drawing room, nervous energy coursing through her veins as she clutched her phone and waited for Nina to give her answer. She stared up at the family portrait and her mother's smiling eyes gave her the confidence she needed to remain positive, even if it was a crazy suggestion, now she thought about it.

'I think it's a marvellous idea, Olivia. I've always wanted to visit Scotland and I know how it inspires you, so maybe it will inspire me too! I say yes. Can I leave you to organise things at your end if I arrange for the models to be available?'

Olivia silently fist-pumped the air and danced around in her stockinged feet while simultaneously keeping her voice even and calm. It was no mean feat. 'Of course. That's great. Thank you so much, Nina,' she replied as calmly as she possibly could.

'Don't thank me, it will be a pleasure, I can assure you. And, of course, Harper will come too. We'll need someone on our team to photograph the occasion.'

Olivia stifled the squeal begging to escape from her chest. 'I don't think you'll get any arguments from her. She loves Scotland. I really appreciate this, Nina. I owe you, big time.'

'Not at all. We're in the UK anyway, so it will be a nice little sojourn before we return to real life. I have been meaning to contact you anyway, so it's good that you called. I have a proposal for you.'

Olivia's interest was piqued, and she flopped down on the sofa. 'Oh? What's that then?'

'Once you are done with the castle, I was wondering if you would consider working for the company on a remote basis. We can do so much over the internet these days and we can hold meetings online. This way, I get to keep one of my best designers and you get to still have a hand in with something you love. You can come over to New York a couple of times a year, so you still get your fix of the Big Apple too. Plus, you can stay in Scotland and be as involved as necessary with Drumblair.'

A wide smile spread across Olivia's face and tears welled in her eyes. 'You'd do that for me?'

'Olivia, darling, you are missed here! Your latest sketches are brilliant, so of course I would do that for you. There's no rule saying you have to be here in the office. And anyway, I make the rules. It's my fashion house, so I say hell yes, you can work remotely. I wanted to suggest it when you first returned to Scotland but knowing the amount of pressure on you, I couldn't ask. So, I waited.'

'Well, I accept!'

The sound of Nina's laughter echoed in her ear. 'You can think about it, you know. I don't expect an immediate answer.'

'Nope. No need, I accept. I get the best of both worlds that way and I couldn't be happier!'

'That's settled then. I'm so glad!' Nina sounded genuinely pleased.

As soon as the call with Nina ended, Olivia dialled Harper's number and relayed the conversation.

Harper squealed. 'Yay! I get to go to Scotland; I get to hug my bestie!'

'I can't wait. I think the next couple of months will simply drag,' Olivia said.

'I bet they fly by! I'm so proud of you, Olivia. The photo updates you keep sending are so awesome. You've pulled off a miracle and your mom would be so damned proud of you too.' She paused. 'How is Kerr about everything now?'

'You'll never believe this, but he actually told me I was doing a great job. He encouraged me to contact Nina about the fashion show too.'

'Awww, honey, I'm so glad. I hope this is a turning point for the two of you.'

'Me too, Harper. Me too.'

'And how about the new man in your life? How's that going?'

Olivia smiled. 'Owain is lovely. So sweet and funny. We laugh a lot.'

Harper paused. 'That's great and all, but does he turn your insides to Jell-O?'

Olivia rolled her eyes. 'I'm not looking for that, Harper. It doesn't last. Lust is fleeting. I'm looking for something stable and safe.'

'Ugh! And boring as hell! You need someone whose clothes you wanna rip off. Someone who excites you. Does Owain do that?'

Olivia sighed, a little annoyed with her friend's unrealistic ideals. 'We haven't slept together yet. He's happy to take things slow. But he makes me laugh so much. I really like him. I think... I think he could be the one.'

'Oh, wow! *Really*? Are you sure? I mean yeah, he's a good-looking guy. The photo you sent was great. But... I don't know... I just want you to be happy, Olivia. Like *really* happy.'

'And Owain does that for me.'

Harper sighed. 'Okay. Only you know your own heart, honey.'

* * *

Bella was giddy when Olivia announced to her and Uncle Innes that Nina was going to come and put on a fashion show for the press and local businesses in the new year.

'Oh, my word! What will I wear? I don't have anything design-ery. But I'll have to look smart. I can't believe I'm going to meet Nina Picarro. Wait until Skye hears about this!'

'I'm sure I have something you can borrow, Bells, so don't worry and it's a while off yet.'

'I hope my wrist is healed by then,' Uncle Innes said thought-fully. 'Is she still single?'

'Is who still single, Uncle?' Olivia asked, trying to hide her smirk.

'Your lovely Nina. I've always thought she carries herself with such grace for a lady of a certain age.'

Olivia couldn't help laughing. 'Got yourself a wee crush there, have we?'

Uncle Innes's cheeks coloured cerise. 'No, no, nothing like that. I just respect strong, talented women, that's all. And Nina Picarro epitomises that so well.'

Olivia nodded and Bella giggled. 'Oh, come on, Innes, you've clearly got the hots for Nina.'

Uncle Innes stood. 'Erm... I think I heard my phone ringing. I... I... left it on charge in the kitchen. I... I'd better go check in case it's something important.'

As he walked out of the room, Olivia and Bella burst into giggles. 'Bless him. He's lovesick,' Bella said.

'Speaking of lovesick. Are you ready to tell me about your mystery man yet?'

'Nope. After he bailed on me that night he said he'd planned something special, I was ready to throw in the towel. But... let's just say he convinced me otherwise.'

He had bailed on Bella on the night of the ball, and she had been so disappointed she had walked around like a bear with a sore head but still wouldn't spill the beans. 'Oh, really? So come on, spill it, Bells!'

Bella shook her head. 'My lips are well and truly sealed for now. He's away at the moment anyway. So, I'd rather wait until he returns before we make anything public.'

Olivia's heart skipped. He's away? Like Brodie? And Brodie was at the ball with me which means... it can't be... not him... Surely he would have mentioned something? But then again, she had berated him for supposedly flirting with other women at the ball, so no, Brodie probably wouldn't have said anything. And it made sense that Bella wouldn't admit to it, knowing his marital status.

'I'm just worried about you, Bella. I hope he's not a married man or anything like that.'

'Pfft,' was all that Bella could utter before gathering her notepad and handbag and saying. 'Better dash. Lots to do!'

Olivia's heart sank and her mind was filled with a kind of dread that she had only encountered on two occasions in the past. Neither of which had ended well.

She picked up her phone and typed out a text to Brodie.

Hey MacLeod. Where the Dickens are you? I know you took holiday time but we've heard nothing from you in days and that's scary. You have friends here that are worried, you know. And if there is something you need to tell me, something about you and my friend Bella perhaps, you can just tell me, you know. I know I seemed a bit judgy before when we were at the ball, but I'm not really like that. I just want you to be happy. And safe of course. Just message me, okay?

As soon as she had finished typing, she reread her words, sighed heavily and promptly hit the backspace button. She couldn't possibly send it, could she?

She just knew that this was one occasion where she really and truly hoped that two and two didn't make four.

* * *

Days were passing at a rate of knots but there was still no word from Brodie. One day, when Olivia was wandering through the grounds with Marley, she ended up on Dougie's doorstep again.

'Still no word, Lady Olivia. But as I said before, he'll be fine. I suspect he just needed to clear his head. He has down times when things get tough. But he's a fighter. Mentally, I mean. Not physically. He's a good lad, my Brodie. But I know you know that.'

She smiled. 'I do know that. If you do hear from him, please tell him I'm concerned for him. He can always just message to say he's okay. It would put my mind at rest.'

'If I hear from him, I'll definitely pass on your message.'

'Thank you. And in the meantime, is there anything I can do for you, Dougie?'

He smiled warmly. 'You're just like your mother. Putting everyone else above yourself, even when they don't deserve it. And no, I think I'll be fine. But thank you. I appreciate you asking.'

* * *

Two days to go to the Christmas Countdown Fayre and Owain had insisted he take Olivia out to calm her nerves. He'd booked a table at Bella Italia restaurant again but that only managed to make her think of Brodie. Of course she ordered the mushroom *agnolotti* with truffle oil, how could she not?

Once their main courses were finished, Owain chatted away about his latest piece that was taking up the whole of his studio. He had driven them to the restaurant so she couldn't even blame the wine for his over-exuberance on this particular evening. She heard the words *landscape, series, seasons* but had drifted off, her mind elsewhere.

'And the aliens loved posing for me, even though I don't usually tackle portraits. It was hard to get the right shade of green, too, but I did my best.'

Olivia's eyes shot towards him. 'Aliens?'

Owain laughed. 'So, you were listening to parts of it, at least.'

Olivia shook her head. 'Gosh, I'm so sorry. I don't know where I went.'

Owain took her hand across the table. 'You're ever so quiet, Olivia. What's wrong?'

She forced a smile. She hadn't mentioned Brodie's disappearance to him at all. Nor her suspicions that he was seeing Bella behind his wife's back. 'Oh, nothing. I'm just exhausted. The fayre has taken all of my energy, I think. I tend to get grumpy when I'm tired,' she lied.

'Well... I may have something that will cheer you up.'

Olivia straightened, willing his words to be true. 'Ooh, that sounds good. What is it?'

'Okay, so you know I said I was going to buy you the best Christmas gift ever?'

She grinned. 'I do remember that. Very clearly.'

'Right... so... god, my palms are sweating. Okay... So... I think as you need cheering up and as it's almost the festive season anyway, I figured I would give you your gift tonight.' He reached into his inside pocket and pulled out a small package wrapped in gold paper and a red ribbon. 'I've had it on good authority that you'll like it. Well, my mum and my sister thought so, anyway. And I know it's probably not what you were expecting, but I saw it and I just knew. I only hope I knew correctly, of course, but I think so. I'm usually a good judge of taste and, of course, yours is impeccable. God, I'm rambling. Okay, so here you go. Just open it.'

He handed her the parcel and she tugged at the ribbon, eager to see what delights lay inside. She opened the wrapping and took out the cardboard box, opened the lid on that, and found something quite unexpected inside.

She gasped and glanced up at Owain. 'What is this?' Her heart thumped at her ribs and her mouth dried out rapidly as she pulled out the small velvet box.

Owain's eyes were fixed on her. 'Go ahead, open it,' he whispered.

She swallowed, mixed emotions vying for dominance and her heart almost stopped when she lifted the creaking lid and caught sight of the diamond ring sitting in the little velvet cushion, the facets glinting in the candlelight.

'Oh, my goodness.'

He reached across and took her hand. 'Now I know this seems stupidly fast, and insta-love is something only usually found in romance novels but... I know how I feel about you, and I know that being married to my best friend would be the most wonderful thing ever. So... Olivia MacBain, would you do me the honour of being my wife?'

She opened her mouth to speak, but as she did so, her phone rang. She glanced at her bag, unsure what to do. But it was almost 10 p.m., so it was obviously something important.

'So?' Owain asked, a wide, hopeful smile still fixed on his face as he slipped the ring onto the ring finger of her left hand. 'What do you say?'

The phone continued to ring. 'I— I should maybe get that. It might be important.'

Owain straightened up and smoothed down his tie. 'Of course. Of course you should.'

Shakily she reached into her bag and pulled out her phone. 'Hello?'

'Lady Olivia?' a familiar voice asked, but it sounded strangled with emotion.

'Yes, this is she. Who's calling?'

'It's Dougal... Dougie MacLeod.' He sniffed and his voice cracked.

Olivia's blood ran cold. 'Dougie? What is it? What's wrong?'

'He's... he's in a bad way. He's... he's asking for you.'

'Oh my god, what's happened? Where is he?'

'He's at Raigmore Hospital. He was taken there by ambulance after the campsite owner found him out in the woods at Rose-markie that surround the site where he'd been camping. He said he was walking his dog and heard another dog howling and whin-ing. It was Wilf. The man called an ambulance and took Wilf to his friend who's a vet to get Wilf's chip scanned. The dog's regis-tered to my address so he turned up here with Wilf and explained what had happened. We got here as soon as we could. Wilf is at home, poor thing.'

'Which ward is he in? I'll be right there.'

19

The drive to Raigmore took a matter of minutes but it still felt too long. Nervous energy coursed through Olivia's veins and her leg bounced as she chewed at the skin around her thumb. Her suspicions that something was very wrong were now confirmed in the worst possible way. What the hell had happened to Brodie?

Owain reached up and took her hand. 'Hey, calm down. We're almost there. He'll be fine. He's a tough guy, from what I've seen.'

He was right, in a way. Brodie was tough on the outside, but it wasn't his exterior that she was worried about.

She nodded and squeezed Owain's hand. 'Thank you so much for this. And I'm so sorry to cut short our evening.'

'Honestly, it's fine. I would be exactly the same if one of my friends wound up in hospital.'

He pulled the car into the drop off space outside the hospital. 'Right. Message me as soon as you know what's happening. I can come back and pick you up, it's not a problem.'

'Thank you again, Owain, but I have no idea how long I'll be. It's probably best that I call a taxi.'

He unclipped his seatbelt, reached across and hugged her.

'Well, the offer stands. You're a good friend and I know he'll appreciate you being there.'

She loved that there was no sense of jealousy, no anger that she was abandoning him. But she felt guilty for that very reason. She had run away from a man who had just proposed to her to go to a man who she wanted but couldn't have. Where was the sense in it? Deep down, she felt she was betraying Owain's trust in quite an underhanded way.

Once inside the hospital, Olivia made her way to the floor that Dougie had mentioned. Everything was quiet apart from the odd nurse or orderly traversing from one location to another with clipboards or bedpans. The sound of distant footsteps and low chatter were all that she could hear as she made her way to the ward.

After she had been buzzed in, Olivia stood at the nurses' station, her whole body juddering and her heart pounding so hard she could feel the throbbing in her head. She explained to the nurse why she was there at such a late hour.

'I'm afraid it's family only and as it is there already two people in there. Visiting hours were over a while ago and I can't just let anyone in,' the petite red-haired nurse told her apologetically. 'We have rules about these things. I'm so sorry.'

Olivia nodded. 'Okay, I understand, I do. It's just that Brodie's father called me and said he'd been asking for me.'

The nurse's eyes widened. 'Oh, are you Lady MacBain?'

Olivia nodded. 'I am.'

The nurse pointed down the corridor. 'In that case, he's in room two. My apologies. He *was* asking for you and I was told to make an exception when you arrived.'

Olivia smiled, relieved. 'Thank you so much.' She inhaled a deep, calming breath and walked towards the room, the heels of her boots clip-clopping loudly on the hard floor, echoing around the otherwise quiet hospital ward. She didn't like hospitals as it was, but at night, they seemed extra eerie, like some sinister scene in a horror movie, and she shivered involuntarily.

She knocked lightly on the door, and it opened a matter of seconds later.

'Lady Olivia. Thank you so much for coming,' Dougie said, holding out his hand. His eyes were bloodshot and his face pale. Olivia pulled him into an embrace. 'Of course, Dougie, and please, it's just Olivia.'

Mirren stood and crossed the room too, a crumpled tissue in her hand. 'Bless you for coming, dearie.' She hugged her tightly.

Dougie gestured to a chair. 'Please, come and sit down. I'll go and get you a coffee.'

'Thank you, Dougie. I think I could do with one.'

Dougie left the room and Olivia walked over to the bed where Brodie lay hooked up to a heart monitor, the blip-blip thankfully stable. She sat and Mirren followed suit, taking her hand.

'I bet Dougie's glad to have you here with him,' she said to Mirren.

She shook her head. 'He was in bits, Olivia. Absolutely heart-broken. I couldn't let him drive here in that state.'

'Of course not. You did the right thing.'

They fell silent and watched Brodie as he lay there in slumber. His eyes were swollen shut, and he had bandages covering patches on his arms. Another bandage wrapped around his head and his hair was greasy and matted. A splint covered his nose, which was bloody and bruised. His hospital gown was pulled down at the neck and the pads for the monitor were stuck in between bruises on his chest. His chest rose and fell naturally, meaning his breathing pattern was, thankfully, steady. But seeing this tall, muscular man lying there in such a fragile and vulnerable state made her angry and sad simultaneously. How could another human being treat him like this? What possible reason could there be?

'Do you know what happened to him?' Olivia asked Mirren.

'I... I can't say, sweetheart. Dougie asked... Well, you know, it's quite sensitive and it's probably best it comes from Brodie.' Mirren stood and walked over to the window. She sniffed and dabbed at her eyes. 'He's like a son to me and I hate to see him like this.'

The anguish in Mirren's voice made Olivia's heart ache, her eyes welled with tears, and she covered her mouth with one hand. 'Oh, my goodness, Brodie. What on earth happened to you?' She pulled herself closer to his bedside his bed and took hold of his hand. 'I wish you'd tell me. I just want to help.' He looked as though he had been beaten up or run over. She wasn't sure which, but it was clear that something horrific had happened. And while she was frustrated that Mirren wouldn't tell her why he had ended up here, she understood too. It wasn't her story to tell. And there clearly was a story here.

'Ol-Olivia?' Brodie croaked. 'D-don't cry,' he whispered as he tried to reach for her.

Her heart tripped over itself. 'Yes, Brodie, it's Olivia, I'm here. It's okay. Just rest.'

'I'm sorry. I'm so sorry,' he whispered as he squeezed her hand.

'Shhh, don't try to speak. Just sleep now. I'm not going anywhere.'

Dougie returned a few moments later and handed her a cardboard cup of coffee. 'It's not the best, but it'll do the trick,' he told her.

'Dougie, can you tell me what on earth has happened? He looks like he's been attacked.'

Dougie nodded and his lip trembled. 'Aye. Broken ribs, broken nose, cuts, a split on his head... He didn't even try to defend himself. Who'd have thought it?' Mirren walked over and took his hand.

Olivia glanced between the two older people. 'Who'd have thought what? Dougie, please tell me what's going on.'

Dougie shook his head. 'I *cannae*. It's for him to tell you, no me. I'm just ready for it to be over now. It's been going on too long. He *doesnae* deserve this.'

Olivia closed her eyes and sighed. 'Look, why don't you two go home and get some rest? I'm happy to stay at his bedside. You both look exhausted.'

Dougie wiped his eyes. 'Aye, I'm exhausted, all right. But I don't want to leave him. He's my only son. My only child. I *wasnae* there for him enough when he left with his mother, so I'll no abandon him now.'

Mirren rubbed his arm. 'Olivia's right, love. You're not abandoning him. And you can't help him if you're ill from tiredness and stress. And poor Wilf will wonder what's going on. Please, let's go home. Olivia will call us if anything changes, won't you, dearie?'

'Of course I will. I won't leave him, so if there's any update, I'll call right away.'

Dougie scrunched his brow and nodded. 'Aye... aye, okay. But you must ring me. It *doesnae* matter what time.'

Olivia reached out and squeezed his arm. 'I promise.'

Dougie walked over and kissed his son's head. 'I'll be back soon, son. I love you.' He smoothed the matted hair back from his face. 'You're loved, Brodie, do you hear me? This has to stop now.'

He wiped tears from his chin and crossed the room to Olivia. 'Thank you, Olivia. I know you had your issues in the past, but your friendship means such a lot to him and he thinks a lot of you. I'm grateful for you being here.'

Once Dougie and Mirren were gone, Olivia turned her attention back to Brodie. 'When you're ready, you can tell me anything.

If I can help you, I will. It doesn't matter the cost. I hope you know that.'

* * *

Olivia was woken by movement on the bed, and she lifted her head, confused for a moment as to where she was. The muscles in her neck were spasming and she reached up to rub a sore spot.

'Sorry to wake you, Lady Olivia. I just had to come and check his vitals,' the red-haired nurse from the previous night informed her.

She straightened up and moved her head this way and that. 'That's okay. How is he doing?'

'Oh, he's doing well. At least, he's doing as well as can be expected. Everything is functioning as it should be. He's just going to be sore for a wee while. Lots of healing to do.'

In more ways than just physical, Olivia thought.

Olivia turned to face the nurse where she stood at the foot of the bed, making notes on Brodie's chart. 'I don't suppose you know what happened to him, do you? He's in such a state.'

The nurse smiled kindly. 'I'm sorry but I'm not allowed to divulge that. If he chooses to tell you when he wakes, that's up to him, but I'm not at liberty to discuss it with you. I'm so sorry.'

Olivia nodded. 'Of course. No worries.'

'I'm Rowan. If you need anything, just let me know. There's a coffee machine at the end of the corridor and a snack vending machine beside it. I'm on 6.30 a.m. so if you get worried about anything, just shout... or whisper loudly,' she said with a smile. 'In the meantime, why don't you move to the chair by the window? It'll be comfier. And you didn't hear this from me, but there's an extra blanket in the cupboard.' She winked and left the room.

Once Olivia was alone with Brodie again, she grabbed the

blanket and relocated herself as suggested. She rested her head on the wingback of the chair and drifted off once again.

* * *

Olivia's phone buzzed, waking her once more. She retrieved it from her bag to see a message from Owain, asking how things were. She texted off a quick reply before turning to face Brodie.

His eyes were still closed, but the swelling seemed to have subsided a little overnight. She stood and stretched her arms above her head before peeping out of the blind towards the waking suburban landscape and across to the Kessock Bridge in the distance. The large metal structure was dotted with white lights that reflected in the ripples of the Beauly Firth beneath. The sky was a mottled purple and pink and the sun was just making an appearance over the buildings out to the east of the city.

'Olivia, you came,' Brodie said in a husky, dry voice, and she swung herself around and rushed to his bedside.

She pulled up a chair as close to the bed as it would go and sat, leaning on the bed with her elbows. 'Of course I did, your dad said you were asking for me so I came as fast as I could. How are you feeling?'

'Like I've been beaten to a pulp.' He gave a laugh but grimaced with the pain of it.

'Oh, you don't look too bad,' she lied.

He laughed. 'I could always read your face, Olivia MacBain.'

'I'm just going to get the nurse and call your dad to tell him you're up. He'll want to come back in, no doubt.'

She dashed into the corridor but instead of Rowan, there was a male nurse at the desk. She explained that Brodie was awake, and he thanked her and asked her to wait outside the room while he went in to check on his patient.

She dialled Dougie's number, and the call was answered in record time. 'Olivia? Is everything okay? I should have come in before, I'm so sorry.'

'Dougie, everything's fine. You needed your sleep. I'm just calling to let you know Brodie is awake and lucid. I'm sure he'll want to see you.'

'I'll be in as soon as I can. Thank you, Olivia.'

She ended the call and the nurse left Brodie's room. 'Everything is looking good. You can go back in now.'

She walked back into the room and took her seat by Brodie's bed again. 'Can you tell me what happened? Who did this to you? Have you spoken to the police?'

He scrunched his eyes as tight as the swelling would allow. 'No, no police. It was my fault. I deserved it.'

Olivia's eyes stung with unshed tears. 'Don't be daft, Brodie. No one deserves this.'

He swallowed. 'I never learn, that's my problem. I should just keep my mouth shut.'

Frustration and worry fought to escape the confines of her chest in a growl, but she bit back on the sound and clenched her teeth. 'About what? With whom? Come on, Brodie. You can tell me. If I can help in any way, if I can do anything at all—'

He turned his head; his eyes were open a little more now and he stared at her. 'You can't do anything. You can't help. No one can. It's my problem and I'll deal with it,' he insisted. 'There's no one to blame but me.' He shook his head and tears escaped the corners of his eyes, soaking into his hair. 'I was warned. I didn't listen.'

Olivia took his hand in both of hers. 'Brodie, you're not making sense. Who warned you? And about what?'

'My behaviour. My attitude. Everything. I was warned, but I carried on as normal. I didn't try hard enough. I'm just stupid and weak and pathetic,' he said through gritted teeth.

Olivia shook her head. 'You listen to me. You are *none* of those things. *None* of them. And whoever has been telling you that is wrong. So bloody wrong. Now you tell me who did this and what reason they gave, and I will use every bit of influence I have to see that they are brought to justice, Brodie, I swear they won't get away with this. I'm here for you, okay? Me and your dad and Mirren and everyone at Drumblair. We're all here for you. We will all support you. And we *will* get to the bottom of this. What they've done to you is a criminal offence. They won't get away with it, I can promise you that. I just need you to tell me who did it. You *will* be protected, I promise. Just tell me.'

'I can't,' he pleaded at her with his expression. 'Please don't ask me to do that. I just can't.'

'Brodie, this can't go on. It's getting worse every time it happens. You have to let me help you. You need to tell me!'

'Mags!' he blurted and covered his face with his bruised arm. 'Mags did it, all right? I'm pathetic and useless and she knows it. *She* did this to me,' he sobbed. 'My own wife.'

20

Olivia sat there, staring in shock, her eyes wide and her hand over her mouth. Brodie's admission still rang in her ears and waves of nausea washed over her repeatedly.

'Brodie...' Olivia was lost for words.

'See, you think I'm pathetic and weak too now. That's why I didn't want to tell you. That's why no one can help.'

'I think nothing of the sort. She's the weak one, resorting to violence to get her own way, Brodie. *She* is the pathetic one.'

'It's not all her fault,' he insisted. 'She gets angry. I make things worse. I don't... I don't try hard enough with her. I should be better. Make better decisions. And she doesn't mean it. She always says sorry.'

Olivia shook her head as tears escaped and left cold damp trails down her cheeks. 'Brodie, you can't live like this. She needs help and you need to leave.'

He clenched his jaw. 'I did leave. When I came to Drumblair to help Dad, the time you came home from New York. I left and swore I wasn't going back. But she was so distraught. Said she couldn't live without me. I... I couldn't leave her to do something stupid because of me.'

Olivia reached and took his hand. 'No, Brodie. You are *not* responsible for any of this. This is her problem, not yours.'

Brodie fell silent and stared at the ceiling. 'I don't even love her,' he whispered. 'Not any more. Not really. I think I stopped loving her the third time she hit me. We'd only been married a year the first time it happened. I put it down to being a tiff and presumed it wouldn't happen again. Then I had a night out with some friends in Edinburgh and when I got home, she was waiting in the dark for me. She swore she could smell perfume on me. Threw a toaster at me that time. Thankfully I dodged but that pissed her off even more. So, she punched me and broke my nose. I've never been unfaithful to her, Olivia. That's not who I am. And I don't know why she thought that I'd do that to her.

'After that, I stopped going out with my mates. It was easier that way. It kept the cart on the wheels, so to speak. Things settled down for a while and I thought we could make a real go of it. I thought maybe she'd changed like she'd said she would.' He sighed and closed his eyes. 'Then we started trying for a baby. And it didn't go according to plan. She accused me of having an affair, saying that's why my sperm count was low. We didn't even know which of us had a problem, if either of us even did. She punched and kicked me so hard that I had to try and restrain her in order to protect myself but then she accused me of hurting her. Said she was going to report me to the police and that they would believe her over me because she was a woman, and no one would believe a man had been hit by his wife. Men aren't victims of domestic violence, apparently. Sadly, I believed that she was probably right and that I'd be ridiculed and maybe even put in jail for her crimes. That killed any feeling I had left for her. I was hurting too about the baby situation. And yet she still managed to turn it all around on me.'

Olivia squeezed his hand. 'I'm so sorry that happened to you.'

'After that, I just went through the motions. There were glimpses of the woman I fell in love with but so infrequently they may as well have not even happened.'

'Why didn't you just leave?'

He shrugged. 'Because I was made to feel like the bad guy. She threatened to take her own life if I left. Said she'd tell everyone I was abusive, and again that everyone would believe her because she was so petite and fragile. Then she begged me not to leave her. Swore she'd really change this time. But then it turned to mind games. Insults. I was weak, just like my sperm. I was pathetic because I was punched by a woman and did nothing to retaliate. I was weak because I wouldn't hit her back. She used to fly into these rages and dare me to hit her. That's not love.'

Olivia swiped at the moisture on her face. 'No, it's not. And your dad? Did he know what was going on?'

'Not at first. I hid it pretty well. But eventually he figured it out. I got Wilf and decided to move back to Dad's. I even registered Wilf to my dad's address, that's how determined I was. He asked me outright if she was hitting me and I lied. Said I'd been mugged. But there are only so many times you can use that excuse before you look like the unluckiest, most ridiculous person on earth.' He laughed lightly but there was no hint of humour. 'Then he would ask me to leave her. I know I broke his heart every time I went back. But I'd made a vow. I didn't take that lightly. I couldn't just give up without knowing I had tried everything to make it work. And stupidly I still clung on to the hope that she'd change, and we'd be happy again. That my feelings for her would return.'

'And this time? What happened this time? You look like you were set upon by a gang.'

He slowly shook his head. 'Nope. All Mags. Well, Mags and a cricket bat.'

Olivia gasped and covered her mouth again. 'Why? What the hell possessed her to treat you that way?'

'I'd rather not say.'

'Come on, Brodie. You can tell me anything.'

He winced. 'I was camping up at Rosemarkie. It's such a beautiful spot and I wanted to clear my head, you know? Take a break and figure out my next move. Anyway, a mutual friend, or so I thought, told her where I was, and she turned up. At first, she was sweet telling me she had missed me and that she was sorry I felt like I had to hide from her. Then she asked me about the work I'd been doing at the castle. I told her I'd all but finished the first part but that I was probably going to move back in with Dad. That it was for the best. That we'd run our course. I was as calm and nice about it as I could be. But then she asked if it was true that I was working for you. I hadn't mentioned you up to that point. Only ever talked about Innes. But again, this so-called friend told her that my boss was a wealthy, beautiful woman. I tried to lie about it, but it made no difference. She'd already made her mind up we were having an affair. I explained that you were with someone else but that didn't help. She said she was leaving and went back to her car.

'Next thing I knew, Wilf started to go crazy and something hit me in the head. I collapsed. When I woke up, she was looming over me with a cricket bat. Wilf was barking but he was terrified. He kept lunging at her but he's a puppy, poor thing. She was yelling that it was all my fault that I should have been honest with her. That I'd ruined everything. The truth is, by lying, all I did was delay the inevitable beating. Next thing I knew, I was being placed on a stretcher and stuck in the back of an ambulance. Mags was nowhere to be seen.'

'My word, Brodie. Mags is a danger to herself and others. You need to contact the police. Please. She can't get away with this.'

'I feel such an idiot, Olivia. What kind of man am I?'

Olivia stood and placed a hand on either side of his face. 'You are the strongest man I know. You could have hit back. You could have mirrored her actions, but you didn't. That takes strength.'

He gazed up at her and placed his hands over hers. 'You don't think I'm spineless?'

Olivia scoffed. 'Absolutely not. But I do think you need to speak to the police. Domestic violence against men *is* a thing. It's recognised. You need a restraining order and to leave her for good. The cottage by your dad's is vacant since Rab didn't come back to Drumblair after Kerr fired him. You can move in there with Wilf and get on with your life. Even if it's temporary. Please just say you'll think about it.'

He nodded and as he did so, he must have caught sight of the diamond ring glinting from her left hand. 'Oh. He proposed? And you said yes? That's... that's wonderful, Olivia. I'm so happy for you.'

With wide eyes, she stared down at the ring. She had completely forgotten about it in all the panic. She opened her mouth to speak but the door opened, and Dougie and Mirren walked in.

'Brodie, lad! It's so good to see you awake!' Dougie said as he strode across the room and hugged his son.

Mirren hugged Olivia. 'Has he told you anything?' she whispered.

Olivia nodded. 'Everything.'

'Good. Now you go on home and get some rest yourself. Poor Owain must wonder what's going on.'

Olivia glanced over at Brodie where he sobbed into his dad's shoulder. She needed to leave them to spend some time together.

She returned her attention to Mirren. 'You'll call if you need me?'

Mirren nodded. 'Of course we will, dearie. Thank you for being here. Dougie was exhausted and I was so glad you managed to convince him to go home. Now it's my turn to do the same for you.'

Olivia turned to look at Brodie once more. He smiled, raised his hand and mouthed the words 'Thank you' before she turned and left.

* * *

Olivia walked back into the castle, where several contractors were milling around, putting finishing touches to the signage for the Christmas Countdown Fayre. She wandered into the peaceful sanctuary of the kitchen and flopped into a chair at the table. She gazed down at the ring on her left hand and twisted it so it sparkled in the artificial lighting. It was such a beautiful piece of jewellery, but what it signified terrified her, and she wasn't sure she should even be wearing it. She cared deeply for Owain. He was perfect for her in almost every way. But she couldn't help the doubt that niggled in the back of her mind. She always said she wouldn't marry for status but for love. But did she even know what love was? Owain wanted to commit to her, but everything had been so chaotic the night before that she hadn't even given him an answer. He had been patient with her. Treated her with respect and kindness. So why was she struggling to come to a decision about the engagement?

'Ah, there you are. I was beginning to worry,' Innes said as he walked into the kitchen. 'Is everything okay? Mirren said you were at the hospital with Brodie, but she wouldn't say anything else.'

'Hi, Uncle. Yes, I'm fine, thank you. Brodie will be too.'

'Ah, good, that's a relief. That daft dog of his is out there with the gardeners, digging holes and getting covered in mud. Dougie didn't want to leave him cooped up. But I think he may regret that decision when he gets home. Thank goodness our Marley is calmer.'

Olivia laughed as she kept her gaze fixed on the ring.

'Ah, so it's true then? Mirren said she caught sight of a rock on your left hand. You do know he's married, don't you? And not in a position to offer you anything. You'd be better with Owain McPherson.'

Olivia looked up at her uncle as he sat opposite her at the table. 'I'm sorry? What do you mean?'

Uncle Innes leaned forward, a concerned expression creasing his brow. 'Brodie is married. I thought you knew that?'

Olivia scowled. 'I do know that. It's Owain's ring.'

Uncle Innes's face relaxed. 'Oh! That's wonderful news! And as you're wearing the ring, I presume you've said yes?'

Olivia shook her head. 'I haven't actually given an answer yet.'

Uncle Innes's brow crumpled again. 'But why? You seem to get on so well.'

'We do get on well. He's wonderful. But last night when he asked, everything suddenly went a little crazy. I got the call about Brodie, and I had to leave. And I just... marriage is such a huge commitment and we've known each other for a matter of weeks.'

Uncle Innes chuckled. 'You've known him all your life, Olivia.'

'No, I've known *of* him all my life but in reality, as an adult, I've known him for weeks.'

Uncle Innes sighed. 'Look, Olivia, Owain McPherson is a fine man. His family are well known and well liked. He has the stability to stand on his own two feet, meaning your inheritance and this place,' he gestured around him, 'are safe. You could do a lot worse. He understands your responsibilities because he pretty much has the same ones. He clearly adores you; I mean, look at the size of that stone. You have so much in common. I understand that it's all very quick. But maybe a long engagement is just a waste of time? You have more to think about than just being in love, Olivia. You have people depending on you. People whose livelihoods are your responsibility.'

His words angered her. 'And that's why I didn't want any of this. That's why I wanted to steer clear of this lifestyle. I wanted a life where I was free to marry for love and love alone.'

Uncle Innes sighed and reached out for her hand. 'But you accepted this life, Olivia. You knew the consequences when you agreed. You could have walked away once. But not any more. Owain will make you happy. He's the right man for you. And he's not already married,' he said with a knowing look. 'Trust me on this.'

* * *

Harper answered the phone after only one ring. Her face was contorted with evident worry. 'Hey! Are you okay? Is Brodie okay? When you messaged to say you were at the hospital, I freaked out.'

Olivia smiled; it was so good to see her best friend even if it was on a tiny screen. 'Hey, yes, we're both fine. I can't really go into details, but he's had a rough time and he was asking for me. I'm home now. And I really need your advice.'

'Okay. Fire away. What's up?' Olivia held up her left hand and Harper's eyes almost fell out of their sockets. 'What the hell! He proposed to you from his hospital bed? Is that why he was asking for you? But he's married, Olivia. This is so confusing. Why are you wearing the ring, girl?'

'Whoa, whoa. The ring isn't from Brodie. It's... it's from Owain.'

Harper slumped back into her chair. 'Oh. Wow. And you're wearing it.' The distinct change to her tone wasn't lost on Olivia.

Olivia nodded. 'Owain is the right man for me. In every single way. I know it but... would I be silly to accept?'

Harper leaned forward again. 'Sweetie, if you love him with all your heart and he makes you happy, then no, of course it wouldn't be silly.'

Olivia nodded slowly and glanced down at the ring that weighed heavily on her finger. 'I really do care for him. I think I could learn to love him. But ours is a different kind of relationship. It's based on friendship first and that's important.' She shrugged.

Harper shook her head. 'Okay. And friendship *is* important, of course. But Olivia, am I the only one who remembers how determined you were to marry for love? How adamant you were not to do something like this out of duty? And now here you are doing a total 180. Honey, we're in the twenty-first century. There's absolutely no need, in this day and age, for you to marry someone unless he makes you happy beyond your wildest dreams. I feel like we've already had this conversation and so you know my thoughts. The fact that you called me tells me you're having doubts.'

Olivia pursed her lips for a moment, trying to find the words to explain her U-turn. 'Not doubts as such. I just... I really like him. I find him very attractive. He's a good kisser.'

'Still no sex?'

Olivia growled with frustration. 'God, Harper, there's more to a relationship than sex!'

'Maybe when you're old, yeah. But you're twenty-eight.' She frowned. 'Is this about Brodie?'

Olivia scoffed. 'No.'

Harper gave a knowing look and tilted her head. 'Really? So this has nothing to do with the guy who's held your heart since you were a teenager?'

'It was a crush. My first love, I suppose. But that's it. He's going through enough at the moment and believe me when I say I'm pretty sure a new relationship is the last thing on his mind.'

'Maybe for now. But what happens when you've married Owain, and Brodie is suddenly single again and ready to make a go of things?' Harper had no idea how insightful she was being.

'Then it'll be too late. And I don't even think he has feelings for me in that way. But I have to think about what's right for me, Harper. I can't wait around hoping that some day he'll realise he has feelings for me. What if that never happens?'

'So, you're gonna rush into marrying a guy you've known for a couple months? Why do you feel the need to go barrelling towards marriage all of a sudden?'

'I don't want to fall out with you over this, Harper. I need your support.'

Harper sighed and closed her eyes. 'And you have it. Of course you do. Always. Just don't put your happiness on hold. If Brodie is who you want, maybe make sure he definitely *doesn't* feel the same before you make a huge decision that could ruin your life. I know he's married but from what I'm gleaning from his time away to clear his head, it can't be a happy union. What would you do if he suddenly did leave his wife? But if Owain is the one you want and who you can see a future with, then go for it. Only you can decide. But think of Owain in all this too. You run the risk of breaking his heart if you marry him out of some misguided sense of duty and you don't really love him. That's all I'm saying, honey.'

Olivia regretted making the call. She could see Harper's points. All of them. And she knew she was right. Marrying for love had always been Olivia's intention. But that was before she became Lady MacBain.

21

Saturday was bright and chilly and by 10 a.m., the designated parking was full. Olivia was awash with a sense of pride at seeing so many people wandering around the castle grounds and the gift fayre.

Skye and Ben arrived and hugged Olivia. 'This looks wonderful, Olivia. Well done!' Skye said before tugging Ben's hand. 'Come on, let's go find my Christmas prezzie!'

'I totally blame you if I end up bankrupt!' Ben called over his shoulder.

Olivia laughed and waved after them. 'Catch you guys later!'

She stood at the entrance to the long gallery and greeted people as they walked in. She loved that so many people were excited to see the inside of the ancient building. Even though this was a practice run, and people could only see tiny glimpses of the castle interior, she'd already heard people saying they couldn't wait to do an official tour.

Most of the gardening staff were there. They had a stall in the grounds just by the steps that led to the gallery and were selling some of the excess stock they had grown in the greenhouses over the summer. The stall was busy, and people were already rushing back to their cars with arms full of leafy, verdant plants.

She walked through the gallery and unlocked one of the doors that led through to main building, then stepped into the drawing room for a moment to gather herself. She stood before the family portrait.

'Well, Mum... Dad, this is only the beginning, but it looks like it will be a success. I hope you're happy with me. I hope I'm doing you proud. And Mum, I really hope I have your approval for all of this. I know you gave me free rein to do what I thought best but I hope this is close to what you had in mind. I miss you both more than words can possibly express. And I love you.'

'Oh, there you are!' Uncle Innes appeared and popped his head around the door. 'Is everything okay? You're not crying, are you?'

She dabbed at her eyes. 'A tiny bit. Just feeling a little overwhelmed. But it's all good. I can't believe we've pulled this off in such a short amount of time.'

Uncle Innes grinned and wagged a finger on his good hand. 'That's teamwork for you, Olivia. And you have a great team here.'

'I certainly do. Seeing this place so full of people is bizarre. It's taking some getting used to.'

He nodded but gave an encouraging smile. 'The guided tours won't be quite as intense as this, remember. There won't be as many people all in here at once. But at least people have shown up. I'm very proud of you. You have fit into your role so well. And your mum and dad would be...' His voice cracked. 'Overjoyed with what you've achieved.'

Olivia's throat tightened with emotion. 'Thank you. That means such a lot to me.'

'Now, why don't you get yourself out there and enjoy the day? Have a look around some of the stalls. I hear there is a homemade gin stall. I happen to know your uncle is quite partial to a gin and Christmas is just around the corner.'

Olivia laughed lightly. 'Noted. And I will get back out there. Don't worry.'

Uncle Innes left her alone and she stared up at the portrait again. 'Let's hope Kerr and I have turned a corner too.'

As she left the room, she bumped into her brother. 'Ooh, that's spooky. I was just talking about you to Mum and Dad.'

Kerr's brow crumpled. 'Eh? How?'

She smiled. 'Oh, just their portrait.'

'Oh. Right. Did they offer any sage advice?'

She rolled her eyes at him. 'How come you're here anyway? I didn't expect to see you.'

'I came to offer my congratulations. I heard on the grapevine that you're engaged.'

She glanced at the ring on her finger for probably the hundredth time. 'I haven't given him my answer yet.'

He scoffed. 'Oh, come on, Olivia. But you're wearing the ring. That usually means you've said yes.'

'I know. But things have been... complicated.'

Kerr's brow crumpled. 'Hasn't he been chasing you down for an answer? You have his life savings on your hand. Surely he must be worried.'

He was right. Most men would probably be badgering a woman after their proposal. 'Owain's not like that. Thankfully he's patient; considerate.' *More reasons to love him*, she thought.

Kerr shrugged. 'I don't see the problem. He's a prize catch. Eligible bachelor and all that. Plus, the McPhersons have got pots of cash. No need to take ours. I mean *yours*. Much more desirable member of the family than that gardener's son if you ask me.' Olivia was about to retaliate, figuring he was being snide, when he interrupted her train of thought and said, 'You've pulled off a

miracle here, sis. Look at all those people. You've really put this
place on the map already. Just think what will happen next year
when it opens to the public officially.'

She narrowed her eyes. 'Is that a good thing?'

He shrugged. 'Well, it's what you wanted, so I suppose yes.
Well done.'

Once again surprised by his candour, she kissed him on the
cheek. 'Thank you, Kerr. Really, thank you.'

* * *

Olivia walked back through the bustle of the long gallery with a
wide smile on her face. Every stall at the Christmas Countdown
Fayre was taken. The place was filled with happy Christmas shop-
pers and the sound of carols over the newly installed sound
system. The fragrance of cinnamon, hot chocolate and pine filled
her senses, and she stopped by the huge marble fireplace to watch
and take stock for a moment.

There was a stall selling handmade Christmas stockings where
the stall holder was hand embroidering on names to personalise
them. Next was a candle stall with the most incredible scents of
lavender, spices and cloves that lifted her spirits every time she
walked by it. A local toymaker was there with the most gorgeous
hand-painted traditional items on display. And a tombola took up
another space. It was being run by the village school to raise funds
for essential repairs to their hall ceiling. In addition, there were
tons of other sellers with wonderful gift ideas and treats to offer.
Olivia couldn't remember feeling this festive since her childhood
and it warmed her heart.

'Isn't it wonderful?' Mirren asked as she appeared beside her,
her green, red and white elf outfit and her painted-on rosy cheeks
making Olivia giggle.

'All the better for seeing you dressed like that,' Olivia replied, not even trying to hide her amusement.

Mirren performed a twirl. 'Oh, I don't mind making a fool of myself for the kiddies. Santa's Grotto is full and they're queuing round to the dining room. I just needed to nip to the loo, so Bella has stepped in dressed as Mrs Claus for a moment.'

'Well, I appreciate you all making such an effort, Mirren.'

Mirren wagged her finger. 'Oh, no, no, my name's Merry the Elf today!' she said before almost skipping off towards the library, where Santa was set up in one of the big wingback chairs beside yet another elaborately decorated and lit tree.

Olivia had worn a Santa hat and a Christmas jumper that lit up when Rudolph's nose was pressed. The place was buzzing with festive cheer and Olivia couldn't have been happier. If this was the shape of things to come, then being open to the public wouldn't be half bad. She'd had her concerns about having this 'practice run' but so far it was working out splendidly.

* * *

As Olivia was admiring the jars of local honey on one of the stalls, she turned and spotted Dougie and Brodie at the other end of the long gallery, and she immediately made a beeline for them.

'Brodie! You're out of hospital so soon! Are you okay?' Olivia asked, concern knotting her stomach on seeing her bruised and battered friend.

He nodded. 'I'm doing good. I wanted to come and see you. Can you take a break for a while?'

'Absolutely.'

Dougie gestured towards the library. 'I'm off to check out that rather lovely elf that's helping Santa.' He wiggled his eyebrows and headed off in the direction Mirren, aka Merry, had recently walked.

Olivia and Brodie walked out to the stable block café and sat at a secluded table in one of the old horse stalls. 'So, were you allowed to come home, or did you check yourself out without permission?' Olivia asked, her eyes narrowed suspiciously.

Brodie chuckled. 'Don't worry, I was allowed. I just need time to heal now, mentally and physically, but I can do that better at home. I've got some counselling sessions booked, too, which I'm hoping will help, although I can't say I'm comfortable pouring my heart out to a total stranger, but we'll see how it goes.' One of the waiting staff placed two mugs of steaming hot chocolate down on their table with a smile and a little curtsy. Brodie smiled at her gesture and shook his head as she walked away. 'See, you're like royalty. Anyway, I have something to tell you.'

Olivia stirred her drink and licked the spoon. 'Oh?'

Brodie nodded. 'I spoke to the police just like you said, and I filed a restraining order against Mags. After they saw my injuries and heard my story, they sent out a BOLO and she was arrested in Edinburgh this morning.' He winced. 'They've charged her with GBH, Olivia. I'll probably have to testify, but I know it's something I need to do. She needs help for sure, but she can't keep getting away with that kind of behaviour. I see that now. If it's not me, it'll be some other poor bloke and I can't have that on my conscience.' He took a deep breath and released it. 'And finally, Dad has spoken to a friend of his whose son is a lawyer, and he has agreed to talk me through divorce proceedings. It's a lot to face, to be honest, but I know I can't go on like this. I've blamed myself for too long. Made excuses for too long. I can't keep doing that. And I can't keep expecting her to miraculously change. And even if she did, our relationship would always be stained by what's happened in the past. Our marriage ended a long time ago. Now all we're really left with is a legally binding document that connects us.'

'Oh, Brodie.' She reached out and hugged him gently on account of his bruising. She tried to ignore how good he smelled now he'd had the chance to shower after his last ordeal. 'I'm so proud of you. I know it must have been difficult and it took a lot of courage, but you've definitely done the right thing.'

When she pulled away, his eyes were fixed on her. 'I have you to thank. A lot of what you said really sank in, and I realised that she doesn't love me. Probably never did. She just wanted to control me and that's not love. You were so right and I'm not sure why hearing it from you made me see things for what they are when Dad has been trying for years but... I'm so grateful to you. Dad is too.'

He leaned closer and took her hand in his. 'In another life, I would have never left Drumblair. I have so many regrets, Olivia. One of which is leaving with my mum when I would have been much happier here. The other is taking out my shitty feelings on you. Mum and Dad's divorce really did a number on me, and I think I hit out at everyone I cared about. Especially you, and for that I'm truly sorry. If I'd behaved better, you and I could've stayed friends and maybe that would have eventually developed into more; grown like those oak saplings we planted; maybe it'd be my ring on your finger today. But now, I'm just grateful that you forgave me for how I treated you back then, and that we can be friends now. Because right now, I really do need my friends around me. And you're one of the best.'

His gaze was sincere, and she felt caught up in it, lost to him for a moment. Her heart rate increased and the feel of her hand in his made her insides turn to jelly, just like Harper had mentioned. But this was the wrong man to elicit those feelings. She stared down at their interlinked fingers.

He fiddled with the ring on her left hand. 'Now, Owain is a good guy and I know he will make you so happy. Yes, it's happened quickly, but he's decent. He's right for you. I can feel it. And he's nothing like Mags. I think you and he will have the most amazing life together. And I know he'll treat you right. I just know it.' She watched as his eyes became glassy. 'You deserve to be happy, Olivia. You deserve the best of everything, and I know Owain is the one to give that to you. So, I want to congratulate you on your engagement and wish you every single ounce of happiness.' He shook his head and wiped his eyes. 'God, look at me. I'm an emotional wreck since the incident.' He laughed. 'But I'm sincere, Olivia. You're going to make the most beautiful bride.'

Olivia wanted to say more but couldn't find the right words. 'But Brodie, I—'

'Owain is someone who gets what you're going through better than anyone could. He understands your lifestyle. Moves in the same circles. Understands what's required of you now. He knows how to support you in it all. And that's massive.'

Olivia's chin trembled. 'Brodie, you deserve to be happy too.'

'I think I'm going to stay away from romance for a very long time. And marriage is not something I'll ever go through again. I've already decided that. One failed marriage under my belt is plenty, and I think maybe I'm not cut out for it. But I just know you and Owain have got what it takes to be successful.' There was a deeper meaning to his words, Olivia could sense it, but she had no idea how to broach the subject when he was so keen on wishing her all the best for her future with another man.

She squeezed his hand. 'Don't give up on love, Brodie. Promise me you won't. Not everyone is like Mags. There's a woman out there who will love you more than anything in this world.' *I just wish it could be me.* 'And that's worth holding out for, don't you think?'

He scrunched his nose and shook his head. 'Nah. Like I said, I've had my shot and don't really want to face another heartbreak. I'm happy to go it alone for a while. I think it's what I need. And I have the most amazing people in my life, yourself included. And, of course, I have Wilf. And now I can live vicariously through you.' He gave a light laugh. 'Seeing you happily married is enough for me. I'll be the first to throw confetti, provided I'm invited to the wedding, that is.'

Olivia fought back tears. It felt like he was saying goodbye. She supposed he was. He was definitely saying goodbye to any chance of them becoming anything more than friends and that hurt more than anything.

'Of course you're invited,' she told him before hugging him again and memorising what it felt like to be in his arms for what would probably be the last time.

* * *

Olivia stood listening to the village school choir singing carols in the foyer of the castle as a finale to the event. Each had their own Santa hat and Christmas jumper just like she did, and she couldn't help the wide smile that was fixed on her face.

'Congratulations, my love. You did it,' Owain said with a kiss to her cheek.

'Oh, hi. How long have you been here?' she asked.

He tapped his nose. 'Long enough to do a little Christmas shopping of my own. So, just the clearing up to do and then we can head to mine?'

She nodded. 'That would be lovely.'

'I thought we'd order a Deliveroo and crack open a bottle of Bolly to celebrate, how does that sound? I mean, I'm hoping we have other things to celebrate than the Christmas Fayre.' He lifted her left hand to his mouth and kissed the back of it.

She smiled. 'We may have.'

His eyes lit up. 'Are you saying yes? I mean, we didn't really get a chance to talk properly on the night I proposed. And I didn't want to push the issue, but of course I would love an answer. I feel like it's yes because you're still wearing the ring, but... an actual verbal yes would be good.'

She glanced around the room, but Brodie was nowhere to be seen. With her attention turned back to Owain, she nodded. 'It's a yes.'

Owain beamed at her before sweeping her off her feet in a warm embrace. 'Amazing! I can't wait to tell everyone. But just so you know, my mother will want a big engagement party. And she'll probably suggest something like Christmas Eve for the event. Grand gestures and all that.'

Once again, Olivia felt a little steamrolled into things, but there was no point holding onto any hope of having a future with Brodie, and Owain made her happy. She knew that given the chance, her love for him would grow and be unstoppable. It would just take time. She'd held onto an unrealistic dream of Brodie for so long that it would take some getting out of her system, but she knew it would happen.

It had to.

* * *

Owain's apartment was a wing of Dores Manor, and it was fairly small considering the size of the main mansion, but it was neat, clean and tastefully decorated. His own artwork adorned the walls and each time she had visited since they had reconnected, she had noticed something different in each piece.

Owain was in the kitchen, opening the bottle of promised Champagne. 'Where would you like to live once we're married? I was thinking Drumblair might be better than this little cramped place, but I can totally understand if you'd rather keep your work separate from your home life.'

Olivia stood before a painting of Loch Shiel, admiring the brooding landscape with its dark grey sky and menacing clouds. 'I hadn't really thought about it, to be honest. But Drumblair is probably fine.'

He walked through to the living room with the bottle in one hand and the glasses in the other. 'I think Drumblair is bigger, so we would get more personal space there. Here we'd have my mother breathing down our necks all of the time. And who'd want their mother in their face constantly?'

Olivia turned and looked at him. 'I wouldn't mind having my mother there all the time.'

Owain closed his eyes and placed down the bottle and the glasses. 'Shit. I'm so sorry. That was stupidly thoughtless of me.' He walked over and enveloped her in his arms. 'I'm sorry, sweetheart.'

Olivia gazed up at him. His lips were so close to hers and she wanted to feel something other than confusion and frustration. She reached up and kissed him, running her hands through his hair. She slipped her tongue into his mouth and moved one hand slowly down his chest. His buttons opened easily and before long, she was able to gently touch the smooth skin of his chest. She feathered kisses from his chest up to his neck and he stepped backwards, laughing lightly.

'Hey, come on. Let's drink this champers before it goes flat.'

Olivia felt foolish. 'What's wrong? I thought you might like to... you know...'

He took her hand and led her to the sofa. 'Of course I'd *like* to.

But... I'm a good Christian boy.' His cheeks flushed and he rubbed at the back of his neck. 'I've been brought up to believe in no sex before marriage. I know that's a bit old-fashioned in this day and age, but I hope you can respect my wishes. It will make things all the more special on our wedding night. Don't you think? Let's leave some mystery, eh?'

Olivia covered her face with her hand. 'Oh god, I feel like an idiot. I've never made the first move before and now I know why.'

He pulled her hand away. 'No, don't feel bad. I maybe should have made things clearer at the start. It's just... it's important to me.'

'Of course. I totally understand. I hadn't realised you were so religious. I'm so sorry.'

He cupped her cheek in his hand. 'Don't be. It's flattering that you feel so strongly. And our wedding night will be so special.'

She nodded and smiled. 'Yes. I suppose it will.'

22

Olivia sat with Skye and Bella in the Victorian Market in Inverness. The café was set out a little like a Victorian parlour with tea served in proper teapots with china cups and saucers. There were even little silver sugar tongs in the lidded sugar bowl. A range, which was built into the wall, was the main source of heating. It was like stepping back in time and the place had always fascinated Olivia. On this occasion, however, she had other things on her mind than how pretty her surroundings were. She had asked them to meet her to get their opinion on something she felt was pretty major, and after disclosing it as they sipped their tea, she waited for their responses.

The two friends shared a glance before Bella chipped in, 'I think it's sort of romantic, really. At least you know it's not all about sex. He obviously really cares about you if he's willing to wait until after you're married. Although I think it would drive me batty.'

Skye nodded an emphatic agreement. 'Yes, it would definitely do my head in. Me and Ben can't keep our hands off each other, so there'd be no chance of us waiting. But having said that, I can see

Bella's point. It's just quite old-fashioned, I suppose. Not really heard of these days.'

Olivia sighed and sipped her Earl Grey. 'I know. I had no idea he was even religious. He's never made any assertions that way. I'm guessing it's his parents' doing. I mean they're lovely and they seem to really like me. But I was hoping for a bit of passion, you know?'

Bella leaned over and touched her arm. 'Do you think he's the right man for you, Olivia? I mean, are you sure you're not making a huge, catastrophic mistake?'

Skye whacked her arm. 'Bells! Be more supportive!'

Bella rubbed her arm and scowled at Skye. 'That's exactly what I am doing. I would hate for Olivia to marry this guy and realise he was frigid or celibate or something. As her friends, we have to vet him maybe, before it goes too far.'

Skye scoffed. 'Says the woman who won't even introduce her man to her best friends.'

Bella rolled her eyes. 'That's different and you know it is. He can't afford negative press, that's all. He has loose ends to tie up before we can be officially together.'

Skye turned to Olivia. 'See, I'd be more worried if I was in her position. At least Owain is happy to be out in public with you.'

It was Bella's turn to whack Skye now. 'Hey! He is happy to be with me. We're just not rushing things. Pretty much the same as you and Owain really.' She looked to Olivia for some support.

Skye leaned backwards and glared at Bella. 'So you're telling me that you and Mr Mystery haven't made the beast with two backs?'

Bella scrunched her nose. 'What a vile way to put it.'

Skye pressed on. 'Well, have you?'

'I've had sex with him, yes,' Bella hissed.

'So nothing at all like Olivia and Owain then!'

Bella tossed her head. 'I'm a young woman with needs.'

'Hmm, of course you are,' Skye said. She turned to Olivia and took her left hand. She examined the large diamond closely. 'I think he adores you, Olivia. I mean, look at this rock. It's twice the size of mine. I honestly can't see you having anything to worry about. And just think how hot and spicy your wedding night will be.'

Bella smirked. 'Either that or it'll be over in a matter of seconds due to all the pent-up sexual frustration.'

'Don't listen to her, Olivia. Honestly, I think you'll be fine.'

Olivia chewed her lip. 'I hope you're right because you're invited to our engagement party... on Christmas Eve.'

* * *

If she didn't know better, Olivia could be forgiven for thinking Brodie was avoiding her. She hadn't seen much of him since the Christmas Fayre, and when she had spotted him in the grounds playing with Wilf, he always seemed to be walking in the opposite direction. He had, of course, sent the obligatory engagement congratulations card that she had stood in her room.

It was early evening on 20 December and Mirren brought the local paper in with the rest of the shopping delivery and placed it in front of Olivia on the kitchen table.

'Have you seen this yet? You do make a lovely couple. Look at you both,' Mirren said, pointing to the posed photograph of Olivia and Owain on the front page with the headline:

A LAIRD TO BE AND HIS NEW LADY... IN WAITING

In the picture, they were standing in the entrance hall of Dores Manor. The obligatory shot of the happy couple, her hand strategically placed on his chest to best show off the expensive ring. Laird McPherson's friend, a photographer for *The Scotsman*, had come to photograph them a week after the Christmas Countdown Fayre. She had worn a pretty knee-length pale blue tea dress and ballet pumps, and Owain had worn a cream V-neck sweater with a pale blue shirt beneath and grey and blue tweed trousers. The photos had come out beautifully, but the headline left a lot to be desired. She understood the intention behind the 'joke', but it made her sound like his servant and she didn't like that one bit.

'Aww, yes, that's a nice photo. It was my favourite out of them all, so I'm glad they went with it. You are coming to the engagement party, aren't you?'

Mirren went about putting away the shopping delivery. 'Of course, dearie. Dougie and I will be attending together.' She paused and placed her hand on Olivia's shoulder. 'It's all *awfy* fast, dearie. Are you sure about it all?'

Olivia turned to face her and patted her hand. 'Perfectly sure. Everyone seems to think I'm rushing into this, but Owain and I are right for each other and that's all that matters.'

Mirren nodded but her eyes still held a look of concern. 'So long as you're happy, Olivia. I feel responsible for you now your parents are gone. I just want to make sure you're not being bamboozled into this marriage.'

Olivia put on her best, brightest smile. 'No need to worry, Mirren, honestly.'

'What are you doing this evening?' Mirren asked, seemingly satisfied with Olivia's answers. 'You look dressed up like you're heading out.'

Olivia sipped her Earl Grey tea. 'Owain is taking me to the Italian again. It's a wee private celebration, I suppose.'

'He likes his Italian food, doesn't he? Let's hope he keeps trim, though. Nothing worse than a middle-aged man with a huge wobbly belly.'

Olivia almost snorted her drink. 'Mirren! That's a bit mean. Owain is in great shape. He works out regularly and he watches what he eats most of the time. This is just his guilty pleasure.'

'Aye, well...'

'Who's got a guilty pleasure?' Brodie said as he walked into the room. Olivia sat up straight and smiled. He looked well. Really well, in fact.

'That fella of Olivia's. He likes his carbs a bit too much if you ask me,' Mirren informed him.

'Well, we can't all be studs like my old dad, can we?' he said as he squeezed Mirren and kissed her cheek.

She flailed at him, grinning all the while. 'Och, away with you, you wee dafty.'

'So, you're going out tonight?' Brodie asked Olivia.

Olivia eyed his features. The facial bruising was almost gone now but he still had hints of dark shadows under his eyes. 'Yes. Just a little celebration of our own before the engagement party. Are you coming, by the way?'

Brodie scratched his head. 'Oh... erm... I don't think I can make it, I'm afraid. I have a... erm... date on Christmas Eve.'

Olivia was shocked at his admission. 'Oh. I thought you were avoiding romance for a while.'

'Aye, so did I, but I got a call from that woman I met at the McPherson ball. Matilda, remember?'

Olivia remembered vividly and a rush of heat travelled through her veins. Matilda was the brunette with the perfect teeth, pert breasts and curves to die for. *No one should be that perfect*. She expected to look down and see that her flesh had turned green. 'Oh, yes. I remember.' She had absolutely no right to be jealous but it didn't stop her clenching her jaw and her stomach roiling with the deadly sin.

'Aye, well, I have to get used to being a man of today when attractive young women make the first move, I suppose.'

Olivia nodded and tried to keep her smile even. 'Ah, yes, well. Things have certainly changed.' She paused and fought mental images of him with slinky, sexy Matilda. 'It's a shame you can't attend the party. Maybe you should bring her.' *Shit, why the hell did I say that?* 'Although that might be a bit much. Christmas Eve already seems a bit intense for a first date.' Brodie glared at her in disbelief as she added insult to injury. 'I mean, you'll certainly remember it if it all goes wrong.' She laughed and then realised how bitchy she must have sounded. 'Sorry, that came out wrong.'

Brodie's expression remained serious. 'It's fine,' he replied through gritted teeth. 'Well, I'd better let you get going. Don't want to keep your fiancé waiting.'

* * *

By the time they reached the restaurant, Olivia had put herself in a foul mood. Not only was she angry at how she had spoken to Brodie, but she was upset that he was getting back out on dates after telling her he intended to steer clear of romance for a while. And yet again, she reminded herself she was not in a position to be jealous. Nor judgemental, seeing as she was marrying a childhood friend she had only recently reconnected with.

Niccolò sat them at their usual table. 'I'll bring Champagne on the house. You have much to celebrate,' he said before heading off to the bar.

'Don't you ever fancy going somewhere else?' Olivia said, almost thinking aloud.

Owain scrunched his face. 'I thought you liked it here.'

'I do. It's just that we seem to have spent almost every date here apart from an odd night at the cinema or watching a show at Eden Court.'

He reached across and took her hand. 'Next time, you choose where we go. How's that?'

She nodded. 'Thank you. I will. Perhaps Thai or Spanish.'

'I don't really like Thai and I can't eat seafood because I'm pretty allergic. I wouldn't want to end up dead on our date.' He laughed.

'You're allergic to seafood? I didn't know that.' She was beginning to realise there was more she *didn't* know about him than what she *did* know. 'Gosh, we really should get to know each other as adults a little better, don't you think?'

'We'll have our whole lives for that, don't worry.'

Her stomach knotted. 'But I do worry, Owain. I worry we're getting married, and I don't know what might kill you on a night out. These are things that should be of paramount importance, don't you think?'

He counted off on his fingers. 'Shellfish, dogs, cats, some white wines, cough syrup and pork. There you go. You know now. Although I'm pretty sure we're not going to encounter cats or dogs on our dates so...'

Her heart sank. 'But that means we can't have Marley to live with us when we get married.'

Owain laughed again but this time he sounded a little nervous. 'But he loves Innes. He'll be fine living there. And you'll still see him.' Her facial expression must have clearly demonstrated her disappointment as Owain continued, 'You're not going to break our engagement just because we can't have Marley, are you?'

Yes! Her mind screamed at her as she thought of Duke and Wilf and Marley, not to mention all the dogs in rescue centres needing homes. 'No, of course not.' She was aware she sounded like a sulking teenager. And she was determined to find a way she could have Marley to live with them. He was her family, after all. And perhaps there were allergy tablets Owain could take? She'd definitely be doing some research.

'Phew! Anyway, you know this engagement party is turning into an event as big as the annual charity ball, don't you? Has Mum been in touch with you about the dress code?'

Olivia's palms began to sweat. 'Erm... no, she hasn't. Why?'

Owain cringed. 'Don't be mad, but she's suggesting black tie with it being Christmas Eve.'

Olivia sighed and tugged at the neckline of her top. 'How many people have even RSVPd to say they will come, with it being on Christmas Eve anyway? I'm expecting only a handful of people will turn up and that would be fine with me. I hate being the centre of attention as it is.'

'Quite a lot have said yes at the last count. But don't worry, she's made some concessions. For example, there will be a hot buffet which is a little more casual than the sit-down meal Mum wanted. I managed to get her to meet me halfway there at least.'

'Great,' Olivia mumbled.

Niccolò returned and placed down their bottle of bubbly and two glasses. 'There you go, my two favourite lovebirds. *Auguro a entrambi ogni felicità,*' he said with a flourish of his hands before walking away again.

Olivia must have looked confused, because as soon as Niccolò had left, Owain smiled. 'He said he wishes us every happiness.'

'Oh, right. Nice.'

Owain picked up his menu. 'He's a really great guy. A good friend. Anyway, what do you fancy for dinner tonight? Maybe you could have something other than the *agnolotti* for a change.'

Olivia glared at him over her menu. 'Maybe I will when we go somewhere different.'

Owain placed his menu down. 'Are we fighting? Because I'd like to know if we are. I have clearly annoyed you or upset you tonight. I apologise for bringing you here again. I just really like it and Niccolò knows about my allergies, so I know I'm safe to eat here.'

Olivia's stomach knotted again but this time with guilt. 'Of course. That's reasonable. I apologise. I think I'm just a little overwhelmed by the engagement. It's become this huge thing that I wasn't expecting.'

Owain laughed. 'Once you're better reacquainted with my mother, you'll realise that everything has to be a huge occasion. She'd throw a party when we get a new toaster if Dad would let her.'

Olivia smiled. He didn't deserve her negativity. He'd done nothing but try to please her and make her happy and she was becoming a spoiled brat; something she had never been. 'I'm sure it'll all be lovely.'

'I'm glad you think so because they want me to bring you home tonight so they can have a drink with us to celebrate.'

Olivia scowled. 'But that's what the party is for, surely?'

'You'd think so, eh? But remember what I said about my dear mother and the new toaster? There'd be a pre-celebration for that too. She'll have a field day with our wedding gifts.' He laughed.

Olivia sipped her Champagne and inwardly panicked.

* * *

Later that night, Olivia lay awake in Owain's bed as he slept on the sofa in his lounge area. Sleep evaded her, her mind whirred with images of Brodie and Matilda. They made a stupidly attractive couple, and she hated that fact.

Fiona and Hamish had been so warm and welcoming earlier.

She regretted being so negative about everything. Owain and his dad had been off drinking whisky at one end of the vast living room and Fiona and Olivia were sitting by the roaring fire.

'You've made us all happy by saying yes to Owain,' Fiona had informed her. 'He just adores you, and he was so worried that it was all too fast, but Hamish and I were a whirlwind romance too and we're almost thirty-five years married this year. We must get together after the party to go wedding dress shopping. I know that's something you would rather do with your own mother, but I hope I will be a good substitute.' She had reached out and squeezed her hand and Olivia's eyes had begun to sting. The realisation sinking in that neither of her parents would be there at the wedding. No dad to walk her down the aisle. As if reading her mind, Fiona had said, 'I'm sure Hamish would be honoured to walk you down the aisle if you'd like. Unless you have someone in mind, of course.'

Olivia had cleared her throat and tried to compose herself. 'That's really lovely but I think perhaps I'd like my Uncles Innes to do that.'

Fiona smiled. 'Of course, my dear.'

'Would it be okay if Mirren comes dress shopping too?' Olivia asked.

Fiona's brow crumpled. 'Your housekeeper?'

Olivia nodded. 'She's so much more than that to me.'

Fiona pasted on a smile. 'In that case, of course she must accompany us.'

Now here she lay, staring at the ceiling, imagining how different it would all be if her parents were still alive. Would she even be getting married? She wasn't sure, and that thought scared her.

23

The day before Christmas Eve was dull and rainy. There was sleet in the air and Olivia spent most of the morning wrapping Christmas gifts in her room. Mirren knocked on her bedroom door at around midday.

'You've a delivery. Look at the size of this box! It was just dropped off by that nice courier chap. Anyway, I'll leave you to your wrapping... and unwrapping!'

'Thanks, Mirren!' She closed her door and took the parcel to her bed.

Mirren was right, it was huge, and it had a USA postmark. Olivia eagerly ripped the paper off and opened the box beneath it. She pulled out the most stunning black velvet dress. It immediately brought to mind Marilyn Monroe and the fifties.

She held it up and gasped. 'Oh, Nina, you've outdone yourself again!' After she had placed the dress down, she took out the card that accompanied it.

To our dearest Olivia
We are so sorry we can't be there to celebrate with you, but

we wanted to send a little piece of us to be there in our stead.
We hope you adore this dress that was designed especially for
your engagement. We know that you will look like a movie star,
and we can't wait to see photos!

Much love to you and your husband to be.

Nina and the team

Olivia covered her mouth and immediately picked up her
phone. It was around 7 a.m in New York and she risked waking
Harper, but she didn't care.

'Hello? Olivia?'

'Harper! Oh, my goodness, I've just opened the dress! It's stunning! I'm guessing you knew all about it.'

'Ah, that's great that it arrived in time. When I hadn't had a
message from you about it, I was getting worried. I'll let Nina know
later today. So, how are you feeling? Excited?'

'Nervous more than anything. Tomorrow makes it all official.
And I'm sad that you can't be here for the party.'

'Oh, honey, me too. I wish I could have made it, but I'm
spending Christmas with my mom.'

'That's absolutely fine. I know Christmas Eve is a strange day
to have an engagement party, but it was Owain's mum that
arranged it all.'

They chatted for a while about what they had both been up to
and it simply compounded how much Olivia missed her best
friend.

'Summer has asked if I'll go meet her folks over Christmas.'

'Wow, things are getting serious with you two, eh?'

'They really are. She's amazing. So funny. You're going to love
her. I think she may be the one, Olivia.'

'Aww! That's wonderful. I can't wait to meet her in person.

Video calls are nice, but it'll be good to meet her properly. Is she able to come over in February with you?'

'We're trying to work something out. It'll be so good to see you. Anyway, I'd better go wrap some more gifts.'

Olivia was suitably impressed and surprised at her words. 'Wow, you're wrapping gifts at seven in the morning?'

'I sure am. I fell asleep wrapping last night, and I have tons to do before I head to my mom's place. Have an amazing party and a wonderful Christmas. I'll call on Christmas Day. Love you.'

'Love you, Harper. Bye for now.'

She tried on the dress and unsurprisingly it fit like a glove. It was a gorgeous off-shoulder design that nipped in at the waist and flared out. There was a stiff petticoat for underneath and just as the letter had said, she felt like a movie star. At least that was one less thing to worry about.

* * *

Christmas Eve was crisp, and a layer of frost covered the castle grounds. Olivia went for a walk outside to clear her head and Marley tagged along. Once again, she thought about the prospect of not having him to live with her and it made her heart ache. Since being back in Scotland, he had been a constant in her daily life. Always there for cuddles or to offer a reassuring paw or lick. There must be a way to have him with us, she thought to herself.

As she wandered down to the chapel by the loch shore, she stopped and stared out at the water as Marley investigated a large rock at the edge of the water. A gentle breeze rippled the surface; something she used to think was a sign that Nessie was lurking there somewhere. She smiled as she remembered learning to skim stones there with Brodie and Dougie. She'd been reluctant at first, concerned in case she bonked Nessie on the nose. But Dougie assured her that Nessie was fast and could dodge them without much effort. Although she deliberately performed badly to begin with, just in case Dougie was wrong. She didn't want to upset Nessie.

She also remembered a long hot summer when Brodie rowed them out on the little boat that always stood on the shore. They had ended up going round in circles for half an hour before they gave up and waded through the water to get back to dry land. The boat had eventually washed up on the beach with a bit of damage and had stood there ever since. These days, it was a favourite spot for birds who perched on it for a rest.

'Hey, I thought you'd be out walking today,' a voice said from behind her and then the expected paws in the middle of her back almost knocked her off her feet. 'Bloody hell, Wilf! Get down!'

'Hi, Brodie. Hey, Wilf,' she said, bending to fuss the happy canine. 'Yeah, I just wanted to get some fresh air. I'm quite nervous.' Once Wilf had said hello, he ran off towards Marley and the two dogs chased each other around the water's edge.

'Nervous? How come? You're already engaged, so this is just the official celebration. What's there to be nervous about?'

Olivia stood and stared out at the water again. 'I don't know. Just last-minute jitters, I suppose. It's a big step.'

Brodie nodded. 'Aye. But if you're happy, that's all that matters. He does make you happy, Olivia, doesn't he? I mean really happy?'

She turned to face him and saw genuine concern in his eyes. 'You don't need to worry. I'm fine. And yes, I'm very happy.' As the words fell from her lips, she doubted them but gave a slight shake of her head to dislodge the intrusive thoughts.

'Good. I'm happy for you. And I'm sorry again that I can't be there.'

Olivia shrugged. 'It can't be helped. I'm sure you'll have a lovely evening with Matilda.'

Brodie scrunched his nose. 'Yeah... I'm having doubts about that. I think I was a bit rash to agree to a date. I should have stuck with my original plan of steering clear of romance. I'm definitely not ready.'

Olivia's heart skipped but she tried to ignore it. She had made a commitment. 'Well, if you end up not going out, you're still welcome to come to the party.'

Brodie stopped and fixed his gaze on her for a moment. 'I'll bear that in mind. Thank you. And if I don't see you tomorrow, Merry Christmas. Come on, lad,' he called to Wilf and turned to leave. 'Oh, by the way, I've left you a wee gift under the tree in the drawing room. It's nothing much but I thought you might like it.'

'Oh! But I didn't get you anything, I'm so sorry.'

'Nah, *nae* bother. Anyway, Merry Christmas, Olivia.'

'Merry Christmas, Brodie.'

* * *

'You look absolutely stunning,' Owain's mum told her as she greeted them at the door. 'That dress is gorgeous.'

'Thank you, Fiona. Nina designed it especially for tonight.'

'Well, you certainly have the best friends! Now come along, both of you, you're a bit late and lots of people are already here. Niccolò has set the food out in the dining room. I'm not a fan of buffets but it does smell rather divine.' Fiona turned and gestured for them to follow.

'So Niccolò's catering this party?' Olivia asked, surprised.

'It was supposed to be a surprise, but then I was worried about telling you after what you said the last time we were at his restaurant. I hope it's okay?' Owain cringed.

Olivia plastered on a smile. 'It's absolutely fine. I just never imagined Italian food as buffet food.'

Owain put his arm around her shoulders. 'Oh, he can do anything where food is concerned. Just you wait and see.'

The great hall was alive with chatter and when Laird Hamish spotted them, he took to the centre of the room and clinked his glass. 'Ladies and gentlemen, I'm so happy to announce that our guests of honour, Owain and Olivia, have arrived. Please join me in welcoming them!' A round of applause travelled the room as Olivia and Owain stood there, like fish in a bowl. All eyes on them.

Once the applause died down, a ceilidh band began to play music from the corner of the hall and a few of the children in attendance started to dance around, much to the adults' delight. Olivia was relieved to have the spotlight located elsewhere.

'You do look beautiful,' Owain said with a kiss to her forehead. 'And that dress is a masterpiece. I must thank Nina when I meet her in February. How are the plans for the soft launch going?'

Olivia nodded. 'Really well. Bella has been amazing. She has everything running like clockwork. I really don't know what I would have done without her. I'm so glad Brodie suggested I get an assistant.'

'Oh, yes, Brodie. Where is he? I thought he'd be here?'

'He has a date,' she said and immediately took a sip of her drink and gazed around the room. 'Oh, look! Bella and Skye are here. I must go and say hi.'

Owain kissed her and then wagged a finger at her. 'You're mine for a dance later, though.'

'Absolutely!' She hurried off to her friends.

'Wow! Look at you! You look like Marilyn Monroe in that frock,' Skye said as she hugged her.'

'She's right and I don't like to agree with her,' Bella said with a wink. Skye pulled out her tongue. 'And this place is rather swanky, eh? You know how to pick 'em.'

'Thank you both for coming. There aren't that many people here that I recognise. I definitely need more friends.'

It was true. As she glanced around the vast space, she didn't see many people she knew. Owain had a lot of friends but most of them couldn't make it due to prior commitments, so the majority of people at the party were friends of Fiona and Hamish. It appeared that Owain had been right about his mum and her parties. Olivia was shocked at how many people had turned out on Christmas Eve, but then the McPhersons were definitely known for their hospitality, so their engagement party was probably just a Christmas do to most people in attendance.

Uncle Innes was standing chatting to Laird McPherson and Kerr was there, with Adaira fussing over him, much to Kerr's evident annoyance. It was clear their so-called relationship wasn't going to last much longer. Mirren and Dougie looked lovely all dressed up. Mirren was in a gorgeous dress that Olivia's mother had given her a few years earlier. And Dougie was wearing a kilt and jacket. He looked very dapper and a lot like an older version of Brodie, she thought. There he was, popping into her head again. In a way, it was a good thing he wasn't here. She would only be reminded again of how handsome, sweet and kind he was these days. It would almost have been easier if he'd still been an obnoxious shit.

* * *

Everyone was having a wonderful time. The music was now playing over the fancy sound system that Owain had insisted his parents get installed a few years prior. It was music that was certainly more to Olivia's taste. She had spent most of the evening with her friends, as Owain had been off mixing with people she didn't know. Olivia was sipping on her third or fourth glass of

Champagne on an empty stomach and bobbing up and down to Fleetwood Mac's 'Gypsy' while remembering what Brodie had said about watching her dance all those years ago. Skye had gone off to the loo and Bella had gone dashing after her a few seconds later.

She felt a tap on her shoulder and when she turned around, she came face to face with Brodie. Her heart sank before it began to race.

'Oh. You came.'

He nodded. 'I hope that's okay? I decided to cancel my date. Definitely not ready for all that. Not yet.'

'Ah, right. Was she okay about it?'

He bobbed his head from side to side. 'Not especially. She said I'd messed her around. Which I suppose I had. Hey, have you heard what's playing?'

'Fleetwood Mac...' She nodded. '"Gypsy",' she said with a smile.

'Ballerina Olivia, my very own gypsy.' His smile was tinged with sadness.

'Ah, Brodie! You came. Put it there, old chap!' Owain said as he held out his hand.

Brodie shook it. 'Aye, couldn't miss it.'

'Well, you're very welcome. Olivia darling, I just have one little job to sort with the catering and then I'm going to make a speech, I hope you're ready.' He grinned.

'Oh, you don't need to make a speech, Owain,' Olivia said, her cheeks already heating in embarrassment.

He patted his breast pocket. 'The deed is already done. I won't be long. I'll leave you with your friend here for a little bit.' He kissed her cheek and walked away towards the dining room.

'Sorry to ditch you too but I could really do with going to get a drink,' said Brodie. 'Can I get you one?'

Olivia nodded. 'Why not? More bubbles on an empty stomach.

What could possibly go wrong!'

Brodie laughed and headed off towards the bar.

'Are you okay, darling girl?' Uncle Innes asked as he arrived beside her.

She nodded and forced a smile. 'I'm fine. In fact, I'd like to ask you something.'

Innes nodded. 'Of course. Anything.'

Olivia inhaled and straightened her spine. 'You're so very dear to me and as Mum and Dad can't be here, I was wondering... would you do the honour of giving me away at my wedding?'

Innes opened and closed his mouth as Olivia observed his eyes becoming glassy. He cleared his throat. 'Really? I would be absolutely honoured. Thank you for asking me. I hope I can do you proud.' He pulled her into his arms, and she closed her eyes briefly. He pulled away. 'I must go and... I mean... I think I have something in my eye.' He turned and dashed away. Olivia smiled as she watched him go, happy that he'd said yes.

* * *

A few moments later, Bella and Skye returned. 'Sorry about that, Bells was being chatted up by this guy who was old enough to date her Granny Isla.'

Bella laughed hysterically. 'Oh, god, he had this hair piece that reminded me of my old boss. I think if the two toupees got together, they could have really cute baby toupees!'

Olivia joined in with their laughter and felt herself relaxing. It could also have been the copious amounts of Champagne, but who knew?

There was a clinking of glass and Hamish's voice could be heard loud and clear this time. When Olivia turned around, she saw he had a microphone.

'Ooh, here we go, Olivia, speeches!' Skye said with a nudge to her shoulder.

'Good evening again! Now that everyone is here, I think it's time we made things official. My son is around here somewhere, aren't you, Owain? I know he has a few words to say, but as I have the microphone, I think I'd like to take this opportunity to say a few words myself.'

There was the sound of loud chatter somewhere out of the hall, but it wasn't possible to hear what was being said.

'Whoever that is, you'll get your turn soon enough,' Hamish said with a chuckle. 'Now, on to my daughter-in-law to be. Fiona and I were delighted when Owain and Olivia reconnected. They had always been so close as youngsters.'

Hmm, that's not exactly true, Olivia thought.

'And to see them together now, it's like they have never been apart. Their deep love has a strong foundation in friendship and that's how the strongest marriages are made. I would like everyone to raise a glass to Lady Olivia MacBain!'

The whole gathering raised the toast and looked towards Olivia, who was now as hot as a furnace and no doubt the colour of Mars.

'Dad, my turn,' Owain said, snatching the microphone rather harshly from Hamish's hands. 'Olivia! Come and join me,' he said with urgency. She glanced at Bella and Skye and scrunched her face, confused at his command.

'Better start as you mean to go on!' someone in the crowd shouted and everyone laughed.

Olivia arrived by Owain's side. He was red-faced and a little sweaty. 'Darling Olivia. Since I met you all those years ago, I've felt drawn to you. I'm so glad we reconnected and that you agreed to be my wife. I can't wait to have a future with you and to make lots of babies.' Whistles and cat calls sounded. 'To my fiancée, everyone!' His words were rushed, and he sounded out of breath.

Everyone raised their glasses once again and toasted Olivia for the second time that evening. She hoped that this meant it was over and she could go back to blending in.

As the chatter died down, Brodie came running in from the direction of the dining room, followed by two of the waiters.

'Stop! Olivia, you can't marry him!'

Olivia turned to Brodie and gasped.

Owain gripped her tighter. 'Can someone show this man out, please? He's had a bit too much to drink and he's making a nuisance of himself.'

The two waiters stepped forward and grabbed Brodie by the arms and manhandled him, but he was digging his heels in.

'Owain, what the hell is going on? Brodie hasn't even had a drink yet!' she hissed. 'Let him go!' she shouted at the waiters and tried to release herself from Owain's grip, but she couldn't.

'Olivia! He's been lying to you! Please, you have to believe me!' Brodie shouted.

Owain turned to the gathered guests who were all gawping, open-mouthed. 'This man is in love with my fiancée and is doing his best to disrupt our evening with lies. He's just a jealous man with a vendetta, please ignore him and carry on enjoying the evening. The bar is still open!'

Confused and concerned chatter travelled the room as everyone tried to figure out what was going on.

Brodie broke free from the men who were holding him back and ran to Olivia's side. He placed a hand on each of her shoulders and after glaring at Owain, he leaned to whisper in her ear. 'Olivia, I don't want to shout this out in front of everyone, so please listen to me. He's lied to you. I promise I'm telling the truth. Olivia, Owain is gay!'

24

Olivia watched in horror as Brodie was dragged, kicking and flailing, from the building. Dougie and Mirren followed, with Dougie shouting, 'Get your hands off my lad! I'll kick your arses! The lot of you! Get off him!'

Owain grabbed Olivia by the wrist and dragged her through the gobsmacked, silent gathering and into an anteroom. He slammed the door and locked it.

'Owain, what the hell is going on?' Olivia asked, tears streaming down her face and her head feeling swooshy. 'Please tell me.'

Owain ran his hands through his hair until the product that was once smoothing it down now made it stand on end. He looked wild-eyed and a bit crazy. 'Look, he thought he saw something that he didn't see. And then he got the wrong end of the stick. That's all. But I was right. It's jealousy that's driven him to this. I could tell he was in love with you the first time I met him.'

'This isn't making sense. What did he think he saw?'

Owain bent and punched a cushion. 'Shit! Shit!'

'Owain?'

He stood up straight and face her. 'He saw me and Niccolò hugging. Then he put two and two together and made five. Idiot.'

Things were still not adding up. 'Brodie isn't stupid, Owain, if he saw you hugging, he would just think you're friends. Friends hug. And Brodie isn't a vindictive person.'

'How do you know? You haven't seen him in years!'

Anger rumbled inside of Olivia. 'The same could be said of me and you!'

Owain jabbed a finger towards the door. 'So you're going to take his side, is that it?'

Olivia slumped onto an antique chair she was pretty sure was too old and valuable to be sat on. 'Owain, please be truthful with me. I deserve that much.'

'I'm not lying. Niccolò may have kissed me on the cheek, he's European, they do that!' He lifted his arms and let them drop violently to his thighs.

'Brodie would still understand that. I don't get why he would say such a thing without reason.'

There was a hammering at the door. 'Owain! This is your father. Come out here right now and explain to me what the hell is going on!'

Owain flinched and then sat on the other antique chair. 'Oh god. It's all gone to shit.'

'Owain!' More hammering.

'Give us a bit of time, Dad, for Pete's sake!'

Olivia stood and walked over to crouch before him. 'Owain, please tell me the truth.'

He lifted his chin and tears were cascading down his face. 'What have I done?'

She cupped his face. 'Just tell me.'

He nodded. 'I'm... I'm in love... with Niccolò.'

Olivia's heart leapt, but not in an angry way. She felt sorry for Owain. He was clearly in anguish and in a lot of pain. 'Okay.'

'I never meant to hurt you, Olivia. But I knew that deep down you didn't love me. It's clear you love Brodie. I thought we could have one of those best friend marriages of convenience where we both get to spend time with the ones we really love. Brodie was married, so I envisaged you having an affair with him and that I would continue to see Nic. I've loved him since I met him at his family's home, Olivia. I had never felt like that about anyone. But Dad is so...' He growled. 'So old-fashioned and homophobic. I knew he'd disown me or kick me out if he found out the truth. I needed a decoy.'

'You wanted me to be your *beard*?'

He lifted his chin and said, 'We hate that phrase, just so you know.'

Olivia couldn't help giggling. 'Sorry. But I'm right, aren't I? You wanted me to be your fiancée for appearances only.'

He nodded and laughed. 'I'm so sorry. But I'm right about you not being in love with me, aren't I?'

Olivia closed her eyes and nodded. 'I'm sorry too. I was being told how good we'd be for each other. How we made such a lovely couple. And how you understand my life, so you'd be perfect husband material. I do care deeply for you, though.'

Owain took her hands. 'And I you. I think you're such a wonderful person. That's partly why I chose you. I thought if I had to spend loads of time with a woman, it had to be someone I really liked.'

'What does Nic think of all this?'

Owain sighed. 'He was the one who had the idea for me to marry at first. He thought it would be a good distraction. But the more things went on, the more he began to doubt my love for him. But I love him with all my heart, Olivia.'

'I think you need to be honest with your mum and dad, Owain. They love you so much and I think they will accept you as you are. You just have to give them a chance.'

'But my dad and his awful gay jokes... I just don't know...'

She squeezed his hands. 'You should give them a chance to know the real you. Because I think he's a pretty special man and I think they will too.'

'You're not angry?'

She shook her head. 'Not really. We were both to blame here. You're right about my feelings for Brodie. But he's just announced that he cancelled his date because he's decided he isn't ready for romance again yet.'

'Ah. That sucks. But you can always wait for him.'

She smiled. 'I could if I thought he felt the same about me. I think maybe he did once. But not any more. So, I'll just go back to being single and I'll meet someone eventually, I'm sure. I'm not over the hill yet.'

Owain pulled Olivia into his arms. 'Thank you for not hating me.'

She patted his back. 'Thank you for being honest with me.'

They stood and Owain unlocked the room. 'I'll call you a cab.'

'It's okay, I think Bella will have waited for me.'

'But how do you know?'

She lifted her phone and grinned. 'Because she's texted me to say she's waited for me.' They laughed and hugged again.

Owain opened the door, and his parents were standing outside with Niccolò. 'I'm so sorry for all the drama, Dad, Mum. I think I have some explaining to do.'

Hamish pulled his son into an embrace. 'If it's to do with Niccolò, he's told us everything.' He held his son at arm's length. 'We're so confused, Owain. We presumed you were gay when you brought Nic home the first time, but then all of a sudden you were dating girls and then the next thing we knew you were getting married to Olivia.'

Fiona dabbed at her eyes. 'Why you ever thought you couldn't be honest with us we just don't know, darling. If it's because of your dad's stupid jokes, he doesn't understand half of them anyway! But he's no homophobe. And he loves you. We both do.'

'You were always too clean to be straight anyway,' Hamish said with a chuckle.

'Stereotypes, Dad.'

'Sorry, son. Now come here.'

Olivia watched for a moment as Owain's parents hugged him. Then she almost burst into tears when Hamish grabbed Niccolò's arm and pulled him into the embrace. She walked away silently, leaving Owain to his moment of real acceptance.

She grabbed her bag and headed outside. Sure enough, Bella and Skye were waiting in Fifi. Bella got out and walked around to hug her.

'Are you okay?'

'I'm fine.'

'Want to talk about it?'

'Nope.'

* * *

Olivia slept late on Christmas Day. She felt she needed the extra sleep after the drama and copious amounts of Champagne of the night before. When she arrived downstairs in her fluffy pyjamas along with her equally fluffy canine companion, the house was quiet. A note on the kitchen table said:

Olivia dearie,

I'm away to call on Dougie just now but I'll not be long. We can exchange gifts when I get home unless you don't feel up to it, in which case we can wait. It's up to you. Innes is coming around at 1 p.m. for lunch. And Kerr may or may not turn up. Who knows with that boy? I will see you very soon.

Love

Mirren

She was all alone on Christmas Day.

She made herself a breakfast of hot chocolate and cookies and took them through to the drawing room. The fire was lit, and the room was toasty warm. Marley sat and drooled on her slippers as she munched away and stared at the tree lights, which had been set to twinkle mode. She usually hated that but on this occasion, the setting was quite slow and soothing, so she let it continue as she moved her attention to the fire and stared into the flames in the grate. She missed her parents so much that silent tears trickled down her cheeks and dropped off the end of her chin into her lap. Sensing her sadness, Marley laid a paw on her lap, and she bent to bury her nose in his fur. Her heart ached as she thought back to the Christmases her family had shared. There were some wonderful memories.

She remembered that Brodie had mentioned a gift, so she placed down her mug and plate and walked over to the tree to look for it. There, as promised, was a little box with snowflakes printed on and a blue glittery ribbon tied around it. With intrigue, she tugged at the ribbon and let it fall beside her as she opened the box.

She gasped and fresh tears fell when she lifted out a silver necklace with an acorn pendant hanging from it.

'Just like the one he bought me for my eleventh birthday.'

The door to the drawing room opened. 'Want me to fasten it for you?'

She turned to see Brodie standing there. He wore the most gaudy Hawaiian Christmas shirt she had ever seen. Santa was on a surfboard wearing a thong, then in another scene Santa was drinking a huge cocktail, and in another he was riding a motorbike, all on a bright, almost fluorescent green background, and she couldn't help laughing.

He glanced down and then twirled on the spot. 'See, you're not the only one with a brilliant eye for fashion, MacBain.'

'Oh, I love it! So tasteful. And yes, please, could you?' She held out the necklace.

He came and stood behind her and grazed the back of her neck with his fingertips. A shiver travelled through her whole body.

'There you go. Beautiful,' he said as he stepped back and appraised her. 'Especially the fluffy PJs.'

'I thought I'd make an effort,' she replied.

'So, how are you doing? Do you hate me?' he asked with a crumpled brow.

'Not in the slightest.'

'I saw them kissing out by the bathroom and I couldn't bear the thought of you getting hurt. Not you.' He shook his head.

'We talked it all through. I had to admit that I didn't love him either.' She stared down at the pendant. 'I think my heart's been taken for a while.'

'By who?' Brodie asked.

She held the little silver acorn between her thumb and finger. 'It doesn't matter. He's not available.'

Brodie nodded. 'Oh, right. Well, if he isn't available to *you*, he must be mad.'

She lifted her chin. 'Oh, yes, I forgot you used to have a crush on me.'

He took a step closer. 'Used to?'

Her heart skipped and began pounding at her ribs. 'What do you mean?' A lump formed in her throat.

He reached out and touched her cheek. 'I think you know. But I think it's gone way past being a crush.'

Her eyes welled with tears, and she shook her head. 'But you're avoiding romance. You cancelled a date with that stunning woman. You're not ready, you said so.'

He closed the remaining gap between them until his face was inches from hers. His lips were so close. 'I was avoiding romance because *you* were getting married. I cancelled the date because Matilda wasn't *you*. I'm not ready to be with someone who isn't *you*. Now do you see?'

'But...'

He slipped his hands into her hair. 'Olivia, I've loved you for so long. I've waited for so long. I never thought you'd want to be with someone ordinary like me. I didn't think I had anything to offer you, especially now you're Lady MacBain. And I was married, still am, but only on paper, which I know is still massive. But the truth is I'm selfish, so I've decided those things don't matter any more and if you'll have me, I'm 100 per cent yours. What do you say?'

No words were needed at this point. Olivia chose to show him instead. She reached up and slipped her arms around his neck and pulled him down until their lips met. Her insides turned to jelly once again, and the proverbial thunderbolt finally hit. Olivia knew that from this moment on, that would be how every kiss would feel. Because after all these years of loving one man, she could now call him her own.

EPILOGUE

'The first Drumblair wedding! We're getting really good at pulling off things at short notice,' Bella said as she checked out her reflection in Olivia's full-length mirror.

Olivia laughed. 'Yes, but it doesn't mean we should make a habit of it.'

'Oh, don't be a spoilsport. You work great under pressure. Anyway, it's time. Are you ready?'

Olivia checked her lipstick one last time. 'As ready as I'll ever be.'

They walked down the stairs to the foyer, where Spencer was waiting for them.

Olivia shivered. 'January is too cold for weddings,' she said as she wrapped her stole tighter around herself.

'Bit late to be saying that now.'

They arrived at the chapel and hurried inside to get out of the cold. Thankfully it was a very small ceremony. Kerr was already there and being fussed over by Adaira as usual; whenever she reached up to straighten his pocket square or flatten down an unruly hair, Kerr swatted her hand away as if she was an irritating bug and Olivia felt silently sorry for the woman. Mirren was already there and hugged them both. She looked beautiful in her wedding finery.

Olivia's eyes settled on Brodie, where he stood flanked by the two dogs, both sporting fancy bow ties. Her heart melted. He looked so handsome, waiting there at the back of the chapel. He made eye contact with Olivia and smiled. She loved him so much it terrified her.

The organist began to play the 'Wedding March' and Brodie held out his arm. Mirren slipped her arm through it and reached up to kiss his cheek. Bella and Olivia walked down the aisle first with their bouquets of Christmas roses and baby's breath. Marley trotted on behind with Wilf's lead in his mouth to keep the younger dog in check; they looked ridiculously cute, almost like father and son.

Dougie turned and gazed at Mirren; his eyes glassy with emotion as he watched his son walk her towards him. Olivia's chin began to tremble, and Bella handed her a hanky. At least one of them was prepared.

The vicar began the service to marry Dougie and Mirren.

* * *

Back at the castle, the dining room was laid out beautifully. Niccolò had prepared a sumptuous four-course meal for the wedding party and it smelled divine.

'I'm so glad they finally did it,' Olivia whispered to Brodie after they had eaten their main course.

'Me too. It's about time. Look how happy they are together.'

Olivia couldn't stop smiling. The newlyweds were chatting away to each other and laughing. It was a beautiful sight.

'I do love a wedding,' Brodie said.

Olivia turned to face him. 'Really? I thought you were off them for good now.'

He shrugged. 'That depends on who's getting hitched, I suppose.'

She laughed. 'Well, we've got Owain and Nic's to look forward to, and Skye and Ben's.'

'True.'

'I suppose as long you're attending someone else's wedding, you're happy?' Olivia teased.

He fixed his gaze on her. 'I didn't say that.'

'No, but I remember our conversation about you never wanting to go through that again.'

He smiled and reached across the table to the little favour bag. He pulled the ribbon out and took her hand. 'Okay, so let's say I changed my mind, how would you feel?'

Olivia swallowed and tried to keep her breathing steady. 'About getting married? Well, it wasn't me who said they didn't want to do it.'

'In that case... once my divorce is final, there will be a very important question I will need to ask you.'

She stared down at his hands and watched as he tied the ribbon around the ring finger on her left hand. She lifted her chin up and locked her eyes on his.

He smiled and said, 'Olivia MacBain, will you wait for me to be a free man again and when I am, will you consider being mine forever?'

She gasped. 'I will.' They sealed their holding pattern with a kiss.

ACKNOWLEDGMENTS

As always there are so many people to thank for helping me to get to this point. And after a strange couple of years, I'm grateful to still be writing. I'm going to try and keep this short and sweet!

As always, I want to thank my family and friends for their unending support and encouragement. I have no doubt driven you all bonkers stressing over this story. It's been a seed of an idea for a long while now and I was determined to do it justice, but I faltered a fair few times when self-doubt kicked in. You all kept me fuelled, positive and on my toes and for that I will be eternally grateful.

Rich and Grace, Mum and Dad, thank you for putting up with my drama, for talking me out of my sometimes negative frame of mind, and for dog sitting when I needed to write. And thank you to my awesome business partner, Claire, for covering for me at our fabulous bookshop for the same reason. I'm not sure what I would have done without you all.

I have to thank Fleetwood Mac this time around too. I've been a fan for many years but their greatest hits CD was the soundtrack I had playing whilst writing this book and their music inspired so many scenes (yes I am still a CD girl!). I shall always think of Olivia, Brodie, Wilf, Marley and the rest of the characters whenever I hear 'Gypsy' from now on.

Thank you, as always, to each and every person who reads my books. You're the reason I keep doing this and hearing from you when you write to tell me you have loved one of my stories is so incredibly uplifting.

I have so much gratitude for Lorella and the team at LBLA. You guys work so tirelessly for your authors, and I hope you know how appreciated you are!

Last but by no means least thank you to the whole crew at Boldwood Books. Caroline, my intrepid editor, your understanding throughout this process has been greatly appreciated and I'm thankful to have you on my side. And to the rest of the Boldwood team who work so incredibly hard, you rock!

MORE FROM LISA HOBMAN

We hope you enjoyed reading *Coming Home to the Highlands*. If you did, please leave a review.

If you'd like to gift a copy, this book is also available as an ebook, large print, hardback, digital audio download and audiobook CD.

Sign up to Lisa Hobman's mailing list for news, competitions and updates on future books.

https://bit.ly/LisaHobmanNewsletter

Dreaming Under An Island Skye, another uplifting and feel-good read from Lisa Hobman, is available to order now.

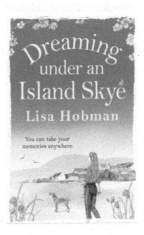

ABOUT THE AUTHOR

Lisa Hobman has written many brilliantly reviewed women's fiction titles - the first of which was shortlisted by the RNA for their debut novel award. In 2012 Lisa relocated her family from Yorkshire to a village in Scotland and this beautiful backdrop now inspires her uplifting and romantic stories.

Visit Lisa's website: http://www.lisajhobman.com

Follow Lisa on social media:

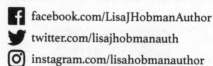

facebook.com/LisaJHobmanAuthor
twitter.com/lisajhobmanauth
instagram.com/lisahobmanauthor

Boldwood

Boldwood Books is an award-winning fiction publishing company seeking out the best stories from around the world.

Find out more at www.boldwoodbooks.com

Join our reader community for brilliant books, competitions and offers!

Follow us
@BoldwoodBooks
@BookandTonic

Sign up to our weekly deals newsletter

https://bit.ly/BoldwoodBNewsletter